Thirteen Tantalizing Tales

Thirteen Tantalizing Tales

Jay Dubya

www.bookstandpublishing.com

Published by
Bookstand Publishing
Morgan Hill, CA 95037
4742_3

ISBN 978-1-63498-883-4

For Ginger

Other Books by Jay Dubya

Pieces of Eight
Pieces of Eight, Part II
Pieces of Eight, Part III
Pieces of Eight, Part IV
Nine New Novellas
Nine New Novellas, Part II
Nine New Novellas, Part III
Nine New Novellas, Part IV
Black Leather and Blue Denim, A '50s Novel
The Great Teen Fruit War, A 1960 Novel
Frat' Brats, A '60s Novel
Ron Coyote, Man of La Mangia
So Ya' Wanna' Be A Teacher!
The Wholly Book of Genesis
The Wholly Book of Exodus
The Wholly Book of Doo-Doo-Rot-on-Me
Mauled Maimed Mangled Mutilated Mythology
Fractured Frazzled Folk Fables and Fairy Farces
Fractured Frazzled Folk Fables and Fairy Farces, Part II
Thirteen Sick Tasteless Classics
Thirteen Sick Tasteless Classics, Part II
Thirteen Sick Tasteless Classics, Part III
Thirteen Sick Tasteless Classics, Part IV
Thirteen Sick Tasteless Classics, Part V
RAM: Random Articles and Manuscripts
One Baker's Dozen
Two Baker's Dozen
Time Travel Tales
UFO: Utterly Fantastic Occurrences
Shakespeare: Slammed, Smeared, Savaged and Slaughtered
Shakespeare: S, S, S, and S, Part II
Snake Eyes and Boxcars
Snake Eyes and Boxcars, Part II
Suite 16
O. Henry: Obscenely and Outrageously Obliterated
Twain: Tattered, Trounced, Tortured and Traumatized
Poe: Pelted, Pounded, Pummeled and Pulverized
London: Lashed, Lacerated, Lampooned and Lambasted
Hawthorne: Hazed Hooked Hammered and Hijacked
Hawthorne Hacked, Shakespeare Sacked & Thurber Thwacked
THEMES

The FBI Inspector
Modern Mythology
First Person Stories
PLOTS
Prime-Time Crime Time
The Psychic Dimension, Part II

Young Adult Fantasy Novels

Enchanta
Space Bugs, Earth Invasion
Pot of Gold
The Eighteen Story Gingerbread House

Contents

Acknowledgement

I would like to thank fellow Hammonton, NJ Lion Bob Delambily for thoroughly proofreading this book.

Introduction

Thirteen Tantalizing Tales is author Jay Dubya's twenty-third story collection. Other fiction and non-fiction short story books produced by this prolific author are The Psychic Dimension, The Psychic Dimension Part II, First Person Stories, The FBI Inspector, Modern Mythology, Prime-Time Crime Time, UFO: Utterly Fantastic Occurrences, Snake Eyes and Boxcars, Snake Eyes and Boxcars Part II, Time Travel Tales, Suite 16, One Baker's Dozen, Two Baker's Dozen, RAM: Random Articles and Manuscripts, Pieces of Eight, Pieces of Eight Part II, Pieces of Eight Part III, Pieces of Eight Part IV, Nine New Novellas, Nine New Novellas Part II, Nine New Novellas Part III and Nine New Novellas Part IV.

"Holiday Hooligans"

The very interesting English word "Holiday" originally pertained to the specific nomenclature "Holy Day" before secularism became the watchword/monitor of modern times. Before School Winter Break, before School Spring Break and before Love/Chocolate Gift Day ever existed, religious celebrations of Christmas, of Easter and of St. Valentine Day were revered Christian "Holy Days" appearing on the yearly calendar.

Chief FBI Inspector Joe Giralo still remains one of those old-fashioned advocates of tradition who wishes that Christmas (and not X-mas) would continue to be a tribute about the birth of Christ and that Easter would not exclusively be about the particular activities of the ever-ubiquitous, egg-distributing, basket-carrying, harebrained, totally juvenile "Holiday Bunny".

At noon on Monday, December 9, 2019 a rather fatigued FBI Inspector Joe Giralo had summoned his three principal agents, Salvatore Velardi, Arthur Orsi and Dan Blachford into his eighth-floor office situated inside the all-too-familiar 600 Arch Street Federal Building, Philadelphia, Pennsylvania. As usual, the curious entrants found their illustrious superior sitting rather stationary behind his massive Canadian oak desk with his brown eyes seemingly transfixed, their superior's large pupils scanning the *Philadelphia Inquirer's* "above the crease" morning headlines. The veteran crime-fighter's ever-vigilant mind was apparently keenly engrossed in much more serious illegal matters than *those* trivial news' stories, which his always-alert cerebral processes were then intensely evaluating. Finally, the Boss recognized the presence of his three loyal underlings.

"Greetings Men!" the Chief nonchalantly acknowledged, lowering the slightly wrinkled newspaper below eye level. "Glad you three somewhat-experienced sleuths were performing your regular duties in the building when my secretary had summoned you' illustrious dynamos from your cramped cubicles. We've got some important business to attend to, but first of all," Inspector Giralo predictably deviated, "I want to know how you men had spent the recent Pearl Harbor Day weekend. It's too bad that December 7th isn't declared a national holiday. Now tell me: what did you do Sal?"

"Well Chief, I took my wife and kids to New York where we enjoyed seeing the terrific Christmas Show at Radio City Music Hall," Agent Velardi disclosed. "Kathy really was impressed with the Rockettes' fantastic performance, and the kids really relished the 'March of the Toy Soldiers'."

"And how about you, Arty? How did you and Carol spend Saturday, Pearl Harbor Day?"

"Well Chief, my wife and I drove east to Smithville Village, which was well-decorated for the Christmas season," Agent Orsi revealed. "We ate a delicious lunch at the historic Smithville Inn, perused the many gift shops in the quaint village and then anxiously motored over to Harrah's Casino to try our luck in Atlantic City. I lost a hundred bucks playing blackjack, but Carol got lucky on the slots and canceled-out my losses. In all, our Atlantic City gambol to gamble was not especially lucrative, but we did have fun!"

"And Dan, what did you and Bing do on Saturday?" Inspector Giralo inquired as if the master detective were conducting a rather important criminal interrogation.

"My wife and I took a really fascinating South Jersey steam locomotive train ride on the 'Santa Express', which is a seasonal branch of the area Cape May Seashore Line," Agent Blachford suavely articulated. "The unique trip was a fifteen-mile fun excursion from Richland to Tuckahoe. Of course, Santa was a mobile passenger on the slow-moving train, and his presence was enjoyed by the many children who had been escorted by their doting parents. And also," Dan Blachford elaborated, "jolly St. Nicholas was accompanied by a host of Dickens-dressed Victorian carolers, and to add to the pre-winter experience, soft background music was provided by a talented accordion player. We savored the scenic ride back to the Richland boarding station; in fact, just as much as we delighted in taking the parallel rails out to Tuckahoe."

"Well Boss, now that you know what we did over the Pearl Harbor weekend," Agent Velardi piped-up, "exactly what sort of caper did you do? Go flying around in a Japanese Zero?"

"If you really want to know, Salvatore," a slightly annoyed Inspector Giralo answered in a feigned, gruff tone of voice, "Gina and I did some preliminary Christmas shopping at the Deptford Mall. Afterwards, my exhausted wife and I consumed a sumptuous filet dinner at the nearby Longhorn Steakhouse."

Sensing that the time for cursory small-talk chatter had expired, Agent Sal Velardi requested to learn about the real reason the three FBI men had been asked to report to the Inspector's spacious office. Joe Giralo reached into the top drawer of his desk and his search produced a commonplace oak-tag folder similar to ones in which school children keep their graded English writing compositions.

"Guys, this is perhaps the most bizarre, eccentric, nonsensical case that I've ever been assigned to investigate," Giralo prefaced. "Our ingenious mentor Matt Riley down at D.C. headquarters dispatched an encrypted communiqué just two hours ago and requested that my team attempt to decipher exactly what is going on."

The Chief quickly distributed copies of the newly transmitted information to his trio of assistants, who then diligently studied the strange contents while their boss provided additional input. "Now Men, these rather insane activities I'm about to describe occur on standard United States holidays. Five nutcases will enter a privately-owned family convenience store," Giralo communicated, "and the queer quintet would be dressed in costumes appropriately related to the particular holiday being celebrated. The five customers would then point their water pistols at the clerk or proprietor behind the counter, and instead of robbing the establishment in question, the five would hand-over a thousand dollars in crisp, unmarked hundred-dollar-bills and then exit the premises and speed-off inside a six passenger van."

"This is some sort of weird crimewave happening in reverse," an intrigued Agent Arthur Orsi noted. "Instead of performing an armed heist with real guns, the tricky intruders use harmless water pistols and then philanthropically give the dumbfounded owner or clerk a bonanza of a thousand smackers."

"Right Arty," Chief Giralo affirmed. "I suspect that the ruse is more pernicious than it appears on the simplistic surface. Now Salvatore, I'd like you to read the first three crazy incidents that are described on the printout-sheet I've just disseminated."

"New Year's Day, Tuesday, January 1st, 2019. Five individuals gaudily dressed as mummers enter a Philadelphia deli and hand-over a thousand bucks to the astonished Quaker City female employee that had been standing behind the counter. The outlandish intruders then evacuate the West Philly business and hop into a van driven by another fellow, who is also dressed in pretentious mummer's garb."

After a moment of exhibiting intense hilarity with his government associates, Agent Velardi read to his alert audience of three that on Tuesday, February 12th, 2019 five bearded men dressed as Abraham Lincoln (wearing high stovepipe hats and black suits) entered a novelty store in Las Vegas, Nevada, gave the shocked worker a cool thousand bucks and speedily departed without ever firing their loaded water pistols.

The third absurd, corresponding incident occurred in Atlanta, Georgia on Sunday, St. Patrick's Day, March 17, 2019. Five merry leprechaun imitators, acting in an outlandish and ridiculous manner, presented the fellow manning the cash register with ten "Ben Franklins" and then anxiously evacuated the corner retail store and next, quickly hopped into an awaiting van that soon accelerated out of its temporary parking space.

Agent Dan Blachford was then designated by the Chief to read items four through seven that had been listed on the printout sheet, and subsequently, Agent Arthur Orsi was assigned to read events seven though eleven. Amidst great amusement exhibited by the four men, here are the incredible results that had been identified on the official communiqué copies that had been sent by Supervisor Matt Riley from FBI D.C. headquarters:

4) Easter Sunday, April 21, 2019. Five individuals in colorful Easter Bunny apparel intentionally hand a thousand dollars to petrified Los Angeles store clerk.

5) Memorial Day, Monday, May 27, 2019. Five men dressed in Army, Navy, Marines, Air Force and Coast Guard garb eagerly point loaded water pistols at an Austin, Texas store employee, and then the impostors gladly hand over a thousand non-counterfeit dollars.

6) Friday, June 14, 2019, Flag Day. Five men wearing typical Uncle Sam costumes enter a Denver, Colorado convenience store and threaten to shoot water pistols at the husband and wife duo standing behind the counter. Instead, the imaginative trespassers generously provide the startled couple with a thousand dollars in cold cash, and then the pseudo-patriotic charlatans rapidly speed-away in a van wildly driven by a sixth Uncle Sam.

"Okay Arty, it's your turn to review occurrences seven though eleven; that is, if you can cease your incessant laughing," Chief Giralo mildly admonished. "Gentlemen, I realize that *this* matter seems to be lunacy to the tenth power, so please try to control yourselves and act professionally as Agent Orsi adequately describes in detail the remaining peculiar episodes."

7) "Thursday, July 4, 2019: Independence Day. Indianapolis, Indiana," still giggling Agent Orsi read out loud. "Five white-wigged gentlemen masquerading as colonial George Washington enter a corner grocery store and deliver a thousand-dollar bonus to the extremely stunned owner."

8) Saturday, August 3, 2019. El Paso, Texas: Watermelon Day. Five muscular males wearing round straw hats and dressed in blue denim overalls, that were held-up by immense, thick matching suspenders, threaten to drench the main store clerk with water pistols but instead, voluntarily deliver ten hundred-dollar greenbacks to the astounded manager.

9) Monday, September 2, 2019: Labor Day. Houston, Texas. Five men imaginatively disguised as pregnant women, having large soft pillows stuffed inside their acquired maternity outfits, provide the store proprietor with a handsome thousand dollars in cash.

10) Monday, October 14, 2019: Columbus Day. Pittsburgh, Pennsylvania. Five males dressed as fifteenth century Spanish ship navigators grant a totally surprised candy shop employee a thousand-dollar reward to be immediately placed into the confectionary business's ancient-looking cash register.

11) Thursday, November 28, 2019: Thanksgiving Day. Irvine, California. Five fascinating men disguised as Mayflower Pilgrims hand-over a thousand bucks to the rattled-and-confused elderly convenience store manager.

After the three assembled FBI agents finally stopped their relentless laughter, Chief Joe Giralo insisted that his humored G-Men ask some pertinent questions designed to help solve the outrageous conundrum that had been egregiously puzzling their investigative minds.

"But Chief, if the prospective bandits give away money instead of pilfering it in an unlawful manner, I don't see how any general or specific crime has been committed!" Agent Velardi volunteered his objective conclusion. "The only aspect of a crime I can determine that might involve FBI intervention is that these similar events have transpired in many different states."

"Sal's absolutely, logically correct!" chimed-in Agent Arthur Orsi. "Has criminal behavior gone completely bonkers and off the rails? This entire oddball scenario we've been scrupulously analyzing, and quite frankly, wasting our precious time upon is preposterously puzzling, to say the least!"

"Well Chief," Agent Dan Blachford began his evaluative inquiry, "do the clever masqueraders demand anything in return for contributing a thousand clams to store personnel once each monthly holiday in various cities all across America?"

"Dan, I'm glad you asked *that* very relevant question," Inspector Giralo commended usually reticent Agent Blachford. "Yes, the five holiday-disguised mimickers do make two distinct purchases each time that they enter a different shop each month."

"And exactly what do the idiotic rascals buy?" a very curious Agent Velardi strongly desired learning.

"Apparently Sal, each of the five prankster-holiday-honoring personages truly possesses a sweet tooth. Every time the candy lovers randomly enter a convenience store on a celebrated holiday, the group habitually purchases two chocolate bars in exchange for a thousand cash bucks: the first a Pay Day Bar, and the second, a 100 Grand Bar," a somewhat addled Joe Giralo replied. "Now Guys, we'll meet again here in my office a full week from today, Monday, December 16 at noon. I want you three Dick Tracy-types to thoroughly research and report back every single iota you detect about this candy phenomenon that has been discussed so far. Something is definitely amiss in this perplexing sequence of loony holiday fiascos," Inspector Giralo hypothesized and concluded, "and I desire learning precisely what is going on in certain urban convenience stores throughout the country on special calendar holidays!"

* * * * * * * * * * * * *

When Agents Salvatore Velardi, Arthur Orsi and Dan Blachford strolled into the first-floor lobby of Philadelphia FBI headquarters at 600 Arch Street at noon on Monday, December 16, the three purpose-minded government officials were casually discussing the amusing theory that their "arcane boss" Chief Inspector Joe Giralo's "uncanny problem-solving ability" was indeed one hundred percent intuitive. The discourse proceeded in the following manner:

"Our distinguished Mentor always reiterates to us that wily criminals and avowed terrorists are people, just like us, and that those same nefarious folks tend to think and behave in observable and measurable patterns, just like *we* do," Agent Velardi accurately declared as the 'dynamic trio' awaited the arrival of the lobby elevator to transport them up to the building's eighth floor. "But truly, the Inspector has the extraordinary capacity to connect formerly unrelated dots that then ultimately lead *us* to interpreting certain enigmatic developments. Our boss calls his fantastic talent 'a simple knack', but I think it's all much more complicated than just that! He seems to marvelously discover the critical missing element that literally always tends to confound and elude the three of us!"

"Yes Sal, I wholeheartedly agree with your depiction," Agent Art Orsi confirmed. "I still think the Chief is more than a tad psychic, although he constantly maintains that all he does is cleverly associate parallel situations. He then uses the process of deduction inside the ordinary 'scientific method of thinking' in order to amazingly verify his authentic theories. I believe that our eminent 'Mentor' is also our diabolical 'Tormentor'."

"Ha, ha, ha!" Agent Dan Blachford cheerfully reacted as the familiar gray metal elevator doors slowly opened. "Of course, Arty, when we quietly enter *his* solemn sanctuary, the Chief will instinctively make us suffer through listening to a barrage of irrelevant small-talk. I hope that you' fellas' are better prepared than I am in regard to explaining the ludicrous stunts being enacted by these very baffling holiday masqueraders."

Upon exiting the elevator at the eighth floor, Agents Velardi, Orsi and Blachford swiftly paced into Chief Joe Giralo's office and immediately noticed their distinguished superior predictably sitting behind his prodigious oak desk and conscientiously examining the front-page newspaper headlines of the morning *Philadelphia Inquirer*. Raising his balding head, the inimitable Inspector was quite pleased upon realizing that his "capable threesome" had punctually arrived to honor their scheduled Monday, December 16 noon conference with their erudite mentor.

"Hi Boss," usually laconic Dan Blachford greeted. "What does the morning paper have to divulge today. It's really yesterday's news, and soon most daily rags will be obsolete just like the Pony Express, Conestoga wagons and the Morse Code Telegraph. If you really want to get what's developing right this minute," Blachford offered, "you need to rely solely on your trusty hand computer!"

"I got bored with the main headlines," somewhat-aggravated Joe Giralo answered, "so I rummaged to page fifteen and read where two altar boys in Spain had put marijuana in the church censer. After burning the censer contents, the Catholic priests who were saying Mass were really fuming!"

"That's one way to get Catholic priests *incensed!*" intrepidly joked Agent Arthur Orsi. "But Boss, you're correct in observing that real news is now mixed-in with pathetic tabloid journalism. I actually think that social media is the true culprit that's wholly responsible for *that* grotesque metamorphosis."

"Needless to say, Boss," Agent Velardi facetiously spoke-up before Giralo could respond to Agent Orsi, "the exasperated Spanish priests soon found-out that there was pot in the pot!"

"Fellas', take your seats," Inspector Giralo announced in an almost apologetic tone, feeling a bit guilty for being drawn into the rather inane conversation. "This will be an abbreviated session for us today because I have an upcoming appointment with several highly-motivated rookie recruits that's slated for 12:30."

"An appointment is always better than a disappointment," jested Agent Velardi.

"Salvatore, you'd better watch your ridiculous sense of humor or else you might be replaced by one of the Bureau's neophytes that I'm about to interview," the slightly irritated Chief chastised his main G-Man. "I think that you might actually fit-in better writing off-the-wall satire and parody scripts for Comedy Central. I could be wrong, but you might even work your way up to organizing hilarious dialogue for South Park!"

"Sorry Boss," the Team Captain candidly indicated. "Sometimes my mouth gets ahead of my brain."

"As I was saying," Giralo proceeded while nodding his head to show that he had tacitly accepted his subordinate's sincere statement of regret, "today I'm dispensing with the regular picayune small-talk about what you three Dr. Watsons had done over the weekend. As for me, I've already completed my holiday gift buying and have erected this year's Christmas tree," Giralo characteristically boasted. "As you dedicated Guys know, I'm a devout miniature-train enthusiast, and I've even gotten my village platform organized early so that the neighborhood kids can appreciate how yesteryear youngsters used to enjoy themselves before this terrible age of sophisticated hand-held computers and i-Pods."

"That's really great Inspector," impatient Agent Orsi half-heartedly appreciated. "But what have you and Matt Riley's stellar committee down in D.C. learned about these conniving holiday mimickers? Honestly, I think we're wandering a trifle off-subject reviewing *your* many mediocre Christmas preparations!"

"Not exactly, Arty. There's an old maxim among newspaper editors that goes, 'Dog bites old man; no story. Old man bites dog; absolutely a frontpage, newsworthy story'," Joe Giralo sternly expressed. "I believe that these bizarre holiday masqueraders are creating a distinct diversion for something more sinister that's happening. Naturally, the moronic media pays attention to the insane, superficial behavior that's in progress while the distracted press obviously usually ignores rather ordinary criminal acts that are simultaneously occurring. Now Arty, kindly give me a non-superficial synopsis of what your recent research has uncovered."

Agent Orsi coughed and then delivered a formal dissertation about how Pay Day candy bars had originated on the retail market in 1932, but the brand name had then been sold to Consolidated Foods in 1938; however, Consolidated Foods later became the Sara Lee Company. "The very delicious peanut and caramel candy bar production and distribution rights are currently owned by the Hershey Corporation," Art Orsi skillfully communicated.

Agent Dan Blachford then orated a brief summary of the 100 Grand Bar created in 1964, which formerly had the title "Hundred Thousand Dollar Bar" until 1986. "The delectable ingredients are chocolate, chewy caramel and crispy rice," Blachford methodically explained, "and the candy bar was a product of the Nestle Company until last year, but now in 2019 Nestle has merged with another confectionery firm named Ferrera Candy Company."

"This is all well and good," Chief Giralo mentioned, "but we still haven't established the evasive motive for these five, devious knuckleheads oddly dressed in foolish-looking outfits giving store personnel a thousand dollars just for two money-oriented candy bars. Now then, before I dismiss this informal meeting," Giralo meticulously specified, "I have something additional to share that Matt Riley and I regard as rather pertinent evidence for you three gumshoes to constructively examine."

Giralo again opened his impressive oak desk's top drawer, removed the same faded oak-tag folder and cautiously handed his men three photocopies of an "essential incomplete word" that the Boss theorized was most definitely a material clue. "Gentlemen, this brief documentation I believe represents a key factor in cracking-open this up-to-now incredulous Holiday Hooligans case."

"This looks like total gibberish to me," complained and protested Agent Velardi. "Why didn't you hand us the Rosetta Stone or maybe some Indian Sanskrit message instead?"

"For your intense scrutiny," the Inspector addressed his competent team, "I've taken the liberty to type-in exact chronological order the first letters of the eleven cities that have thus far been frivolously exposed to the abnormal shenanigans of the five disguised suspects, along with their similarly-dressed van driver accomplice."

"I see a definite connection already," Agent Blachford deduced and verbally shared. "There are eleven letters indicated on this piece of paper, and eleven cities have actually been targeted. I conjecture that the twelfth mystery city will be hit on Christmas Day."

"Dan's right," impulsively verified Agent Orsi. "The twelfth impractical intrusion will mischievously occur on Christmas Day, and our challenging task is to figure-out what U.S. city will be the next setting for these obnoxious, six slippery rogues to visit."

"Now study the eleven letters carefully," Giralo advised his fully preoccupied assistants. "There might be some elusive-but-germane hint embedded within the chronological sequence of first letters starting with alphabet item P."

P-L-A-L-A-D-I-E-H-P-I

"Now Men, I confidently predict that the next candy store exploit will occur with six individuals dressed as Santa Claus on Christmas Day, Wednesday December 25," the overweight man seated behind the oak desk prognosticated. "And I also think that city number twelve will begin with the letter 'H', but it will not again be Houston. We'll meet this coming Saturday at noon inside Andy's Restaurant, Route 54, in Hammonton to further discuss this most fairly sensational case. Until then," Chief Giralo remarked and then smiled, "I strongly recommend that you three crackerjack detectives also actively pursue your regular happy investigations."

* * * * * * * * * * * *

Rural Hammonton and vicinity had for over a century been a prosperous, commercial agricultural hub for Southern New Jersey. In the 1950s, peaches were the dominant fruit crop. Then in the late '60s, blueberries became the area farmers' money favorite. Now in 2019, raspberries, grapes and blackberries have been gaining a solid economic foothold. To remember and honor the community's vital agrarian past and present, Peach Tree Plaza on Route 30 and Blueberry Crossing Mall on the same four-lane highway respectively refer to the '50s and '60s, and now Raspberry Run Shoppes, located south of town on Route 54, alludes to the present summer produce industry. Chief Giralo and his three proficient federal colleagues were scheduled to unite at Andy's Restaurant at Raspberry Run for a pertinent noonday discussion on Saturday, December 21st."

"It was nice for the owners to cooperate and provide an isolated table in the back room," Joe Giralo stated as the four hungry patrons sat-down at the reserved round table. "Thanks to my shiny FBI badge, we G-Men always receive top priority when it comes to accommodations and seating arrangements."

An attractive blonde waitress scurried across the brown tile floor and intended to pass-out menus that included breakfast and lunch entrees. "That's all right Miss," the Inspector pleasantly declared. "Just bring us three cups of hot coffee and three orders of eggs, bacon, home fries and white toast. And please have the chef make the eggs over light!"

"Now Chief," Agent Velardi softly uttered, "Arty, Dan and I have successfully decoded the cryptogram with the letters P-L-A-L-A-D-I-E-H-P-I. You told us that the twelfth missing alphabet letter is a second 'H'. If you rearrange the twelve letters after adding *your* 'H', the city of 'Philadelphia' is formed."

"That observation is only a minor coincidence," Giralo plausibly informed Velardi. "The important factor to note is that the second 'H' city is going to be something other than Houston."

"Well, I'll wager that it certainly isn't Hammonton," Art Orsi surmised and chuckled. "Inspector, I'm pretty befuddled about this whole silly ordeal. What's *your* esoteric theory about the second 'H' city having a variety of convenience stores that could potentially be harassed by a bevy of asinine St. Nicholas wannabes. The next event, or should I say 'fiasco', will be a dumb, foolish Santa Claus intrusion happening somewhere in an 'H' city on Wednesday, December 25th."

Just after the breakfast orders had been graciously served, Joe Giralo then delved deeply into the crux of the matter. "I conjecture that the redundant 100 Grand candy bar purchase is probably the master key that unlocks this entire freaky holiday costume mystery. Certain criminals are so cocky and haughty that they think they can easily outsmart anyone involved in law enforcement," Giralo maintained. "This ongoing holiday candy bar travesty is merely a cute diversion to draw the press's attention away from a crime-in-progress. Reporters and TV news anchors will stupidly divert *their* so-called 'news stories' from describing crimes to writing disgusting tabloid journalism such as imbecilic leprechauns and Easter bunnies fanatically paying a thousand dollars for one Pay Day candy bar and for one 100 Grand candy-bar that will have been obtained at twelve separate stores in a dozen different metropolises."

"Okay Inspector," chipped-in a generally bewildered Sal Velardi, "but how do we determine what the second 'H' city will be that'll have some unfortunate convenience store clerk scared to death by these nutcase holiday hooligans on Christmas Day?"

"You're putting the cart before the horse," Giralo responded by uttering an overused, hackneyed cliché. "Now Salvatore, certain expensive automobiles such as Mercedes-Benz CL Class, top-end Cadillac Escalades and Porsche 911s retail at around a hundred thousand dollars each. I speculate that the 100 Grand candy bar is the real decoding mechanism to be utilized here."

"Holy cow! I think you're positively right, Boss," Agent Blachford confirmed after aggressively consulting related data from his indispensable handheld FBI computer. "Now I believe I understand the entire complicated canard. High-end plush cars have been stolen precisely on the same holiday dates that the weirdo masquerading hooligans had created havoc in all eleven cities that formed most of the letters to the word 'Philadelphia', which if I recall, was the first city existing on the comprehensive FBI list."

After sipping a mouthful of his tasty coffee, inspired Inspector Joe Giralo directed Agent Orsi to research on *his* handheld computer the identities of the next three densely populated U.S. "H cites".

"Huntsville, Alabama is indicated as Number 123, Huntington Beach, California is listed as Number 124 and Hollywood, Florida is not far behind," G-Man Arthur Orsi contributed his valuable input in solving the formerly perplexing holiday hooligan enigma.

"Then it's all settled!" Inspector Giralo sagely proclaimed. "I'll consult with Matt Riley later today and we'll dispatch three separate FBI squads: one each to Huntsville, to Huntington Beach and to Hollywood, Florida. I'm quite sure than our triple 'H' dragnets, all occurring at high-end car dealerships, will ultimately land us with at least several surprised suspects this coming Christmas Day! The clowns that we will apprehend will surely rat on all of *their* criminal accomplices. Bon Appetit, Gentlemen!"

"The Piano and the Organ"

Over the years I've often regarded and prided myself as being quite objective-minded. I believed that in adulthood I have always been a very decent, moral, good American citizen but definitely not a seriously religious-oriented person. In the past, I had habitually practiced obeying the Ten Commandments along with "the Golden Rule" with loyal fidelity. Adhering to St. Paul's philosophy, I had deceived myself into thinking that faith alone was needed for eternal salvation, as opposed to the alternative St. Peter "structured and austere doctrine", which mandated that a good Catholic must attend Mass every Sunday and on every Holy Day of Obligation in order to accumulate enough grace to evolve into the Kingdom of Heaven.

True, over the years I had reluctantly attended church Baptisms, Confirmations, Holy Communions and also innumerable funeral services, but I must confess that ever since I had entered college and was influenced by ultra-liberal university professors as early as age nineteen, I've defiantly abandoned the St. Peter principles of strict subservience to the directives of priests, bishops and church cardinals' teachings (along with the Vicar of Rome's doctrines). Instead, my moral compass soon preferred accepting missionary St. Paul's more lenient creed of eternal salvation by virtue of easily achieving Heaven by means of faith alone. I now fathom that all of *that* sinful, simpler, apostate attitude of mine had drastically changed in eight challenging weeks ever since I had experienced significant encounters with "the arcane dimension".

Yes, up until my major supernatural confrontations, I had been extremely haughty about being a contemporary cynic and a full-fledged twentieth century skeptic. Indeed, I had never even half-heartedly believed in Bigfoot, Alchemy, Sorcery, Witchcraft, Satan, Saints, Angels, the Loch Ness Monster, the Abominable Snowman, or UFOs piloted by bellicose space aliens. I'm still doubtful about everything just mentioned with the non-fantasy exception of Saints, Angels and Devils. Let me thoroughly explain *this* whole extraordinary phenomenon by intelligently reverting-back to the beginning of this totally incredible tale.

In 1975, my wife Joanne, a primary grade public school teacher, accompanied me on an excursion to Germantown Avenue in Philadelphia where we merrily purchased a "surprise upright piano" for our three young sons for the purpose of keeping the vulnerable lads out of trouble through their early teenage years. An open space existed in our living room between two brown armchairs and under a large wall oil painting of a bowl of fruit accompanied by an apple and a banana lying flat on a fancy, elaborate tablecloth.

"The piano lessons along with adolescent sports should keep our junior trio safely away from malicious peer influences," Joanne convincingly insisted. "John, I believe that our musical investment will reap handsome dividends in the form of excellent character development. Don't you agree?"

"You're right Ginger," I answered my wife's sage remark. "The upright piano along with baseball, soccer and basketball will keep Joey, John Thomas and Steve off the streets until they're ready for college. With parenthood comes massive responsibility," I affirmed. "Being a successful stockbroker, I fully know the merits of making genuine, good investments!"

Two years later in 1977 Joanne and I had made a major twenty-by-twenty-four-foot extension to our home's cozy den. To help fill the additional space to the new step-up area from the old den, my spouse and I happily journeyed to a South Jersey mall and cooperatively acquired a small organ as an attractive piece of furniture to finish-off the new interior construction.

"Since our boys are still enjoying their piano lessons and have advanced beyond 'Jingle Bells' and 'Please Release Me'," Ginger articulated, "this mahogany organ certainly complements the terrific idea of expanding their separate musical repertoires."

"Yes Dear," I automatically concurred. "If one knows how to play a piano, then obviously, mastering the organ ought to come easy. Joey is now ten but still gets satisfaction from banging-out the pretty cool oldies' rock songs he's been learning from Mr. Gibson. And John Thomas and Steve are not far behind in developing their talents on the eighty-eights."

A decade and a half later in 1992 our three sons had finally matured into young adults and were attending various colleges while living in campus dormitories. Joe was a graduate student at Delaware University, John Thomas was a senior at Stockton University in Pomona, NJ and Stephen was a sophomore acquiring his advanced education at Rutgers up in New Brunswick.

Now having more free time and less family responsibility on our hands, Joanne faithfully attended choir rehearsals every Thursday night at St. Joseph Church on North Third Street, Hammonton, New Jersey, and I would go to Rotary Club meetings at Joe's Maplewood Restaurant (in the same community) on the White Horse Pike, which specializes in delicious Italian cuisine. These traditional "adult activities" had been happening regularly for over a decade, and my wife and I actually took the weekly obligations in stride. However, rather bizarre and strange events began transpiring a little over eight weeks ago, with the uncanny manifestations starting in early March of 1992. These hair-raising, virtually supernatural incidents have radically altered my whole perspective of my relationship with Nature, and the anomalous sequence of inexplicable occurrences have contradicted most of the "Demosthenes-type ideas" that had been maliciously espoused and communicated to me by my 1960s agnostic and atheistic college professors.

On a Thursday night in early March, I was sitting comfortably in the new den reading a copy of the weekly Hammonton newspaper, when all of a sudden, my auditory perception heard the living room upright piano being expertly played. I turned my head for a more astute interpretation of the melody and chords, and my keen senses immediately recognized the familiar tune as "Galveston", the lyrics originally recorded by singer Glen Campbell in 1969. 'I wonder if one of my sons has snuck into the house and is playing a practical joke on me,' I considered. 'I'll trek through the kitchen and the hall to the living room to acknowledge my son's surprise visit.'

When I had reached the source of the instrumental notes, my eyes were amazingly shocked, and also my legs became weakened and were about to buckle from overwhelming fright. I rapidly comprehended that the piano was weirdly playing itself without any human body occupying the wooden bench behind it.

'This can't be,' I doubtfully marveled and considered out of pure astonishment. 'It's acting just like an old-time player-piano, but the mechanism that we had bought in Philly doesn't have any rotating scroll with punches upon the roll that would indicate the various notes to be played. And I thought that the stock market is crazy!' I related. 'Right now, I feel like I'm having some kind of delusional hallucination and that I'm ready for a quick admission into nearby Ancora State Mental Hospital.'

My thinking was in a stupor. Feeling weak and confused, my body sank down into the left-side brown armchair, and my beleaguered brain commenced reminiscing the time that Joanne and I had flown down to Houston, Texas. We had rented a car from Avis and drove through Galveston on the Gulf of Mexico before motoring-down to South Padre Island to have a pleasant vacation staying at my sister Anne and her husband Steve's residence.

After the piano ceased perfectly playing its splendid instrumental version of Glen Campbell's superhit song, my psyche was still a prisoner of extreme wonderment. 'I won't tell Ginger about this aberration,' I fearfully decided. 'My better half still thinks that I'm off my sanity rocker for building the second larger den onto our suburban two-story colonial house.'

* * * * * * * * * * * *

On Friday morning at my stock and bond financial services place of employment over in Northfield, my group's secretary noticed that my mind seemed to be elsewhere after I had ambled past her desk into my sales office. "Are you feeling okay John?" Mrs. Marie Turner alertly asked. "Your face looks a trifle pallid."

"I'm fine," I falsely and guiltily replied. "I had a bad allergy attack early this morning in front of the bathroom mirror. I think it's the wild change in weather now that we're nearing springtime," my imagination and lips shrewdly invented. "The advent of the vernal equinox will predictably do *that* to me almost every March."

The following Thursday evening, I thought that I would conduct a clever experiment. At eight p.m., I was sitting in the familiar brown living room armchair and watching the casino-bound traffic heading towards Atlantic City passing-by through Hammonton on busy two-lane Central Avenue. Without notice, the now-autonomous piano keys began moving up and down (with rhyme but without reason) playing the smooth rhythm to "Old Cape Cod", which I recollected had been vocally recorded by artist Patti Page back in the early 1950s. My semi-frenzied mind promptly evaluated a horrible realization: 'Patti Page is dead!' But to the credit of having logic triumph over anxiety, I staunchly regained my stronger sensibilities and my normally doubting personality, along with my pretentious mental and emotional composure: 'But unlike Patti Page, Glen Campbell is still alive and performing in the year 1992', I determined with much psychological relief.

My baffled mind drifted into a deep reverie where my memory recalled Joanne and I vacationing up in Cape Cod to celebrate our first year of marriage. We had stayed at a nice motel in Hyannis, patriotically drove around the oceanfront Kennedy Compound mansions (that is as close as our automobile could approach), visited artsy avant-garde Provincetown, and the next dawn, we were enthusiastic foot passengers on a ferry ride over to scenic Nantucket Island, where we excitedly toured a whaling museum and amply enjoyed the "sand dunes and salty air".

'This remarkable piano has somehow become a haunted musical device that's effectively devastating my sense of confidence,' I worried and reckoned. 'My greatest fear is that there exists some kind of invisible ghost playing the damned thing. How am I ever going to keep this terrible secret to myself without eventually sharing it with Joanne? She'll think that I'm crazier than the notorious Mad Hatter in *Alice in Wonderland*.'

When Ginger returned rather fatigued from choir practice at nine p.m., my observant wife immediately perceived my detectable melancholy mood along with my silent grief. "John, are you feeling all right. Your face is a trifle pale. I'll fetch you two aspirins and a glass of cold water!"

"No thank you, Honey," I instinctively and facetiously lied. "I've already had two magic pills and downed-them with plenty of water from the kitchen faucet. Honestly Ginger," I continued my phony litany. "I endured a wicked five-minute sneezing fit about an hour ago. I'm fine right now after going through at least a dozen tissues in the downstairs powder room. My theory is that my delicate nose, throat and sinuses are going through their annual spring adjustments," I weakly equivocated. "But Dear, thanks anyway for your loving concern about my annoying allergy problem."

"On the third Thursday evening in March of 1992, I was quietly sitting upon the living room's red and white striped sofa and conscientiously researching the New York Stock Exchange's expected Friday morning futures when the white keys on the piano started moving up and down and mysteriously producing the 1975 song "Philadelphia Freedom", which had been sung by British singer Elton John. My distracted-but-inquisitive mind recognized at that moment that I was becoming accustomed (and somewhat unfazed) to (and by) the "possessed piano" and that I no longer regarded the object's presence and odd performance with any heightened trepidation. My compromised mind gently imagined that Joanne and I were taking our three fairly compatible sons on educational tours of Philly taking an array of taxis and buses to historic Independence Hall, to the Liberty Bell, to Phillies baseball games at Veterans Stadium and to academic and scientific learning experiences at the magnificent, marble-walled Franklin Institute.

'I can't ever tell Joanne about our piano's oddball, deviate ability, and I can't prevaricate by sneezing and coughing my way out of this sensational, weekly Thursday night musical spectacle. Even though I'm no longer directly afraid of the 'haunted piano', I'm still not going to share my phantom concert engagements with what my anemic mind has great difficulty in understanding or explaining,' I plausibly fabricated. 'Science and rationality have little to do with the peculiar, supernatural forces that are currently perplexing my fathoming of reality.'

The following Tuesday evening I had been listening to a boring guest speaker expounding on the subject of "Relaxation" at the Rotary Club meeting over at Joe's Maplewood, but the true highlight of the session was me savoring a plate of "the World's Best Spaghetti", just as the outstanding restaurant often advertises. When I returned to the safety and security of home, a somber conversation with my devoted spouse ensued.

"Joanne, are you feeling up to stuff?" I diplomatically asked. "You seem to be a bit out of sorts, and your dark Sicilian complexion is now a tad faded. Are you distraught about something negative that happened at choir? Did the new director quit?"

"Like you, my sinuses are acting-up due to the amount of pollen in the air," Ginger verbally returned. "Those allergy tablets we've been taking twice a day aren't as effective as Dr. Nurkiewicz's prescription had promised. Honestly John," my wife continued her lengthy explanation, "I'm beginning to lose faith in modern medicine. Maybe we should consider moving to Arizona or even New Mexico."

"I understand completely," I sympathetically commiserated. "If you can live in South Jersey through all four seasons, I insist that you and I could live anywhere. You'd think we'd have built-up sufficient immunity to combat the radical weather changes by now," I disingenuously enunciated. "If our nasal afflictions become any worse, we might need to spend the upcoming Easter holidays in Miami or West Palm Beach. And if you think the Philly Airport is too hectic," I declared, "Atlantic City features Florida economy flights to Orlando and Ft. Myers."

"Unfortunately, we can't!" my wife sadly stated. "The boys will all be home from college *that* Spring Break week and we'll have to be here to feed and entertain them."

As it turned out, all three studious sons elected to remain in their respective dorms to prepare and cram for their upcoming May final exams. In early April, the mercurial living room piano persisted in producing its random geographic melodies, of which my acute ears (and suspicious senses) were becoming adequately adjusted to appreciating.

All throughout April my ears had become so used to the unsolicited piano interruptions that when they occurred, I just remained sitting stationary inside the larger elevated den and proceeded to casually read a sports magazine or view a television comedy show. After several seconds of introspection, I would soon abandon my former activity so that my influenced mind could contemplate the memorable scenes that my memory associated with the nostalgic song being played.

On the first Thursday of the fourth month in 1992, this targeted "April Fool" was being delighted with the aforementioned piano belting-out the 1961 rock and roll classic "Bristol Stomp", which my still-healthy mind recalled had been recorded by the Dovells. My instant mental retrieval reverted back to Levittown, Pennsylvania where I had lived with my family up until 1959. My "Dogwood Hollow" friends and I would often cruise Mill Street in nearby Bristol while searching for gorgeous representatives of the opposite gender. A secluded-but-sentimental area of my brain reviewed myself as an impressionable twelve-year-old juvenile happily attending St. Mark's Elementary School on Radcliffe Street in Bristol because St. Michael the Archangel School in neighboring Levittown had not yet been completed for educational occupancy.

On the second Thursday evening in April of '92, as I was awkwardly putting-in-place the larger den's summer screens for *our* Andersen windows, I was not at all disturbed that the "player piano" in the distant living room was emanating a novel rendition of Bobby Bloom's 1970 hit titled "Montego Bay". My thought processes were magnetically distracted by the lyrics, which made me reflect on a week's vacation with Ginger at Rose Hall International Resort, conveniently situated between Montego Bay, Jamaica and Ocho Rios. I smiled upon remembering a majestic side trip we had taken by van to beautiful Negril Beach and then later having an adventurous steam locomotive train ride from the Montego Bay station up a steep mountain ridge and next chugging into the island's jungle-like interior to a rum factory located in the center of the lush rain forest.

For my sixth Thursday night musical episode, I again was sitting in the spacious upper den, this time assiduously inserting new batteries into my television's remote control. Without notice, the living room piano creatively selected the notes of "Palisades Park", which I immediately ascertained had been recorded by vocalist Freddie "Boom-Boom" Cannon in 1962. Then with a grin on my face, I fondly recalled motoring up the New Jersey Turnpike and visiting alluring Palisades Park with Hammonton friends John Kryvoruka, Jerry Tomasello and Anthony "Tatar" Bertino. 'At the amusement park, I had spent twenty dollars at a ring-toss game before I had finally won a stuffed kangaroo to present to Joanne for her birthday,' I extracted from my subconscious mind. 'The other three guys teased that I was crazy throwing-away such an extravagant sum of money, and my three friends were greatly amused when I answered their polite criticism, "Guys, what can I say; I'm madly in love!"

The yard daffodils and yellow forsythia bushes were soon blossoming and ready to bloom by the next Thursday in April. I was preoccupied in the lower den rearranging the family photos on the fireplace mantel when my receptive ears instantly identified the catchy tune "California Dreamin'", which was originally harmonized in 1966 by the Mamas and Papas. While feeling drab thinking about Big Mama Cass Elliott being deceased just like Patti Page, my ruminations defensively switched to more positive musings. My newly excavated recollection instantly traveled to the long-gone week when Ginger and I had visited our cousin Tom in Palm Springs and three days later, Joanne and I drove over to La Jolla on the Pacific and then later registered and stayed at a modest motel in downtown San Diego. Without exaggeration, the highlight of the sidebar-Segway was when the two of us nonchalantly strolled through the fantastic interior of the incomparable Hotel Del Coronado, the famed lodge being where many fabulous scenes from famous motion pictures had been filmed.

On Thursday night April 23rd, 1992, I was patiently standing in front of the kitchen sink and admiring the massive backyard pine tree limbs gracefully swaying in the late twilight breeze. Joanne had just left early for her scheduled choir rehearsal, and a minute later, (originating from the living room) I heard the instrumental melody to one of my favorite musical arrangements, "Arrivederci Roma", the eighth special recital presented by the illustrious, 'out of this world' piano. I mentally thanked the rather versatile 'living room musician' for favorably reminding me of Joanne and me vacationing a full ten days in the Eternal City and relishing the Vatican Museum, St. Peter's Basilica, the fascinating Roman Forum ruins, the Tiber River, the inimitable Pantheon, the Spanish Steps and the fantastic remains of the ancient Colosseum.

'I'm no longer apprehensive of my new friend, the mystical living room piano,' I erroneously judged. 'But I still can't tell Joanne about *our* unearthly possession. The independent-minded piano might not play a requested melody on demand, or it might be stubborn and not cooperate and entertain us one iota on any future Thursday night when Ginger's choir practice might be cancelled.'

20

* * * * * * * * * * * *

I must admonish myself for being a snobbish elitist and a hypocritical religious anarchist for the past forty years of my morally-prejudiced life. From relevant circumstances that would evolve upon Joanne returning from choir practice on the following Thursday night, my defective soul would miraculously undergo a marvelous transformation that could best be described as a cathartic, spiritual Renaissance. As a result of my interactions with the living room piano, I now passionately espouse the rigid mandates of St. Peter and his edict-oriented papal descendants. I eagerly attend Catholic Mass each and every Sunday and have absolutely astounded my wife by voluntarily joining the St. Joseph church choir as an inspired baritone. Without further digression, here is how my whole unbelievable 'soul metamorphosis' synthesized with my heart switching from sin to grace.

On Thursday night, April 23rd, I was waiting for Joanne to arrive home from her standard choral routine. My wife parked her Ford Fairlane inside the two-car garage, and soon I heard the right-side electronic door descend to the cement floor. After entering the house through the laundry room portal, Ginger appeared exceedingly exhausted, and my beloved spouse presented herself to me in a heightened, upset and agitated state of mind.

"What's the matter? Did one of your choir members pass away?" I empathized in a low, respectful, reverent tone of voice. "Clearly something bad has happened."

"I have a very important matter to tell you about that I've been withholding for several months," Joanne uttered, almost crying. "John, I'm actually scared to death."

"Okay, I'm a good listener. Take ten deep breaths and then say what's bothering you," I wisely advised. "That's what I always do when a hostile, antagonistic client screams and yells at me on the phone over a major stock market loss."

Joanne heeded my recommendation and went on to inform me that the organ in the larger elevated den was the principle source of her becoming overly distraught. According to Ginger's account, one Tuesday in March when I had been at Joe's Maplewood for a weekly Rotary Club meeting, the organ commenced playing the radio ballad "Devil or Angel" without skipping a note.

"That hit song was recorded in 1960 by Bobby Vee," I recollected and orally conveyed. "The tremendous lyrics have always been amoung my favorites."

"But John, you don't understand what I just said," Ginger announced before sobbing incessantly. "The following Tuesday the demon organ began playing 'You Are My Special Angel' without anyone's human fingers ever touching the keys. I was beginning to think that I was going insane!"

"Holy smokes," I accidentally and clumsily punned. "Bobby Helms recorded *that* smash hit back in 1957, I believe. The wonderful composition marked the revolutionary blending of country and western music with pop rhythm and blues."

"You still don't seem to understand the entire scenario!" Joanne sobbed. "The third Tuesday I recognized the organ blasting-out the notes to 'The Devil Went Down to Georgia', which was written and developed by...."

"The Charlie Daniels Band," I finished my wife's disheveled memory. "That tune first hit the charts in 1979. But I now see the disturbing pattern that's tearing at your emotions. You're laser-focused on death and punishment themes in the hereafter because of the repetitious mentioning of Satan in the three song titles."

After drinking a cup of soothing hot tea, my wife found enough courage to audaciously reveal the other Tuesday night songs that the "other world organ" had generated. Naturally, because of my generally garrulous nature, I had to comment on each selection.

"Fourth was 'Devil Woman'."

"That one is much rarer than the others, but the song was released around 1976 and was suavely done by a singer named Cliff Richard," I expounded, taking great satisfaction regarding myself as a minor twentieth century rock and roll music authority.

"And the following Tuesday the fifth number I recognized as 'Angel in the Morning'. I think that *that* was done by one of my favorite artists Juice Newton in...."

"1981," I offered, filling in the glaring blank in Ginger's recollection. "She really belted-out the powerful lyrics of *that* legendary piece. What's next?"

All the while, I was so enormously enamored with my wife's musical organ song litany that I wholly neglected to tell her about my parallel tune experiences with our very talented living room piano. "What's next?" I reiterated.

"Then there was the instrumental organ '50s number that you always like hearing on oldies radio stations when we go on long trips to either the Poconos or the Blue Ridge Mountains."

"Manhattan Spiritual, recorded in 1959", I uttered, a little too boisterously. "I could listen to that upbeat piece for an hour and not get tired of it."

"Well John; then the next Tuesday I was perturbed at hearing *that* pathetic macabre song "And When I Die" done by…."

"Blood, Sweat and Tears; it was published and issued in 1969 during the height of the anti-establishment Hippie Revolution," I academically added.

"But John, the next appalling pattern the organ played is what has frightened me the most," my addled wife intimated. "The last two Tuesdays the organ played familiar top forty songs specifically and regrettably dealing with the topic of death. The first one that frazzled my emotions I often hear promoted on the Philly oldies radio station, and I think it was done by the Eagles."

"Hotel California!" I ecstatically answered. "That's an authentic rock and roll classic that I predict will be widely listened to a hundred years from now. The story line is about a lost visitor's permanent stay at a haunted desert hotel where all of the insidious residents are ghosts, monsters and ghouls."

"And the last pitiful rendering the organ generated was 'Devil with a Blue Dress'," Joanne revealed while weeping intensely, "and John! I happened to be wearing a dark blue dress *that* night."

Just as my very upset wife terminated her startling organ-death story, the piano and the organ together eerily began playing the same introduction to George Harrison's "My Sweet Lord". Amazingly, the specter of a long-dead TV star Liberace appeared before *us* sitting upon the piano bench. Joanne and I swiftly hastened from the living room into the elevated den and *our* spellbound pupils perceived the apparition of long-dead Door's virtuoso Jim Morrison pounding the appropriate keys to "My Sweet Lord" on the now-mystifying organ. At the completion of the last verse, the pale Morrison ghost (along with the living room Liberace shade) dually initiated playing *their* rendition of Norman Greenbaum's iconic classic "Spirit in the Sky".

"Oh my God!" I impulsively shouted to my wife. "I read in the Atlantic City Press the other day that Liberace had died in 1987, and being a fanatical Jim Morrison and Doors fan, I've memorized the fact that Morrison died in a Paris bathtub on July 3rd, 1971. Joanne," I nervously persisted, "I'm not Nostradamus or Edgar Cayce, but I honestly think that Liberace and Jim Morrison's apparitions are trying to alert us that our lives are presently in some kind of grave jeopardy. We have to get out of this house fast before some obscure tragedy eliminates us from this Earth!"

"John, I think I smell gas!" At that moment Joanne's legs were pathetically paralyzed from fright, and for several pregnant seconds, my lower appendages were equally petrified. Soon we gained the necessary fortitude to frantically sprint through the laundry room and exit into the garage.

With dispatch, I violently pressed the wall button to raise the rear paneled door. I quickly backed my white Chevy Impala onto the newly surfaced asphalt driveway, and after Joanne entered the vehicle on the passenger side, without exhibiting any measurable hesitation, I electronically lowered the garage door and almost spontaneously sped around the home's oval driveway. And after realizing that we had safely escaped suspected danger, I neurotically made a right-hand turn and anxiously accelerated the Impala onto Central Avenue.

Arriving in downtown Hammonton, I navigated my cherished automobile into the 7-Eleven convenience store parking lot, which is strategically situated for business on normally busy Bellevue Avenue. I stopped my Impala and remained stationary with my car facing east. Joanne and I each inhaled a few deep breaths after experiencing *our* rather exasperating "haunted house" ordeal. Acknowledging that we had luckily escaped diabolical terror, my spouse and I next discussed what had recently transpired with our "other world" living room piano and with our arcane "other world" upper den organ.

"I think that *my* living room encounters with the outlandish piano music represented *our past,*" I hypothesized and communicated, "and Joanne, I believe that your interactions with the unworldly den organ were symbolic portrayals, each one illustrating *our present* spiritual situation."

"Well John, what about the *future?* What were Liberace and Jim Morrison's specters attempting to communicate to us by together playing 'My Sweet Lord' and 'Spirit in the Sky'? I didn't know that Jim Morrison could play the organ," my wife astutely remarked. "I thought that he only was the talented lead singer of the Doors."

"Morrison must've learned how to play the organ from Ray Mazarek while *he* was still alive," I replied, my frayed mind still in an extreme muddled quandary.

My erratic brain felt an urgency to honor a sudden impulse. I turned-on the car radio dial and Ginger and I (still scared out of our wits) listened to the first few lines of a now-obscure '50s hit "This Old House" sung by Rosemary Clooney.

"This old house once knew his children
This old house once knew his wife
This old house was home and comfort
As they fought the storm of life
This old house once rang with laughter
This old house heard many shouts
Now he trembles in the darkness
When the lightnin' walks about
Ain't gonna' need this house no longer
Ain't gonna' need this house no
more..."

Right that moment a mammoth distant explosion originating a half-mile away (from Central Avenue) brilliantly illuminated the night sky; the powerful blast forming a bright, red semi-circular glow. That resounding gas detonation constituted the true genesis of me again becoming a devout churchgoer, even vigorously practicing modern-day religion to the extent of willfully joining St. Joseph Church's piano and organ-led choir.

"Realty Reality"

In April of 1966, elementary school teacher Rita Grasso married insurance salesman Rocco Costa in St. Joseph Catholic Church, North Third Street, Hammonton, NJ. In April of 1968, Rita's sister and elementary school teacher Arlene Grasso (in duplicate fashion) married former Air Force Sergeant and present construction company foreman Vincent Bartolone at the same St. Joseph Church. Both wedding receptions were held and celebrated at Buena Vista Country Club in nearby Buena.

The ecstatic Grasso sisters were the daughters of Henry and Laura Grasso, who co-owned a farm-related business that aggressively sold fertilizer, tractors, crop sprayers, vegetable seeds along with blueberry and peach packaging supplies to various growers in the Hammonton-Vineland area. Henry and Laura were prudent partners with David and Emily Grasso, "Dave" being "Hank's" younger, envious brother. However, complicating matters, entrepreneurial Hank Grasso had built a profitable strip mall alongside his two-story Dutch colonial home situated on Route 30, also locally known as the White Horse Pike. The prosperous, popular shopping center soon materialized into a major bone of contention between brothers Hank and David, whose wife Emily Grasso especially resented Henry and Laura's exclusive ownership of the mini-mall, mainly since the sibling-rivalry brothers were fifty-fifty proprietors only of the farm products regional distribution enterprise.

In June of 1975 Hank and Laura's commonplace, two-story Dutch colonial residence was forcefully broken into while the middle-aged couple was preoccupied in the upstairs bedroom dressing and preparing to drive thirty miles east to an Atlantic City casino for a night of revelry and entertainment. Laura was wickedly gagged with a dirty handkerchief stuffed in her mouth, and then the hysterical woman's hands were cruelly tied with a telephone cord to the second floor bannister. In the meantime, Hank was viciously pistol-whipped with three strong blows to his head while having trouble remembering and revealing the exact combination to the bedroom wall safe, which was situated and concealed behind a wall painting of the nearby Grasso Strip Mall. A total of fifteen thousand dollars in crisp Ben Franklin bills along with thirty-five thousand-dollars' worth of expensive diamond rings, ruby pendants, emerald bracelets, sapphire brooches and pearl necklaces were greedily heisted by the four vile masked intruders.

After the brazen armed robbery, Laura became exceedingly paranoid about living and staying in the white Dutch colonial home, and the sometimes-delirious wife had recurrent nightmares about her recent horrible misadventure. The local and State Police were never notified of the terrifying robbery because Hank feared that the bad publicity that would be reported in Atlantic and Camden County newspapers would soon get the attention of an intensive IRS audit investigation, the potential probe seeking skimmed cash being kept secret from the infallible scrutiny of the always-avaricious federal government.

"Hank, who do you suppose had the audacity to commit such a brutal, life-threatening home invasion?" Laura asked her beleaguered husband three days after the major larceny had occurred. "We could've both been killed!"

"To be honest, I think it was Tony "the Brain" DeMarco's gang," Hank replied. "Tony and I were good friends back during the latter 1920 days of Prohibition, and we often took turns driving trucks hauling cheap bootleg whiskey from barn and field stills that were illegally operating on Hammonton farms; both of us were merely trying to make some extra cash during the harsh, difficult winters. Times were really tough back then if you may recall."

"But if you and Tony DeMarco were once loyal friends, why would he now plan such a violent assault and theft on us, right in our own home? That frenetic home invasion was absolutely atrocious!"

"I understand that Tony has a terminal case of cancer and doesn't have long to live," Hank convincingly explained. "His nefarious subordinates have taken over his illicit activities. Those dangerous thugs are ruthless, especially in the Egg Harbor City area."

"I see. The lesser hoodlums are now enacting their misdeeds independent of Tony the Brain. But how did the despicable hitmen know that we had ample cash and jewelry stashed in our bedroom?" the wife wanted to know. "Their out-of-control treachery almost killed both you and me."

"Our spiteful sister-in-law Emily has a vile black-sheep cousin named Frankie "the Whale" Giordano," Henry conjectured and quickly related. "I suspect that either my brother David or his jealous wife Emily, or perhaps both of them had intentionally or accidentally spilled the beans to Frankie," the spouse paused and then resumed his theory. "And next, corpulent Giordano probably organized the coordinated raid on our place without ever getting permission from poor ailing Tony DeMarco. Now Laura, I plan on turning our home-sweet-home into a well-protected fort with a high fence around it;

28

and also, I think I'll be having three vicious Doberman pinschers fanatically patrolling the property's circumference."

"Oh Hank, I'm really afraid of spending another day living in this house where I had been so brutally attacked," Laura Grasso mournfully admitted. "Not even three months in Florida could soothe my frayed and frazzled nerves! And quite frankly, I really miss admiring my beautiful jewelry!"

"Honey, I called Tony DeMarco yesterday on the phone and pleaded that I want your precious jewelry returned."

"And what did your old Prohibition era friend say?"

"The Brain claimed that he had nothing to do with the gruesome larceny, and Tony informed me that he had heard on the syndicate grapevine that your jewelry has already been fenced for cash," the husband sadly articulated. "And if I unwisely replace the gems, Mr. DeMarco believes that there's a good chance that the new precious stones will also be stolen."

"Oh Hank, I absolutely dread living and sleeping in this accursed house another hour," Laura quite candidly confided. "Can't you do something to calm my anxiety? I don't care if it's drastic. Just please do something!"

"I'll tell you what we'll do!" Henry answered, acknowledging an idea that suddenly entered his troubled head. "As you know, our younger daughter Arlene and her husband Vince are building a nice rancher across 'the Pike' that is nestled next to the pond. The gorgeous setting is pretty relaxing and quite peaceful. We'll just swap houses with Arlene and Vince. This Dutch colonial has four bedrooms, and it's enough to accommodate at least three children. And the rancher being constructed across the highway has only three bedrooms, just enough for us and for an occasional relative or friends who wants to stay overnight."

The attractive, under-construction rancher featured a meandering, S-shaped asphalt driveway that marvelously curved its path through eye-appealing clusters of rhododendron, hydrangea, lilac and red-rose bushes. Six circular "treatments" of yellow lilies also embellished the rancher's placid entranceway. Adding to the pleasant landscape, an array of oak, elm, tulip and maple shade trees handsomely bordered the dark green lawn, which majestically sloped-down next to the somnolent, tranquil pond. The well-manicured grass was also well-positioned along the elevated opposite side of the perfectly level driveway.

In September of 1976, Hank's proposed real estate transactions were completed, and Mrs. Laura Grasso then felt much more comfortable functioning in her newly-constructed, exquisite one-story abode. Distress gradually abandoned the woman's psyche, and the formerly distraught woman's mental and physical existence once again became acquainted with necessary serenity and tranquility. The tormented woman's life seemed worth living once more.

* * * * * * * * * * * *

The year 1990 was marked by two noteworthy events dominating the lives of now-elderly Henry and Laura Grasso. First of all, the formerly notorious mobster Tony "the Brain" DeMarco finally died of a lethal combination of lung and pancreatic cancer. Secondly, Tony's erratic and defiant henchman Frankie "the Whale" Giordano clandestinely purchased twelve acres of land that was adjacent to "the Pond", and ironically the new acquisition was inconveniently located five-hundred feet behind Hank and Laura's formerly isolated rancher. Naturally, Henry and Laura were extremely bewildered by the unexpected development, but Hank quietly told his wife that he would not try interfering (in an effort) to stop Frankie the Whale from renting his land to the neighboring Chinese growers.

"Hank, I just read in the real estate section of the Atlantic City Press that our sister-in-law's Mafia cousin Frankie Giordano has obtained twelve acres of land existing directly in back of our rancher," the wife lamented and verbally conveyed in a melancholy tone of voice. "It reports in the newspaper that the deplorable swindler has bought the nearby ground from retired peach and vegetable farmer Daniel Donio for a meager forty-thousand dollars. But Hank, I really feel sorry for David and Emily. Your' brother and sister-in-law truly must regret having such a wicked, heartless criminal flourishing his disgusting evil from within their family."

"You can choose your friends but not your relatives," Hank philosophized and stated in the form of an overused cliche. "I drove yesterday to the Winslow Township tax office and did some basic research. I found that Frankie's deed has an easement in the rear that's touching Wiltsey Mills Road."

"Wiltsey Mills Road?" Laura wondered and asked. "Where on Earth is that? I've lived in the Hammonton vicinity all of my life and I've never heard that name before."

"Yes Honey. That's the new name of the road in Winslow Township, Camden County. The same road in Hammonton, Atlantic County is more familiarly known to us as Third Street. But more importantly as a matter of great concern," Hank emphasized and resumed his relevant narrative, "Frankie the Whale owns a substantial twelve acres of ground that abuts our dozen acres; but ours is nine acres on this side of the pond and the other three acres are located on the Camden or west side."

"Excluding the lot where our ranch home is, we rent most of our twelve aces to the ambitious Chinese farmers," Laura logically declared. "They grow bok-choy and other exotic Oriental vegetables that they ship to wholesale markets in New York and Philly. In many respects, the mannerly Chinese are much better neighbors than villainous Frankie 'the Whale' Giordano could ever be!"

"That special agricultural use saves us a bit of tax money because Winslow Township has assessed our fields as being farmland, and our land is not evaluated as residential real estate," Hank accurately added to the conversation. "I wonder if *that* corrupt crook 'Frankie the Whale' also intends to rent his land to the Chinese."

The advent of the new century after Y2K saw the swift demise of the Prohibition-Depression-World War II "greatest generation" throughout the Hammonton and Winslow Township area, and also all across the United States. In March of 2001, covetous Emily Grasso died after suffering a long battle against colon cancer, and her husband David perished in June of 2003 after experiencing a massive heart seizure. And in October of 2005, strong-willed Henry Grasso finally succumbed to being progressively vanquished by Parkinson's disease at age ninety, and then finally in January of 2006 Laura Grasso, being heartbroken at the passing of her late beloved husband "Hank", slowly perished at age eighty-eight from general old age symptoms in a geriatric facility in Hammonton.

With Henry and Laura now being deceased and buried in Hammonton's Oak Grove Cemetery, the decades-long rivalry between the two Grasso brothers and their respective combative wives ceased, but the emerging threat of conflict between next generation Rocco and Rita Costa and Vincent and Arlene Bartolone had become extremely palpable. Arlene had contracted MS in the early 1970s and by the year 2016, the afflicted woman was virtually bedridden. Arguments and tensions between the Costa and Bartolone female heirs and their spouses dominated the family's "hostile relationship", especially in regard to the settlement of Laura Grasso's estate. The wise maxim "Greed is the root of all evil" was certainly proving its ugly veracity.

In her Last Will and Testament, Laura Grasso, fearing that her son-in-law "Vince" would eventually place daughter Arlene as a patient in a nearby nursing home, stipulated in her "final thoughts" that older daughter Rita would be in charge of distributing monthly money amounts to cover her younger sister's medical expenses and essential home care. Vincent vehemently protested ever abiding by *that* particular clause in Laura Grasso's will, so being intimidated by her brother-in-law's perpetual hostile objections, Rita Costa agreed to obtaining an important change in the will's exact language. CPA/Attorney Thomas Jarvis filed for "a waiver" from the State of New Jersey to allow for the modification in Laura's "final wishes", and *that* lengthy, bureaucratic procedure materializing in Trenton required over a full year to complete.

The total inheritance after providing estate taxes to the state and federal governments amounted to a respectable 5.7 million dollars, which subsequently included the liquidation of the farm equipment and packaging business along with the adequate sale of the still-thriving Grasso Strip Mall. Also, in another a matter of significance, after Henry Grasso had died, the ranch home's deed had not been transferred to Hank's surviving spouse Laura, so *that* fundamental obstacle oversight had created another legal caveat in the successful dispensation of Mrs. Laura Grasso's estate. Finally, female beneficiaries Rita Costa and MS-stricken Arlene Bartolone's bank CDs were readily distributed because those financial entities existed outside of Laura Grasso's will.

Henry and Laura Grasso's hundred-fifty acres of fertile farmland located between Walker and Oak Road could now be sold to the neighboring Chinese farmers for the sum of 1.5 million dollars, and the magnificently landscaped ranch home situated next to the White Horse Pike pond could be put-up for sale for a tidy four-hundred-thousand dollar asking price. The three-room bungalow rapidly became a matter of contention between the Costa and Bartolone families because Laura Grasso had specifically stated in her Last Will and Testament that her elder daughter Rita should exclusively inherit the residence-in-question.

But despite all of the inherent family controversy regarding Laura Grasso's complicated (and originally discriminatory) will, the prospect of inevitable future strife with neighboring gangster landowner Frankie "the Whale" Giordano seemed a definite real estate reality haunting the ever-suspicious minds of Rita and Rocco Costa.

* * * * * * * * * * * *

The all-too-familiar charming pond adjacent to the "Laura Grasso rancher" did not belong to either Rocco and Rita Costa or to notorious Frankie "the Whale" Giordano. Since the fifty-foot-wide narrow body of water was a free-flowing stream that meandered both above and below ground from Winslow Township and then through Hammonton all the way to the Jersey pinelands and the Mullica River twelve miles to the northeast, the State of New Jersey actually owned the in-motion creek under a rare legal statute esoterically titled Riparian Water Rights.

From Friday, April 14th to Sunday the 16th of 2007 a wicked Nor'easter pounded the Middle Atlantic States, and the Hammonton-Winslow Township region was severely deluged with nearly eight inches of torrential rain, which had created massive flooding. The picturesque pond next to the superb rancher had overflowed its banks, with the darkish water advancing-up to the serpentine asphalt driveway. In addition, the heavy inundation had prominently drenched the vulnerable three-acre "Chinese vegetable field" on the opposite side of the landmark creek. At ten a.m. on April 16th Rita and Rocco engaged in an impromptu conversation inside their 699 North White Horse Pike home's kitchen.

"Rocky, I heard you get out of bed around six this morning, and then you abruptly left the house. Did you bravely drive over to the local WaWa convenience store for a cup of coffee and a Danish?"

"No, Rita. The savage storm was really horrendous and we were lucky to still have power and have our landline and cell phones working," the husband remembered and politely stated. "I drove across the street to your Mom's rancher to inspect the property for any damages. A few shade trees were down in the back yard, but overall tree and shrub wreckage was not-at-all extensive."

"Did the pond overflow and drown-out the rhododendron and hydrangea bushes? That would be my principal worry. Mom positively loved her shrubs and flowers!"

"No, fortunately for us the water surge stopped just short of touching the bushes," the man of the house disclosed. "But as you may recall, Frankie Giordano has a small dingy moored to a wooden mail box post several hundred feet down the free-flowing stream behind your Mom's rancher's boundary line. The decrepit old boat somehow had drifted from its post and then floated all the way past the bungalow. The renegade aluminum skiff eventually wound-up positioned sideways, resting against the cement culvert going under Route 30."

"That explains why the New Jersey State Highway Department keeps the culvert clear of debris resulting from serious storms. You managed to beat the highwaymen to the culvert before they could ever begin cleaning-out the branches and snags. But what about the shabby old rowboat? Was the dilapidated thing still salvageable?"

"Apparently, the strong winds along with the high-water rise had dislodged the boat's rope from its flimsy mooring," Rocco revealed, "so I immediately called our brother-in-law Vince, who as you know likes SCUBA diving and occasionally goes snorkeling in the Egg Harbor River and also in the Atlantic. I told Vinnie to bring along his canoe paddle. The rowboat had two oars for me to use."

"I'm surprised that Vince would help you in such a sudden unplanned rescue mission!" Rita replied. "But I must confess. Our volatile and impetuous brother-in-law takes very good care of my ailing sister."

"Our 'volatile and impetuous' brother-in-law told me that he is perfectly willing to let bygones be bygones ever since learning that he and Arlene are to get their inheritance money promptly in one lump sum. Both Vince and your sister now appreciate the fact that you had filed a waiver to release half of your Mom's inherited stock and bond portfolio for their benefit instead of you, being the executor of your mother's will, allowing monthly installments that had initially been designated to pay for your sister's care and general health maintenance."

Then Rocco proceeded to describe in detail precisely how Vince had jumped into the eight-foot-deep water with his goggles and snorkel apparatus intact and how the junior aquanaut had deftly guided the renegade "dinky-dinghy" back to the eastside pond embankment. The pair of volunteers then stepped inside the primitive mode of transportation and awkwardly rowed and paddled the archaic boat back seven-hundred feet to its singular home-base on Frankie Giordano's property. The repossessed object was next swiftly tethered to its mooring mailbox pole by Vince, who then instinctively submerged into the dark water and fastened the second shorter rowboat rope to an underwater tree stump, where the wayward dinghy had probably previously been tied, judging by of the length of the shorter second rope.

Rocco and Vince together reasoned that the two ropes had become detached when the pond water had ascended to a height of four-feet above normal depth; apparently, the loops that had secured the rowboat to its two terminal points had raised above the mailbox post and also above the underwater vertical tree root. Consequently, the boat became loosened, and it soon separated from its two improvised hitching points.

"Obviously Rocky, when Frankie will check his little Winslow Township woodsy empire for storm damage later today," Rita plausibly assumed and summarized, "he'll never for one second realize that his precious dinghy had broken free earlier this morning and had drifted all-the-way-down to the culvert running under the Pike. You and Vince are to be congratulated for secretly performing a Good Samaritan job well-done."

The husband-wife dialogue was suddenly interrupted when the kitchen wall phone shrilly rang. CPA/Lawyer Thomas Jarvis was on the other end ready to convey some rather startling news.

"Hi Tom," Rocco commenced his salutation. "Missed you at the Lions Club meeting last Tuesday. Did you get much storm damage yesterday and early this morning? We just have a few trees down; one white pine and two oaks were uprooted. Of course, there's the usual branches and limbs scattered on the ground that need some gathering and removal."

"Only three roof shingles and two lengths of vinyl siding," Tom announced. "Other than that, everything else seems copesetic."

"Well then, what's up?" Rocco curiously inquired. "You ordinarily make your business calls on weekdays and not on Saturday or Sunday."

"I suggest that you sit-down and grab ahold of your chair," Jarvis emphatically recommended. "Yesterday at noon, I endured the heavy downpour and ventured over to the Hammonton Post Office to check my mailbox. Much to my surprise, I had received a letter from none other than that insufferable rogue Frankie 'the Whale' Giordano. Momentarily, I was in total shock."

"Does the worthless punk want to sue me for once trespassing upon his cherished property behind Rita's Mom's rancher? I wouldn't put such a shenanigan apart from the wily thug! I was only pursuing Rita's runaway house cat."

"Not exactly," Jarvis indulgently laughed. "Believe it or not, Giordano wants to buy your inherited home for a plump four hundred thousand bucks. He indicates in his typed letter that he desires to purchase the abode for his one and only deadbeat son. But honestly Rocky, I wonder if his purchasing money has been legitimately earned."

"But the only improvement to the rancher was putting-on a new roof, which was added a half-year before my father-in-law died," Rocco Costa recollected and related. "There needs to be at least a hundred thousand dollars-worth of repairs and renovations to be done. For example," the recipient of the phone call divulged, "the entire place needs new hardwood floors, new front entrance doors, new cabinets and new floor tile in the kitchen, and the 1970s wallpaper and accompanying walnut paneling both in the den and in the office has to be stripped-off the walls. And finally, Tom," the astonished son-in-law honestly vociferated, "the outside light-brown barnboard siding is faded and needs to be refreshed. And oh yes; let's not forget that the whole place truly requires brand-new rain gutters. Is slippery Frankie Giordano fully aware of these numerous maintenance problems?"

"Yes Rocky, and the portly Sicilian guy wishes to meet you and Rita in my Fairview Avenue office at ten-thirty this coming Wednesday morning to have a preliminary discussion about him procuring Mrs. Grasso's former home. Needless to say, our little rendezvous should prove quite interesting! I've notified your real estate friend Jim Perna to also sit-in and to give legal input."

"Okay Tom. Rita and I will be there. I only hope and trust that this whole matter we're discussing is not some sort of colossal hoax! Starting with my wife's parents, Mafia punk Frankie Giordano has caused hundreds of other South Jersey victims a ton of grief."

* * * * * * * * * * * *

At quarter past ten on Wednesday morning Rocco drove his new pearl white Lexus SUV out of his two-car garage. Both the man-behind the wheel and his stoic-minded wife were busily exchanging views about their hastily scheduled meeting with reputable CPA/Lawyer Thomas Jarvis, with established real estate broker James Perna and with local junkyard tycoon and infamous syndicate scoundrel Frankie "the Whale" Giordano. As the impressive automobile exited the two-story home's U-shaped driveway onto four-lane Route 30, some pertinent observations were shared between the classy vehicle's inquisitive occupants.

"It's rather weird that our home is only five hundred feet east of Mom's rancher," Rita prefaced, "yet we live across the Pike in Hammonton and Mom and Dad had lived next to the pond in Winslow Township."

"Not exactly true," Rocco clarified. "Our side porch is in Camden County and the remainder of our home is situated in Atlantic. Your parents owned a hundred feet of ground in Hammonton that no one ever knew about. Fortunately for us, your

Dad was influential among the local tax assessors back in the 1970s, so Old Hank arranged that we would buy another hundred feet of his frontage in Winslow Township to form an acceptable building lot existing in the two jurisdictions. Actually," the husband stressed, "our side porch is in Camden County and the rest of our dwelling is in Hammonton," the driver accurately reviewed. "Our friend Chris Dobbins was the surveyor who had discovered Hank's hundred-foot Hammonton section, upon which your parents had never paid taxes. So, both political entities were happy to receive *our* new-found tax revenues."

"Now I remember," the wife confirmed. "All of that legal maneuvering occurred in the early '70s before the Pinelands Preservation Act became law. It could never happen in *this* hectic day and age. The Environmental Commission would never approve of our two-county deed. Thank goodness we are grandfathered-in!"

The on-a-mission driver headed east in the direction of Atlantic City, but upon reaching the traffic light at the Fairview Avenue WaWa convenience store, Rocco made a right-hand turn onto the congested thoroughfare. After her husband had negotiated the "hard turn", the garrulous wife continued their conversation.

"I still remember how Mom and Dad suspected Aunt Emily's thug cousin Frankie Giordano as being responsible for robbing them back in 1975 during a wild and violent breaking and entering. Mom's mental health carried emotional scars for many years after that ghastly incident. Honestly Rocky, I feel very uncomfortable selling Mom's rancher to a genuine Mafia hood who had assaulted and robbed her, causing *my* family such great emotional adversity."

"Honey, you're one hundred percent correct. Giordano is a four-hundred-pound fat slob who is a certified menace to human civilization. If you recall, in the '70s, Frankie was associated with Tony 'the Brain' DeMarco's gang of dangerous small-time creeps. Our mercurial backyard neighbor Mr. Giordano is certainly no model citizen by any stretch of the imagination. In my opinion, we're just showing-up at today's meeting out of courtesy for my friends Tom Jarvis and Jim Perna. Here's the Third and Fairview light just ahead," Rocco alertly uttered before skillfully navigating his expensive Lexus into the CPA/Lawyer's parking lot. "Look Rita, over to your left! There's our bully nemesis's black Chevy Suburban parked near the office's main entry. We're gonna' see Frankie the Whale in the flesh; I mean in a lot of flesh!"

After entering the brown-brick building and being cordially recognized and accepted by secretary Janet Adamucci, the new arrivals were then escorted through a side portal leading into the straight-shooting attorney's bailiwick where obese Frankie Giordano had already been seated at an enormous oval conference table alongside James Perna.

"Welcome aboard," greeted Tom Jarvis. "I presume you two already know Frankie and Jim."

"Yes, certainly!" Rocco replied with a casual wave of his right hand. "Jim served with me on the Hammonton Board of Education, and Mr. Giordano happens to be a distant relative of my wife's now-deceased Aunt Emily. Everyone who is third generation in the Hammonton area is somehow related in one respect or another!"

"Won't you two find a pair of chairs so that our little parley can commence," the CPA host amiably suggested. "This introductory session should take less than an hour, and we should wrap-up all of the vital details by noon."

After several minutes of small-talk minutia, the high-standards' accountant advised that the principal participants should "get-down to brass tacks". "That pond next to the rancher is a fluid stream that flows above and underground from Winslow Township all the way to the Mullica River," CPA Tom Jarvis professionally began the group consultation. "The water rights really belong to the State of New Jersey, but the twelve acres that Mrs. Costa has inherited from her mother Laura will soon officially be *her* property. Nine acres including the rancher are on the eastern Hammonton side of the pond, and the remaining three acres are located on the Camden County western side. Now Frankie, are you' fully aware of *those* geographic and legal details that *I've* just outlined. If you have any questions, please offer them now!"

"Yes, I learned about those special facts when I had purchased from Daniel Donio the back tract of land that also borders the pond," Giordano proudly declared. "I happen to like water, and the available rancher is about the only quiet property around that's located near a creek or lake."

"You have very good taste, Mr. Giordano," commented real estate broker James Perna. "I've performed a credit check on you and apparently, you're quite qualified to purchase Mrs. Costa's splendid ranch home."

After James Perna's loud uttering of those rather complimentary words (which evidently represented a verbal signal), three Hammonton policemen with weapons drawn unexpectedly burst through the side entry door into the spacious office. The law enforcers spontaneous intrusion had alarmed and frightened everyone in the room except already knowledgeable Tom Jarvis and James Perna.

"Okay Frankie, put your hands up!" commanded Captain Jake Frederico while brandishing a sophisticated rifle aimed at the well-known area culprit. "You're under arrest."

"I'll get his gun," volunteered Lieutenant Ted Slimm. "Ah, here it is inside the shoulder holster."

"What's this silly fiasco all about?" Frankie demanded knowing. "Are you three idiots rehearsing for next year's high school play?"

"Sergeant Santora, please read to Mr. Giordano his sacred Miranda Rights. Go ahead Eddie."

> "You have the right to remain silent. Anything you say can be used against you in a court of law. You have the right to speak to a lawyer for advice before we ask you any questions. You have the right to have an attorney with you during questioning. If you cannot afford a lawyer, one will be appointed for you before any questioning, if you wish. If you decide to answer questions now without a lawyer present, you have the right to stop answering at any time."

"This set-up scam is an insult to my dignity. I ain't answerin' nothin' until I have my lawyer present," Frankie prodigiously insisted. "This trick is a freakin' abuse of police authority. I'll report you all to the Human Civil Rights Commission."

"We've been after you Frankie for over a decade," Captain Frederico verified, "and now we're gonna' take you into custody and have you transferred over to the Winslow Township Police Department. Sorry we had to startle the daylights out of *you* folks sitting there, but this was the perfect opportunity for us to successfully apprehend dastardly Mr. Giordano," apologized the head arresting officer to Rita and Rocco.

"I'll sue the pants off of your whole lousy department," threatened and boomed Giordano. "You're making a false arrest. None of you' moronic pansies are a witness to anything that I've never done wrong!" Frankie nastily maintained. "You still haven't given me the charge? Make an accusation, damn it! This ain't Russia, ya' know! What's the damned charge?"

"Patrolman Colasurdo, please carry-in the abundant evidence that's been gleaned," Captain Jake Frederico sternly bellowed. "Mr.

Giordano, I want you to know that this coming demonstration of reliable proof will afford me great law enforcement pleasure."

Young Officer Ken Colasurdo obeyed Captain Frederico's direct order and gingerly entered the conference room carrying a fairly large three-dimensional black metal container. The patrolman next gently placed the extraordinary-looking item squarely upon the center of the huge, mahogany, oval conference table. Much to Frankie Giordano's utter shock and dismay, Captain Frederico meticulously opened the large metallic box, and the high-ranking cop soon provided his still-awed audience with a fantastically spectacular dissertation.

"Officer Colasurdo, please gently remove the black waterproof container's contents for our general inspection." After the patrolman complied with the Captain's exceptional request, Jake Frederico competently explained that the container held five hundred thousand bucks in hundred-dollar bills, or "five thousand Benjamins." Besides the lucrative cash cache, the black container also held eight half-kilo bags of cocaine, each one having five hundred grams (17 ounces) of the deadly illicit powder.

"There's enough physical evidence hear to indict and convict you Mr. Giordano of flagrant drug-pushing and of the illegal possession of lethal contraband. And I'm sure that the IRS and the FBI will want to get in on analyzing your many fraudulent criminal activities, too! Now Frankie, there's no doubt in my mind that you're egregiously guilty of practicing Interstate drug trafficking and also of committing blatant money laundering! Uncle Sam doesn't like *that* stuff! Today's revelations are only the beginning of a series of racketeering investigations that'll certainly bleed-over to implicating your numerous Mafia cohorts and colleagues!"

"This is entrapment! My lawyers will get me off the hook in no time!" Frankie angrily predicted. "Defense attorneys make plenty more money than prosecutors do because they're much smarter about legal technicalities. I've been set-up; plain and simple! You amateur cops aren't even good enough to be cartoon detectives!"

"Escort Mr. Giordano to the patrol car that just pulled-into the parking area!" ordered Captain Frederico to his four loyal subordinates. "Ken you drive, and Ted, you'll ride along and serve as security. It's a good thing we had hidden our two squad cars behind the rug and tile business across the street."

"This is outrageous! It's totally absurd! Where are you uniformed jerks taking me!" Frankie yelled. "I'm being framed!"

"You're being arrested and conducted to the Winslow Township Police Department over on Route 73," Captain Frederico calmly communicated. "Chief Barnes knows all about your planned arrival. And Frankie; you'll also have a chance to consult with your expert defense attorneys while behind bars. We've taken the time to notify your team of lawyers, also! Put the cuffs on our belligerent guest Ken and remove our enraged prisoner from these premises!"

* * * * * * * * * * * *

After the Hammonton policemen adroitly escorted Frankie "the Whale" Giordano out of the CPA/Lawyer's black leather chaired conference room along with the replenished black, metal evidence chest, the four seated individuals bartered remarks about the uncommon events that had recently transpired. The accountant, after regaining his full composure from "the Whale's" recent arrest, was first to make a remark.

"Wow! That whole thing went according to Hoyle!" Tom Jarvis praised and lavishly evaluated. "Mr. Giordano got caught with both his chubby hands stuck inside the cookie jar. I'm glad I had the opportunity to witness justice in action!"

"And thanks for having me participate in this magnificent ruse," real estate broker James Perna congratulated and asserted. "This definitely was more exciting than watching Al Capone, Bugs Moran, Lucky Luciano and Ma Barker being taken into custody on *The Untouchables* cable TV reruns!"

"We didn't even have to cast aspersions on Frankie Giordano's faulty character!" a very euphoric Rocco Costa objectively opined. "The overwhelming evidence actually prevented 'the Whale' from being able to clumsily brag and nervously disparage himself. I speculate that the black container holding the hundred-dollar bills and the plastic cocaine bags could eventually lead to breaking-up the whole Mafia network that's been operating over the years with almost complete impunity in Hammonton and vicinity."

"Okay, now that the police have arrested Mr. Giordano," Tom Jarvis reiterated to his shell-shocked audience of three, "we'll now mull over how this entire escapade unfolded. I still think that there are several missing pieces to this intricate jigsaw puzzle."

"But how did the black box with the laundered money and the cocaine bags come into the picture?" wondered and asked Rita Costa. "Rocky, you never disclosed to me *that* unique aspect of today's peculiar meeting with Frankie?"

Rocco confidently described to his three listeners that after he and his brother-in-law Vince Bartolone had rowed and paddled Giordano's runaway dinghy from the White Horse Pike culvert back to its mooring on "the Whale's" pond embankment, "Vinnie", wearing his wetsuit, first attached the longer rope (tied to the left oarlock) to the old mailbox post that had been cemented into the ground. Next, Bartolone donned his diving goggles and then expertly submerged into the murky pond water with the second shorter rope. In several seconds, the athletic brother-in-law surfaced and after diving again, very capably re-tethered the second shorter rope to the opposite right oarlock. After doing *that* job, the diver went down a third time and proceeded to connect the looped end to an underwater two-foot-high tree stump, thus completing the clever reattachment scheme that would capably present to the unsuspicious hefty Mafia inspector a contrived scenario where nothing out of the ordinary had ever occurred.

"There usually is plenty of algae floating at Frankie's end of the pond due to the fact that the general water level back there is usually on the average only four-foot-deep," added Rocco. "The more-shallow the water, the more sunlight penetrates down to the bottom. As a result of this natural scientific process, algae growth thrives and multiplies, and ultimately, over time, it rises to the surface. But the formidable Nor'easter had dispersed the clogged-together algae and later allowed Vinnie to easily tie the ropes to their original positions," Costa theorized and shared. "The black metal container had become separated from its underwater anchor point when the pond level rose from four-foot to eight feet deep during the fierce Nor'easter. The rise of the water level also made the other rope loop move above the wooden mail box post and then naturally detach."

"Ha, ha, ha," guffawed real estate broker Jim Perna. "If Frankie had been less frugal and had shrewdly invested in heavy-duty metal chains instead of getting cheap hemp at Wal*Mart or at Home Depot, his disobedient dinghy would've never drifted afloat, dragging the metal box all the way past your rancher to Route 30! The wooden tub was like a miniature tugboat! Ha, ha, ha!" the real estate broker again loudly laughed. "Even an inexpensive marina store anchor would've served the simple purpose of better securing the ramshackle rowboat. It never pays for a doltish, dunce-headed ignoramus the ilk of Frankie G. to be overly parsimonious, ya' know! Ha, ha, ha!"

"Well, something's definitely missing here," insisted and declared Rita Costa as the abbreviated male levity simmered-down.

"This is what I don't, pardon the expression, *fathom*. How was the black metal box connected to the dinghy if you previously said that it had been fastened to the tree stump below the surface?"

"You're perceptively right," admitted Rocco after Tom Jarvis and Jim Perna ceased their incessant laughter at Rita Costa's humorous-but-inadvertent pun. "Vince and I soon detected a circular, dark-painted metal ring that Frankie G. had welded onto the black box," related Rocky. "The second oarlock's thinner rope had been tied through and then around the welded ring several times in a sailor's knot, and next, the same narrow second rope again was tethered to the underwater tree stump ten foot from the side bank. When the second rope freed itself from the tree stump, probably after the first longer rope had escaped the resistance of the mailbox post on the pond bank, the old rowboat pulled the whole kit and caboodle downstream all the way to the culvert running under the Pike. The old skiff always was resting right in the center of the pond, which was the deepest depth that would conceal the black metal box from a stranger's incidental discovery. The heavy black box was sort-of its own anchor. That's precisely why the longer oarlock rope was used while being attached to the mailbox pole and then extending the entire distance to the pond's middle," Rita's husband concluded and assessed. "Of course, Frankie's little boat was too large to enter the concrete culvert's opening, so his tawdry 'cruise ship' also served as an obstacle limiting the amount of water flow under the highway."

Changing the subject of discussion, CPA/Lawyer Thomas Jarvis then persuasively made a rather surprising, unorthodox commentary. "I've prepared a legal affidavit for sleazy Frankie Giordano to sign while in jail. Mrs. Janet Adamucci will serve as the valid Public Notary and Jim here will be the signing witness. I believe that the reprehensible fellow just arrested will cooperate with my proposal within a month."

"What is the language included in the legal statement?" Rita inquired. "This real estate deal is becoming more fascinating and intriguing with each passing moment. Is it an admission of guilt on Frankie's part? A bona fide confession?"

"Well, the statement is not exactly in reference to the laundered cash and the stashed cocaine," Tom Jarvis orally responded and then momentarily paused. "But the typed paragraph does in essence constitute a confession about another matter! The specific nomenclature alludes to the year 1975 when Frankie and the rest of Tony DeMarco's pugnacious henchmen pilfered cash and jewelry totaling fifty thousand dollars from your parents' Dutch colonial home. Now Rita, I'll be in touch with the Camden County prosecutor's office and will vouch for Mr. Giordano's vowed admission of guilt to *that* former crime, which would show validation of some remorse on Frankie's behalf. If the mobster signs the document and agrees to reimburse you fifty thousand dollars for your parents' substantial loss, then the affidavit will be used as a legal tool to slightly lighten Frankie's prospective jail sentence. The affidavit will also serve as a functional Promissory Note," attorney Jarvis further indicated. "Now I've already checked 'the Whale's' financial stock holdings over at UBS in Northfield, and the evasive con artist has more than enough liquidity to cover the fifty-thousand-dollar debt that I predict will be paid to you in full. In fact, I've clandestinely researched additional financial information and learned that the clumsy thug's strategic stock and bond investments are owned by him outright and that the rogue's prolific assets have not been acquired or borrowed on stock margin loans!"

"Well Rita," Rocco addressed his spouse with a forced smile, "it looks like we've just lost the opportunity of selling your Mom's home to obnoxious, now-incarcerated Frankie Giordano. But as a dedicated mariner once told me, there's plenty of fish in the ocean."

"Yes Hubby," Rita Costa concurred with a mild frown expressed on her countenance. "Our three sons will have to wait a while for their cash bonanzas that we've earmarked for them from the anticipated rancher sale. Oh well, there's always the notion of finding another buyer. I'll say a silent prayer in church on Sunday."

"Well now," Tom Jarvis gleefully interrupted the temporarily disconsolate couple. "If you two compatible inheritors reduce your selling price to three-hundred and fifty-thousand, I've learned that Jim Perna has a serious customer ready to bite at your offer."

"That's right," the real estate guru affirmed. "If you two heirs succeed in receiving the sum of fifty-thousand dollars from dishonorable Frankie Giordano to cover your parents' malicious robbery back in 1975, then instead of your four-hundred-thousand asking price," Jim Perna attested with a grin, "you then could come down to three-hundred-fifty. My anxious client is more than willing to meet *that* lower cost. And my client's impetuous wife desires to own perhaps one of the last houses for sale in the Hammonton area that's situated near water. The husband and wife know all about the hundred thousand bucks needed for the ranch home upgrades, and the happy couple will be more than glad to accept assuming those additional expenses."

"Doing Bristol"

Prior to last summer, my personal value system had never placed much faith or credence in what my previous beliefs had regarded as preposterous conjectures in matters like the theory of the time/space continuum, like *Twilight Zone* parallel universes, or like the prospect of actual time travel. So being a born pragmatist, I've either always been rather suspect of such 'wild speculation', or I have been somewhat wary of such 'impractical science fiction fantasy'. But because of my experiencing certain extraordinary events having their genesis on Monday, August 11th, 2014, I've recently learned to respect the powers of certain arcane forces that inexplicably transcend everyday objective scientific investigation and logic.

At 4 p.m. on that sultry summer afternoon, I had dropped-off my wife at the Delta Airlines Terminal of Philadelphia International Airport. Joanne was scheduled to fly to Orlando, Florida and visit her sister Eileen, who would be driving over from her condo' in Vero Beach to greet her. My lovely spouse would be away for an entire week's hiatus, with her flight back to Philly' being scheduled for Monday, August 18th.

After leaving the congested airport vicinity, I drove my silver Nissan Maxima north on I-95 through standard center city expressway traffic, through bustling North Philadelphia industrial zones and soon my vehicle had exited the high-density busy thoroughfare at the Levittown/Bristol interchange. Now in 2014, I have a certain nostalgic memory for *that* particular Bucks County area, for in the 1950s, me being between the ages of eleven and sixteen, my family had lived at 50 Daffodil Lane in Levittown's Dogwood Hollow section.

'I've made arrangements to spend the night at the *Comfort Inn* on Route 13 between Levittown and Bristol,' I neurotically reminded myself. 'I'm glad I've confirmed my reservation this morning before leaving Hammonton and driving Joanne out of Jersey to Philly'. Before motoring to the *Comfort Inn* on Bristol Pike, I think I'll perform a little sentimental tour of Levittown and nearby Bristol.'

I switched on Sirius XM Radio and listened to Chuck Berry's all-too-stellar "Sweet Little Sixteen" and then heard Bill Haley and the Comets' sensational rendition of "Rock Around the Clock," and those most terrific early rock and roll songs immediately resurrected fond recollections from my youth while then living in Levittown. Next I pressed my radio's second button to reminisce 60s' tunes and my ears quickly discerned the Dovells fast harmony lyrics belting-out "The Bristol Stomp", which actually had been a new teen dance that had originated in 1961 at the Bristol Fire and Hose Department Hall, a nifty place where I had attended lively "bobby socks and poodle skirt dances" in 1958 and 1959.

My improvised itinerary around Levittown was quite sentimental-but-melancholy in both scope and sequence. As my Maxima exited left from Route 13 onto Levittown Parkway, my pupils immediately recognized that my revered Catholic high school, Bishop Egan, had been demolished and that a weed-laden, empty lot now occupied the landscape where the four-story building had formerly stood.

Then as I carefully made a left-turn into what used to be the Levittown Shoparama Outdoor Mall, and I was saddened to witness that the former shopping center had been razed and has since been replaced with several large modern-day box stores.

'Wow!' I instantly regretted. 'Even the Towne Movie Theater has been eliminated from existence.' In the mid-fifties my friends and I would frequent the establishment in July and August because *that* then-new structure was about the only special place that featured the amazing revolutionary technology known as air-conditioning, which to us was actually 'a scarce-but-welcomed novelty.'

I next drove through the community's Kenwood section, where all the streets began with a K. I gently turned right into Stonybrook with all its S streets and a half mile ahead stopped my automobile outside where the Brook Pool used to be, but now that former popular recreational facility was also gone from existence along with the side Little League baseball field where I had played for the Meenan Oil team in 1954-'55.

'Holy cow!' I sadly lamented. 'Even the pool's rear basketball court is gone.' I had enjoyed so many teen Friday night outdoor dances there during the mid-'50s Golden Age of Rock and Roll. Kids from Stonybrook, Farmbrook and Greenbrook would frequent the 'Brook Pool' that had been by design sandwiched between those three 'Letter Sections', and the teens there mingled with clean-cut kids but deliberately avoided the tough greasers from Junewood, Kenwood and Dogwood Hollow.

More dejection entered my heart when I piloted my Maxima into Dogwood Hollow and observed how the homes had generally deteriorated over the course of the last sixty years. My former residence at 50 Daffodil Lane looked almost-alien to my eyes with different dull siding and faded roof shingles being viewed. And much to my utter dismay, a ruinous-looking lawn and accompanying inferior-looking shrubbery were evident throughout the now-aged shabby property where I once lived.

My final Levittown excursion had me venturing into Junewood, where for two years I had worked a newspaper route delivering the now-defunct *Philadelphia Bulletin.* 'I was making ten dollars a week profit, which today would be equivalent to a hundred dollars,' I recalled and then smiled.

Driving around Junewood, I stopped in front of my old pal Bob Jalonec's home on Jonquil Lane, and I especially remembered him and his boss green and cream '57 Chevy, and then my cluttered mind mentally reviewed the countless hours "Jokes" and I would spend "cruisin'" the region and listening to disc jockey Joe Niagara, the "Rockin' Bird", playing the latest hits on WIBG Radio 99.

My final connection with my '50s Levittown past was heading east on Haines Road past the now-empty Delaware Canal and after crossing Route 13, I judiciously applied the brakes and halted in the center of a strip mall, my eyes staring at the Eagle Nest Tavern, which has replaced Hal's Delicatessen where I had diligently worked inside the business's backroom kitchen on Saturday and Sunday afternoons to earn additional steak sandwich and pinball money.

My final Bristol Pike visitation was to park my Nissan at the adjacent Dairy DeLite custard stand and actively enjoy devouring a medium-size vanilla cone, my appetite habitually repeating a tasty treat my mouth had savored so often back in the 1950s. As I munched on the soft cone, my eyes glanced next door at a seafood restaurant presently named 'Under the Pier', that in the '50s used to be the fabulous Feed Bag, which was a popular eatery and teenage hangout where Bob Jalonec and I had encountered a myriad of romantic and culinary adventures.

* * * * * * * * * * * *

Continuing on my casual Bucks County jaunt through Bristol, Pennsylvania, population fourteen thousand, I temporarily parked my car in front of the Bristol Fire and Hose Department and soon a mental newsreel of past favorable escapades promptly switched on inside my brain. From Mifflin Street I traveled south to Mill, and at the 'L right angle corner' of Mill and Radcliffe Street my silver Maxima slowly descended a short-but-steep ramp, and I quickly maneuvered my comfortable leather-seated Nissan to a parking lot situated next to a Lions Club Park and also conveniently located near the town boat pier, which Bob Jalonec and I had often utilized as our private *Delaware River* fishing destination.

I departed my vehicle and my elderly feet ambled into the historic King George II Inn, 102 Radcliffe St., which is a landmark Bristol establishment that had originally been constructed in the 17th Century. I nonchalantly sat-down at the bar, ordered a Coors Light draft and a medium-well-done sirloin steak with mashed potatoes, and since I was the only patron seated upon a stool, the affable bartender (who identified himself as "Bill") decided to initiate a friendly conversation.

"Where ya' from Stranger?"

"Hammonton, over in South Jersey," I quietly answered. "It's halfway between Philly' and Atlantic City."

"I know the town well," Bill replied with a smile. "It's called the Blueberry Capital of the World. My wife and I attend the annual festival each late June over at your high school. Quite an event, I must say! We were just there two months ago!"

"The town's farmers grow over ten thousand acres of the luscious blue fruit," I informed the inn's very affable employee. "In the 1950s, Hammonton farm acreage was half peaches and half blueberries, but in the end, the blueberry guys won-out and the former peach growers have admitted defeat. Now *they* almost exclusively harvest the eight-week-long summer blue crop!"

I soon learned that Bill was an avid history and geography enthusiast. "Bristol was named after a city in England," I remarked. "The Pilgrims sailed from Bristol to Massachusetts on the *Mayflower* in 1620," I proudly-but-erroneously stated.

"Not exactly!" the congenial bartender laughed. "The Pilgrims sailed from Plymouth, England and landed near Cape Cod. That's where we get Plymouth Rock! Lots of places in the New World were named after towns and cities in England. For example: New York, New London, New Hampshire, New Jersey and New Castle Delaware. Your own New Jersey was named after the Isle of Jersey in the English Channel."

"Well then, didn't Sir Francis Drake voyage out of Bristol?" I asked, attempting to redeem my very evident knowledge deficiency in the British maritime history category.

"No Sir!" Bill chuckled and then reflexively coughed. "Like the Pilgrims, Drake also embarked from Plymouth. But Sir, Bristol was the home base of John Cabot, the famous North American explorer who led several important expeditions out of the port in 1496!"

48

Just then, coincidentally, the familiar 'Bristol Stomp' rhythm was heard emanating from the tavern's overhead speakers. I related to my new beer and alcohol acquaintance what represented the true inspiration for the 60s' hit song.

"One of the singing group's members had stayed at the Deauville Hotel in Miami Beach, and that's how the Philly' group got its name the Dovells," I authoritatively informed, again endeavoring to compensate for my obvious lacking in Bristol, England nautical history. "Another band member had heard of a new teen dance started right here in town at the Fire and Hose Hall over on Mifflin, so the song's lyrics were expeditiously composed and the hit number was soon recorded and went national in a hurry."

Bill nodded his head in appreciation of my sage rock and roll commentary, swiftly stepped into the kitchen and soon returned to serve my plate of sirloin and mashed potatoes; then the ambitious young man attended to the thirst needs of another guest sitting four stools to my left. When the pleasant young fellow again arrived to where I had been eating, we mutually resumed our cheerful dialogue.

"Ya' know," I prefaced, "back in the '50s a good buddy and I used to fish off of that pier out there. Of course, we always wanted to come inside for a beer or two but were too young to be served."

"Yeah, *that* landing dock date's back in 1681 when goods and supplies began arriving up the Delaware from Philly' to Bristol," the encyclopedic bartender deftly explained. "Those Pre-Revolutionary War colonial days must've been something else!"

I glanced-up at the inn's liquor shelf and noticed bottles of Jack Daniels, Jim Beam, Southern Comfort, and Seagram's Seven displayed among other whiskey favorites, all lined-up and ready for public consumption. "Say Bill, since I'm here in good old Bristol, why don't you give me a glass of that Harveys Bristol Cream up there on the liquor rack?"

"Good choice!" the bartender commended my selection judgment. "It's a dessert sherry nicely blended ever since the year 1880, but the famous distillery was first begun by Mr. John Harvey and Sons in Bristol, England in 1796."

"Your impeccable and impressive knowledge of British history is absolutely amazing!" I generously praised. "I guess you know plenty about the blue bottle too?"

"It's referred to in the trade as Bristol blue glass," Bill related as the garrulous guy poured the tempting dessert liquor into my glass. "Not too many customers order it. Most prefer chugging-down hard whiskey shots instead!"

"I'm staying the night at the *Comfort Inn* over on Route 13," I revealed, desiring to continue our rather courteous conversation. "Say Bill, when was the last time someone else came in here and drank a glass of this Harveys Bristol Cream?"

"It was a whole week ago today," the bartender reflected and then uttered. "Yes, in fact the fellow swallowed-down two glasses. Apparently, he really liked the smooth flavor."

"Well, in that case," I insisted, "give me a refill. That stuff was positively delicious!"

"Just like yourself'," Bill calmly stated as he recharged my empty glass, "this guy I'm mentioning also lived in Levittown in the 1950s. Junewood section I believe. Said his name was 'Bob' something or other. Was from Florence, South Carolina and was visiting relatives in New York before taking a detour and touring the area before entering the King George. But for the life of me, I can't remember the fella's last name. It began with a J., I think."

My eyes widened and my mouth was then totally agape. "Jalonec?" I asked with subtle surprise.

"Yeah, that's it!" Bill eagerly verified in a semi-excited tone of voice. "Jalonec! Said he' was also staying at the *Comfort Inn* up on Bristol Pike."

"Know the highway well!" I remarked without divulging that gregarious Bob Jalonec was once my closest Levittown friend. "It's below Edgely Road and near Green Lane. When I was sixteen, I was a junior fireman for the Edgely Fire Company and there was a big blaze at Delhaas High School over near the small plane airport on Green Lane. Levittown was really something else back then. Could you imagine? Seventeen thousand brand new homes erected on open land in a mere five-year period!"

"Maybe I shouldn't tell you about *this* incident, Mister," Bill indicated, getting back to our main topic of discussion, "but this guy Bob Jalonec was back in here just an hour or so ago before you entered. Said he was anxiously heading south to Dixie."

"Did he have another two glasses of Harveys Bristol Cream?" I wondered and inquired. "The stuff is delectable! I think I'll buy some at the local liquor store and sample it at home! The flavor could be addictive!"

"No Sir!" Bill mildly exclaimed. "The guy instead asked for a double shot of Jack Daniels on the rocks. He drank it down in three seconds as if he had just crossed the Sahara Desert on foot and needed to quench his parched tongue and throat!"

"Did this fella' Bob J. say anything to you about his seven-day activities between his two visits?" I deliberately asked. "Why was he so thirsty?"

"I reckon the gentleman wasn't nearly as thirsty as he was scared," Bill communicated with a serious expression suddenly appearing upon his florid face. "Ironically, that same 'Bristol Stomp' song began playing and the music seemed to drastically affect the man's behavior. At least that's my impression!" the grim-faced bartender qualified. "He slammed a twenty-dollar bill on the counter, mumbled some barely discernible words about some weird time and space travel incident, and then the perturbed fella' rapidly scurried out the door and off the premises, bolting straight to his car like a frightened jackrabbit!"

* * * * * * * * * * * *

My emotions were a trifle addled on the brief drive from the King George II Inn on Radcliffe Street to the *Comfort Inn* on Route 13. Many random thoughts meandered about inside my head. 'What a remarkable coincidence!' I evaluated. 'I haven't seen nor heard of Bob Jalonec in over a half century and now I just missed him by a matter of an hour. Swell; at least I now know he lives in Florence, South Carolina. Maybe I'll look him up in a telephone directory and get on the horn to have a much-needed talk about our memorable past friendship in 50s' Levittown.'

Being fatigued from the day's various travails, I gathered my wits and checked into the 'cookie cutter lodge', made my way up a flight of steps to Room 201 and slowly unpacked my suitcase. After showering and watching Fox News on cable TV, at eight p.m. I called Joanne on my cell phone to determine how her flight from Philly' to Orlando had gone. My wife reported that everything was "copacetic" and that the daytime climate in sunny Florida was hot and nearly sweltering.

After hanging-up my portable phone, I brushed my teeth and retired to bed early, all the while anticipating my pleasurable ride across the *Delaware* on the Burlington-Bristol Bridge back into New Jersey and then enjoying the scenic forty-mile trip south on Route 206 to agricultural Hammonton. For some remote reason, feeling highly exhausted, I fell asleep upon the bed wearing my designer jeans, a light blue cotton shirt, and contrary to my sleeping habits, I was still wearing my white socks and brown penny loafers.

The following morning, I awoke at daybreak, but incredulously, the entire room, wallpaper, furniture and decorations were all now quite different in appearance. I hastily opened the drapes, peered out the window and much to my astonishment, Route13 was nowhere in sight but instead, a heretofore unknown massive edifice with the designation Wellmont Hospital somehow existed across what was now identified by a street sign as 'West State Street'. A nearby red, white and blue sign surprisingly read I-81. Being fully confused, I hastily dressed, left Room 201 with my plastic key in hand and nervously roamed downstairs to obtain necessary, plausible clarification of my exact whereabouts.

A local tour-guide pamphlet and brochure rack of area sightseeing attractions described such foreign venues as 'Bristol Speedway just off Exit 5 of I-95', 'King College Walking Tours', 'Marvelous Bristol Caverns' and 'Beautiful Skyline Drive Bus Tours'. I turned my head, glanced at the wall logo situated above the main registration desk and then my bewildered eyes noticed that the newfound emblem mysteriously read: 'Holiday Inn, 3299 West State Street, Bristol, Tennessee'.

'I guess I'm no longer in Bristol, Pennsylvania!' my puzzled brain surmised and shockingly realized. 'I'll peruse this pamphlet section and try acting inconspicuous while doing so. Then I'll sit-down in the side room and sort things out over a Continental breakfast!'

One particular brochure showed the colorful photographs of the nearby Comfort Inn, 2368 Lee Highway, Bristol, Virginia. Then my thought processes finally comprehended that Bristol, Tennessee and Bristol, Virginia were sister cities that physically bordered each other in two separate states. For mental security, my hands quickly honored my instinctive reaction. I frantically reached into my back and side pockets and my furious searches, much to my relief, simultaneously confirmed that my wallet and my cell phone were still in my possession.

After consuming my early meal in a rare, perplexed state of mind, I walked-up a flight of steps to Room 201 and after entering, plopped-down on the bed and contemplated my extremely bizarre circumstances. 'I dare not leave the property if I'm under some obscure evil spell or curse. I don't want to be jinxed or be punished by mystical supernatural forces I can't right now clearly fathom,' I dreadfully assessed. 'If I boldly step out of the Holiday Inn, then who knows what my' resultant fate might be?'

I stayed secluded in my room that entire day and later, after regaining my composure, I ordered from room service a hamburger and French fries for supper. My troubled mind was now singularly worried about my arcane time and space travel misadventure. 'Perhaps this 'Bristol visitation phenomenon' is what had caused Bob Jalonec to panic into a frenzy and swallow-down his Jack Daniels double-shot after hearing the Dovells singing 'Bristol Stomp' at the King George II bar?' my mind wondered and suspiciously conjectured.

At nine that evening I sufficiently calmed-down, called Joanne in Vero Beach and was happy making contact with her and hearing her wonderful, comforting voice over my cell phone. My suspicious-minded wife articulated that she could not reach me during the afternoon and that she was becoming somewhat concerned.

"Maybe *my* cell phone is only transmitting and had trouble receiving incoming calls," I cleverly theorized and communicated to my better half. "From now on this week, I'll call you until I have Verizon correct my cell phone's malfunction."

"Okay Honey!" Joanne aptly agreed. "Miss you! Can't wait to be arriving back home in Hammonton next Sunday! Don't forget! Meet me at eight at the Delta baggage carousel! Love ya' Babe! See you then!" Click.

That evening I watched the late-night CNN and local newscasts and finally managed to doze-off around midnight. But after a restless night of tossing and turning, I climbed-out of my queen-size bed at dawn, hustled to the window, but amazingly, my vision saw no Wellmont Hospital across the highway. Instead, I noticed three distinct arrowed road signs, the first one reading I-93 and the second indicating, "Bristol, New Hampshire." I clumsily turned-on the side wall light to further investigate the apparent visual aberration. The third arrowed sign in the far distance read: "Wellington State Forest near Newfound Lake."

'Oh my God!' I imagined in awe. 'I've been vacationing in these parts before. This is no doubt New Hampshire out there. Joanne and I had taken a senior citizen bus trip up here three falls ago to enjoy the splendor of the autumn foliage. The White Mountains are just north of here and Wolfeboro and Lake Winnipesaukee located just southeast. If I accurately recall, Squam Lake is geographically near Lake Winny. That's where the popular 70s' movie *On Golden Pond* had been filmed! In fact,' I remembered, 'friends of ours had moved up here from Jersey and now live not too far away in Meredith. If I had the courage, I'd intrepidly walk out of this *Comfort Inn* and pay

Steve and Nancy a visit in an effort to escape this terrible ongoing Bristol nightmare!'

The following three nights the same type of reprehensible time/space travel pattern had been experienced and again repeated in Hilton Double Tree Hotel and Comfort Inns in Bristol, Rhode Island, in Bristol Virginia, and in Bristol, Connecticut. All the while, fortunately I was able to successfully recharge my cell phone, call Joanne and pretentiously assure her that out of sheer boredom, I had been staying the week in New York City attending 'a spectacular merchandise show' being featured inside a huge exhibit hall near Columbus Circle.

The sixth night I was fretfully staying in Room 201 of the Bristol, Connecticut Double Tree Hotel on 42 Century Drive. Again, I dared not leave the building out of fear of some unintended supernatural repercussions being surreptitiously administered upon me by alien invisible powers. My whole beleaguered psyche was now overwhelmed with abundant dread and apprehension. My spirit and audacity were both indeed being mercilessly challenged.

After I almost-mechanically ate an ordinarily excellent crab cake dinner inside the exclusive Willow Restaurant, I strolled across the Double Tree's lobby and then curiously trekked around the entire downstairs, impatiently examining without any specific purpose the facility's exercise room and large indoor swimming pool, both accommodating amenities enclosed inside the high-end boutique hotel's glass-paneled atrium.

A tall, thin gentleman standing in the main lounge innocently asked me if I had attended the recent Newport Jazz Festival just across the state line in Rhode Island. I quickly answered a little too curtly, "No Sir. I prefer the mid-June Monterey Pop Festival out in California!" I then briskly sauntered away to again be alone in my ascending misery.

'Gee! Now I know why Bob Jalonec was acting so petrified and so psychotic last Sunday afternoon at the King George II Inn!' I genuinely-but-erratically thought. 'And no one at any of the hotels has been charging any fees or expenses to my credit card. All I do is sign my name and tell the waiters and employees my 201room! If I ever get back to Hammonton,' I decided, 'I'm never going to risk my reputation and disclose this hellish tale to anyone, including Joanne! The only person on the face of the Earth whom I might ever consider telling is Bob Jalonec!' I rationally concluded. 'If I ever get back to Jersey with some remaining sanity, I think I'll spend several weeks rehabilitating in Ancora State Mental Hospital in order to recover from this incredibly outlandish and wholly enigmatic Bristol six-state astral journey! Oh well, at least I haven't time traveled across the Atlantic to Bristol, England!'

* * * * * * * * * * * *

Much to my emotional alleviation, on Sunday, August 18th I awoke, hopped out of bed, bolted to the window, opened the drapes and immediately, thankfully perceived that Bristol Pike, Route 13 constituted the wonderfully ordinary outside physical and commercial environment. I quickly turned on a table lamp, examined my wristwatch and was fully elated to note that the time was 6:15 a.m. and that the timepiece's calendar element indeed indicated August 18th.

I next ecstatically paced to the bathroom, removed my harshly wrinkled designer jeans, blue cotton shirt, brown penny loafers and white socks. Next, I showered, shaved my week-long beard (for my small traveling bag had still been kept inside my suitcase), and then I merrily donned my much-needed change in underwear, summer weight black pants, green tee-shirt and new white socks.

'This Bristol Comfort Inn already has my credit card number,' I reasoned. 'I'll just leave a twenty-dollar maid's tip on the bureau along with the room key and furtively exit the lodge. I'll skip the monotonous free Continental breakfast and later eat at a New Jersey diner on the drive back to Hammonton.'

Then I again rushed to the window to confirm that my 2013 silver Nissan Maxima was still there in the lodge's asphalt parking lot. 'Oh yes!' I gladly thought upon performing additional searching. 'My car keys are still in the top bureau drawer, right where I had deposited them last Sunday night!'

I was never so happy to be back in Jersey again after crossing the two-lane Burlington-Bristol Bridge into Burlington City, which like Bristol, was an old Delaware River town dating back to the American colonial era. Somewhere between Mt. Holly and Medford on Route 541, my disheveled mind awkwardly rehashed the exceptionally strange developments that I had inadvertently survived during the past incomparable seven days.

'I refuse to turn on Sirius XM radio and accidentally hear the Dovells singing Bristol Stomp,' I firmly resolved. 'And I'm never going back to the King George II Inn like Bob Jalonec had unfortunately done. And I'm never again going to stay at the Route 13 Comfort Inn either. And I'm never ever again going to drink two or more glasses of Harveys Bristol Cream. And absolutely,' I further rationalized, 'I'll never ever do any combination of those four Bristol-related things on the exact same day!'

After having a pancakes, coffee and bacon breakfast at the Red Barn Restaurant on Route 206, I called Joanne in Vero Beach to see if any time changes had been made for her return flight from Orlando to Philly' International. Truthfully, I was never so glad to hear her soft, feminine voice chatting about simple, nondescript, mundane, every day matters.

On the final leg of the drive home to Hammonton, my mind still futilely tried understanding how I had consecutively time/space voyaged from Bristol, Pennsylvania to Bristol, Tennessee, to Bristol, New Hampshire, to Bristol, Rhode Island, to Bristol, Virginia, to Bristol, Connecticut, and then miraculously arriving full-circle back to the Comfort Inn, Bristol, Pennsylvania.

After gingerly pulling into my all-too-familiar driveway and stopping to obtain my week-long mail, I coyly decided while sitting behind the steering wheel, 'The next time Joanne flies down to Florida to visit her sister in Vero Beach, I'm going to merrily drive down to Florence, South Carolina and have a lengthy chat with Jalonec about our dual week-long Levittown and Bristol adventures. Bob and I will definitely have a plethora of items to converse about. And then,' I imaginatively considered, 'I'll secretly motor further down south to Vero and pay a surprise visit to my unsuspecting wife and sister-in-law.'

"A Photo' Finish"

At 8 p.m. sharp a black 2018 Mercedes luxury S 560 sedan slowly entered the secluded, U-shaped, asphalt driveway enveloping a well-manicured lawn on East First Road, Hammonton NJ. The recently constructed three-million-dollar brick and stone mansion belonged to local wealthy business mogul James Dante Carlino, who that evening was scheduled to meet with the arriving prestigious South-Jersey Central Bank President, Thomas Monastra. In response to recent phone exchanges, the visiting financial executive and the resident real estate guru were slated to discuss an imminent shopping center development project planned for erection just outside Somers Point, across the bay from scenic Ocean City, New Jersey.

"Hello Mr. Monastra," James Carlino warmly greeted. "It's too bad we couldn't meet at the Blue Heron Country Club yesterday for a round of golf. But Mother Nature isn't always cooperative with desired business consultations."

"Very well put!" the bank official aptly answered. "Egg Harbor Township isn't exactly located in Southern California where it seldom rains in the early summer. Living on the West Coast does have its climate advantages. I must admit Mr. Carlino, it's quite a beautiful estate you've imaginatively built here, neatly tucked into the Jersey pines."

"Yes Sir," Carlino appreciatively replied as the investor gestured with his right hand for his suave guest to enter the spectacular chandeliered foyer that featured a magnificent spiral staircase. "I've designed this home myself. In high school, drafting was my favorite class. In my youth I always aspired to becoming an architect. But I suppose now, I'm simply a humble, amateur unlicensed home designer at best."

"Just last week I read in the *South Jersey Gazette* that you had a small-time robbery happen at the convenience store situated on Fairview Avenue and the Pike, I believe," Mr. Monastra stated with a weak smile. "Hammonton has the reputation of being a rather tranquil, rural, safe agricultural community. I was surprised to read *that* particular article."

As James Carlino graciously escorted Thomas Monastra into the enormous home's resplendent study, the multi-millionaire explained that the desperate robbers absolutely needed the four-hundred-dollars that the "idiots" had stolen from the startled store cashier to satisfy another debt the armed criminals had amassed.

"The full details weren't described in the newspaper account," Mr. Monastra curiously informed. "So much for the mediocre state-of-affairs that's lacking in modern-day journalism. Please if you may, fill-in for me the missing specifics of the ugly misadventure that had apparently boldly occurred in broad daylight."

"Well Sir," seventy-six-year-old James Dante Carlino laughed as the newly-acquainted pair continued conducting their preliminary conversation, "the two lowlife ignoramuses involved in the armed gun heist were caught inside the municipal parking lot in front of Hammonton Town Hall; the ridiculous dummies were waiting to have a 3 p.m. court appearance before the town judge for two speeding tickets along with several other citations for attempting to evade police pursuits. Hammonton Police quickly apprehended the knuckleheaded culprits, who amazingly were intending to use the pilfered money from the convenience store armed felony to pay certain accumulated traffic violation fines that very same day in the Hammonton Municipal Court," explained the all-too-humored speaker. "This incredible oddball story has really become a favorite item shared among the town gossipers sitting in local beauty parlor and barber shop chairs."

"Ha, ha, ha!" guffawed the distinguished and well-dressed banking visitor. "Your terrific story about two imbeciles committing a store heist was a classic example of the all-true aphorism 'Crime doesn't pay'! Those two ambitious, moronic fools were really at best dimwitted dunces," the totally amused financial wizard opined. "It's a good thing that Hammonton is not a notorious hotbed for major crime events like Vineland, Millville and Bridgeton are. I'm glad that I live in Mays Landing, which just like Hammonton, is a very placid and serene place to raise a family. But from general knowledge, your wonderful town is such a somnolent small city with a stellar blueberry farm reputation, and it's strategically located right in the preserved core area of the pristine Jersey Pinelands."

Before the garrulous duo stepped forward and approached the huge mahogany conference-table occupying the very center of the vast study/library room, James Dante Carlino paused for a moment to draw his avid listener's attention to an ordinary-looking vintage waist-high stereo/radio credenza tastefully placed along a side wall, the obsolete object instantly creating a mood of sentimental nostalgia to surface in the homeowner's mind.

"This once-popular early 1960s console was mine when I was a naïve teenager, and to tell you the truth Mr. Monastra, I loved playing rock and roll records and eagerly hearing the radio Top 40 hits during my formative adolescent years. My 97-year-old father gave this marvelous piece of furniture to me five years ago before he had been admitted into the Berlin Rehab' Center, and now my dad Pietro permanently shares a room with my elderly mother Angelina. Both of my parents are presently virtual invalids, mom and pop suffering from advanced cases of dementia."

"Sorry to hear such bad news about your folks' declining health!" genuinely sympathized Thomas Monastra. "It's too bad that your mom and dad are unable to enjoy any normal facet of their human existence. My parents have been dead for over a decade now. And I must confess Mr. Carlino, I sure miss them both dearly."

"You can call me Jim," convincingly recommended the rich host. "And let's forget the general formalities that standard etiquette has over-the-years conditioned us with. You don't mind if I drop a cultural norm and call you Tom."

"Not at all!" spontaneously agreed the affable banker. "Before we get down to the nitty-gritty though, please tell me Jim all about these twelve black and white photographs that you've randomly arranged upon the closed lid of your treasured 1960s entertainment console."

* * * * * * * * * * *

"This first picture to your left is that of Aunt Carmella Carlino, a Hammonton transplant originally from South 'Philly," the mansion dweller confidently told Mr. Thomas Monastra. "Aunt Carmella's husband Uncle Lorenzo Carlino was my father Pietro's younger brother by seven years."

"I presume that your father Pietro and your Uncle Lorenzo were partners on the family farm way back in the 1930s,'40s and '50s!" the banker guessed.

"Correct," confirmed James Carlino. "My ambitious father had mortgaged everything he owned right after the Great Depression and bought a defunct peach farm from a man named Horace Priestley, who lost his once-thriving agricultural empire after the infamous 1929 stock market collapse. During World War II, there was a drastic need for food supplies, so the war actually enabled my father and my uncle to get themselves out of debt."

"When did your family switch from peaches to blueberries?" the bank president inquired? "I've read in the papers where today there are over ten thousand acres of cultivated blueberries harvested in this sandy soil area."

"In the 1950s it was fairly evident that the Hammonton growers were hastily switching from peaches to blueberries," James proudly articulated. "The four-hundred-acre peach and apple farm gradually expanded to eight hundred acres of blueberries. The back section that was newly acquired in the mid-60s was often referred to as 'Texas', and that two-hundred-acre blueberry block was given to Uncle Lorenzo as *his* portion of the Carlino family partnership."

"How did you become directly involved in the farm?" Monastra coyly asked James Carlino. "Was there some sort of rift between your father and his brother Lorenzo?"

"Exactly true!" verified and exclaimed the now independently successful entrepreneur. "First my father took a risk and purchased the peach land from Horace Priestley in 1929. Then after my dad and his brother had a major disagreement, my pop bought the 'Texas' ground a second time from Uncle Lorenzo, who then gambled his new-found windfall and went into business as a fertilizer and packages' distributor to area fruit and produce farms, mostly in the Hammonton/Vineland area."

James proceeded to further relate to his all-too-inquisitive guest that in 1977 his father then offered the fertile 'Texas tract' to him and shrewdly took-in the eldest son as a suitable replacement partner. The well-intended arrangement lasted for a dozen years, and in 1989 a truculent Pietro Carlino re-purchased the Texas blueberry block from his son James for the handsome sum of four-hundred-thousand-dollars. "My arrogant father always was an argumentative, stubborn dictator of a man, a sort of unyielding tyrant who never recognized my independent thinking. Pop always wanted to be the boss, whether it was on the farm or playing cards with cronies at the Sons of Italy. In Pop's very limited, narrow-minded understanding, the word *partnership* was only a functional euphemism for *me* being an obedient subordinate to his every command."

"Well now Jim, your father Pietro was definitely aging after you left the farm scene. How did he ever manage operating his huge agricultural empire?"

"Pop immediately made my younger brother Franco his new partner and gave him the aforementioned Texas block as evidence of *his* family commitment and responsibility," James verbally indicated. "But six years later, all-too-sensitive Franco couldn't take the constant daily abuse being administered any longer, so he too departed, being bought-out by Pop for the same remarkable price as I had been. In time my father's mental health eventually diminished to where he exists in his present feeble state. The packinghouse, cold storage and equipment on the once prosperous farm are now in shambles, and the entire operation is debt-ridden."

"And so now Jim, you're standing here and telling me that your obstinate father had obtained the same land four separate times: first from Mr. Horace Priestley, secondly from his brother Lorenzo, thirdly from you and finally, from your younger sibling Franco Carlino. Your dad's once lucrative blueberry empire is now up for auction as I had read last week in the *Atlantic City Press* real estate section," Thomas Monastra accurately expressed. "But please tell me Jim; what ever happened to your attractive Aunt Carmella who is candidly represented smiling in this faded photograph? Is she also deceased?"

"Aunt Carmella became depressed from all of the family bickering being enacted over power and control," James orally conveyed to his astute audience of one. "In 2008 she fell inside her bathroom shower and unfortunately broke her hip. After having a joint replacement operation, Aunt Carmella's troubled-mind went totally haywire. She experienced a severe mental breakdown, became semi-conscious; acting quite erratically, her delirious mind was suffering greatly in a heightened state of agitation. I recollect that on her death certificate it had been bluntly stated that Aunt Carmella had died of dementia and cardiac arrest."

"Are all of these twelve people depicted in these dozen pictures now dead?"

"Yes indeed," James Carlino softly replied. "And I must mention that I was deeply attached to each and every one of them, and quite frankly, better bonded with a few of them more than the rest. I experience emotional anguish every time I affectionately view these twelve deceased relatives. I only wish I could turn back the hands of time and bring them all back to life and again fully value their support, comfort and love once more!"

"Who is this woman in the second picture?" the banker queried.

"This second black and white photo' is that of my older sister, Bianca Carlino. She was a warty-faced, hideous-looking old maid, and she and I never favorably harmonized on any matter that involved the myriad family businesses, including the very productive blueberry farm!" James Carlino paused for a moment, gauged Mr. Monastra's facial reaction to his negative rhetoric, and then resumed his revealing narrative. "Simply for the vile purpose of causing widespread chaos, resentment and disruption, my conniving father deliberately had me work under Bianca's jurisdiction so that I was unable to effectively challenge *his* authority and control. I was the nasty wench's underling in the family packinghouse, on the family roadside market and inside the family cold storage, and I had to endure a litany of belligerent commands from my petulant female superior numerous times each day."

"Then your father obviously perceived you as a direct threat and intentionally empowered your older sister Bianca to neutralize your prowess," Mr. Monastra logically concluded and stated. "He cleverly formed a difficult family alliance against you!"

"That sage assumption you've formulated is right on target!" James Carlino concurred in a feigned melancholy tone of voice. "But outside of the array of family business activities, Bianca was as sweet as could be, especially kind to me during the Thanksgiving and Christmas holidays. That's when the mercurial-tempered witch would bake for me delicious apple and pumpkin pies along with delectable chocolate cakes. My mole-faced sister was like a complicated female version of Dr. Jekyll and Mr. Hyde," James explained. "She was rude and condescending toward me during the summer growing and harvest seasons, but conversely, wonderfully kind and exceptionally courteous to me in November and December. The shrew was neurotic and schizophrenic ever since our early teen years; the nasty hussy was sometimes envious toward me, and at other times, she preferred being dramatically polite and respectful. During the cold winter months," an animated James Carlino expounded, "Bianca's erratic personality was like Mother Teresa in regard to my anemic position in the family enterprises' pecking-order. However, from April to October when she and I had to work together, Bianca's vicious, hostile demeanor was like that of an extremely energized Medusa the Gorgon!"

"How did Bianca die?" Mr. Thomas Monastra wondered and finally asked his ten-million-dollar loan solicitor. "Her overall behavior sounds rather opposed to the well-known maxim, 'Only the good die young'!"

"My mood-changing, hideous-looking elder sister died from advanced lung cancer in April of 2014. Bianca was addicted to nicotine and smoked two packs of cigarettes each and every day, mostly out of perpetual nervousness and tremendous anxiety. Those destructive cancer sticks did her in. I sincerely hope that Bianca's demanding soul is now finally in a passive state and calmly resting in eternal peace!"

James Dante Carlino then used his right index finger to point at the third picture situated atop the waist-high credenza. "This is my Uncle Lorenzo Carlino, married to my Aunt Carmella. As has been mentioned, Uncle Lorenzo left the family plantation and used his new-found profits from the Texas tract deal to own a farm package and fertilizer distribution outlet on West End Avenue in town. His wife Carmella always wanted half of the retail farm market operation, but my mother Angelina refused to share the business with her always-protesting sister-in-law. That was another sticking-point of incessant dispute between my father Pietro and my Uncle Lorenzo. But on the flip side of the coin," James emphasized before taking a deep breath to continue his monologue, "Uncle Lorenzo and Aunt Carmella had a comfortable get-away place in Cape May and allowed me to use it whenever I was having a verbal conflict with my avaricious, egocentric father!"

"How did your Uncle Lorenzo die?" urbane Thomas Monastra deferentially requested learning. "Was it from old age or from natural causes?"

"Uncle Lorenzo was notorious at dining at Hammonton taverns and coincidentally being a chronic alcoholic who after Aunt Carmella had passed away, enjoyed many Southern Comfort Manhattans while having supper, especially at the Maplewood Restaurant over on Route 30. Several times the bar maid had to drive him home in her vehicle while a second bar attendant would follow behind in Lorenzo's trademark red Cadillac," James described and shared. "Cirrhosis of the liver was the principal cause of death as had been documented on the physician's official state certificate. I believe that my seldom-sober uncle drank heavily because of the loss of his devoted Carmella and also, he habitually imbibed liquor as a result of putting-up with my insufferable father's regular abuse!"

"Who is this gorgeous young lady monopolizing this fourth picture? She must have been some sort of beauty queen?"

"Yes Tom, this is my first wife, Lisa Nelson, who was the Hammonton Peach Blossom Queen back in 1966 when peaches were still the dominant crop. My father and mother disliked Lisa with a passion because she was not Sicilian but instead, was of British descent. In retrospect, I think I might've married her just to spite my parents, who suspected that Lisa wanted to nail me in matrimony solely for the love of pelf. I must admit that she was obsessed with money, with expensive cars and with our plush La Jolla, California winter vacation home. Regretfully," James sorrowfully related, "Lisa perished in 1968 when her white Bentley lost a wheel and then careened down a steep canyon near Delmar while speeding on Pacific Highway 101. Learning of that devastating tragedy was one of the most horrible, dreadful moments in my entire life!"

The fifth picture on the furniture console was that of Eleanor Davidson, a second cousin to James who lived with her deadbeat husband Robert in Edgewood, just outside Baltimore, Maryland. "Eleanor always kindly remembered my birthday and sent me cards and small gifts. Sometimes Tom, the little things in life are the most important and memorable ones," James Carlino stressed and insisted to his captive listener. "Poor Cousin Eleanor died of ALS, Lou Gehrig's Disease. If I could somehow miraculously bring dear Eleanor back to life for let's say, a mere million dollars, I would gladly do it in a heartbeat!"

"This sixth photo'," deftly interrupted Mr. Monastra. "Is this your younger brother Franco? Genetically speaking, he looks like he possessed several similar facial characteristics to you, particularly around the eyes and mouth."

"Yes Sir. My younger brother and I were intense rivals throughout our formative years. Franco was jealous of me because I was a better high school football and basketball player than he was. Clearly," James boasted, "I was the more coordinated and athletic brother. Basically, to put our relationship in context, we merely tolerated each other and had several bloody fistfights in back of the packinghouse, of which naturally I had emerged victorious. But realistically, we were valid stockholders in a number of family enterprises such as the cold storage facility in Vineland and the extensive real estate property in Mays Landing alongside the Atlantic City Expressway. Franco was a poor investor outside the prolific family businesses," the prospective mall developer critically commented, "and because of the careless mismanagement of his personal funds, the abominable fool declared bankruptcy in 1993 and subsequently died a year later when his ancient airplane crashed inside the Wharton State Forest while approaching the runway at Hammonton Municipal Airport. Although the FAA investigative results into the landing accident were inconclusive, it's my firm conviction that my cowardly brother had committed suicide."

"Is there a small fond memory or perhaps anything good you could remember about Franco?" skillfully interrogated Mr. Monastra. "You seem to give a very pessimistic impression of your younger brother."

"Yes Tom, Franco was better than me in baseball and made the Cape-Atlantic League All Star squad in high school. My mentally capable brother was also more gifted than me academically, and the educated genius graduated from Cornell University with high honors, but my quixotic younger brother lacked corporate acumen and was not at all practical in formulating sound business judgments. Franco was like an isolated Einstein destined for economic bankruptcy when compelled to venture-out on his own and exploring opportunities outside the familiar realm and safety-net of family corporations."

James Dante Carlino then hesitated for a moment to perceptively interpret the impact of his recent statements upon his all-too-pleasant visitor. "Personally Tom, I detest monotony! I hope I'm not boring you with my bizarre family history. I only wish that I could edify and eulogize my brother's memory, but in all candor, I cannot lie and misrepresent the veracity of the actual facts to you!"

"Oh no Jim," Thomas Monastra genteelly replied. "Truthfully, I find your honest revelations to be most refreshing, fascinating and intriguing, and I think that your descriptive anecdotes concerning each photographed person displayed upon your stereo's lid happen to be most authentic; most interesting. It's rather astounding to me how you have over the years become a prominent, legitimate small shopping center developer," evaluated and enunciated the amiable banker, "considering all of the very evident negative influences that your tough father, your' elder sister and your vindictive brother must have had on your all-too-vulnerable psychological growth. I wish that you would now elaborate on the other six people whose pictures are sublimely exhibited upon your cherished 1970s music and radio credenza."

* * * * * * * * * * * *

"Jim, you've divulged some fantastic family secrets like your father Pietro spending over a million dollars and buying the Texas block of your family's sprawling farm four separate times. But admirably, you've been able to parlay your consecutive investments into an enormous, enviable financial accomplishment. It's not everyone who is able to present to my bank over ten million bucks of tangible collateral to subsidize a new shopping center! I must admit that I admire your determination."

"I'll try to be modest and forthright Tom about my series of achievements," the gray-haired financial veteran euphorically maintained, attempting to contribute an element of humility to the ongoing extraordinary dialogue. "There are plenty of farmers in Hammonton who are worth over three million clams, but hidden beneath the surface those same growers have four million in debts. With a little bit of Lady Luck along the way," Carlino pontificated with a broad grin, "I've managed to accumulate a decent fortune by having and utilizing the services of two very competent financial advisers: my CPA William Tomasello and my Stock Account Executive Richard Palmieri, who adroitly manages my stocks and bonds' portfolio. Without their trustworthy, professional guidance, I speculate that I'd probably be several million in arrears rather than thirty million ahead of the game. I can't possibly brag about my holdings without first extending my utmost appreciation and wholehearted kudos to Bill and Rich."

Then signaling his shift in focus for the bank executive to gaze upon the seventh exhibited photo', James Carlino disclosed that the petite female shown inside the silver frame was Barbara Carlino Grillo, the land investor's favored younger sister, his junior by five years. "Barbara was the one family member who truly loved me without seeking any special remuneration in return. Prior to her death, she and her husband Steve lived in Ft. Myers, Florida, but before then, the couple had made a respectable living flipping houses, mostly in Palm Springs and Palm Desert, California and in South Padre Island, Texas," Carlino lectured to Monastra. "Not only was Barbara very academically smart, being the Valedictorian of her St. Joseph High class, but also she was extremely caring and compassionate toward me. Twice Barbara and Steve flew-up from Florida and visited me in the hospital. First was when I had a polyp surgically removed from my large intestine, and the second occasion was when I had my hip replacement done three years back at Our Lady of Lourdes Hospital in Camden. But I must confess Tom, I'm saddened to relate that my favorite sibling died just last year after courageously battling breast cancer for over a decade."

After taking a very deep breath to demonstrably show his excessive distress, the now-melancholy host next divulged to his indulgent guest that the eighth photo' was that of his second cousin Megyn Carlino Johnson, who had a very tough and miserable early life, being the sixth of seven impoverished children. "Megyn needed a glass eye at the age of five, and I used most of my saved allowance and secretly sent her parents the money to get one. As fate would have it, twenty years later Meg married a construction worker named Fred Johnson, and with my benign help, the industrious pair founded a guardrail business in Glassboro. Over the next twenty years, Meg and Fred eventually lifted themselves out of poverty and did pretty well on the prosperity front. But six years ago, my dearest cousin unfortunately contracted leukemia and died just last November."

The handsome male depicted in picture number nine was James Dante Carlino's best friend, Gary Testa, who had functioned for twenty-five years as an effective local middle school vice-principal. In terms of recreation, Testa became the land developer's loyal bowling partner twice every week at DiDonato Lanes. "Poor Gary passed away in 2012 of colon cancer, a terrible disease that I fortunately avoided when I had eight inches of large intestine removed from my right-side abdomen at Virtua Hospital on Route 73 in Voorhees. Life can be extremely cruel," the talkative speaker added. "After contributing to Social Security for two and a half decades, Gary's wife Lorraine received a mere 255 dollars towards burial expenses. My bowling chum never collected one penny, succumbing and dying at the tender age of sixty-one years before ever becoming eligible for government benefits."

"And who is this dark-haired beauty in Picture Number Ten? That fabulous face could qualify for Miss Universe?"

"Well Tom, that's Carol Sorrentino Carlino, who was my second wife and a daring and adventurous winter weather person. I had built exclusively for her a magnificent lodge up in the Poconos just outside of Bushkill," the prolific investor communicated. "To make a long story short, Carol loved skiing at several tourist resorts near Camelback Mountain, and one day her defective right ski broke in half and my beloved spouse crashed into a tall pine tree. Much to my sorrow and disenchantment, Carol died from multiple internal injuries sustained in her horrible downhill accident."

"Sorry to learn of your second wife's awful demise," the visiting banker empathized. "I remember reading about the incident in the *Vineland News Journal*. Her family owned several cold storage facilities, didn't they?"

"Yes, and that's the connection of how I had met and courted my second wife!" James revealed. "Her family and mine were fifty-fifty partners in three different fruit and produce cold storages in the Vineland-Newfield area."

Carlino then offered a brief preface on the mustached gentleman represented in Picture Number Eleven. "This very serious-faced gentleman is Ben Lucas, a distant cousin who had a severe gambling problem. I felt sorry for him and gave addicted Ben thousands of dollars from time-to-time to cover his atrocious mounting family debts, hoping that he could somehow eventually be reformed and rehabilitated. But during one notable casino excursion at Harrahs in Atlantic City," James Carlino soberly uttered his exposition, "Ben suffered a wicked heart attack and died shortly thereafter at Mainland Hospital in Pomona."

"And who is the alluring-looking lady shown in this final photo'?"

"She is, or should I say 'was' Josephine Lucas, who was Ben's faithful wife right up to the end," elaborated Carlino. "After her husband unexpectedly departed this Earth, feeling obligated, I provided Josie with food and mortgage money along with additional funds to compensate for her talented daughter's college education at nearby Stockton State University. As you can plainly observe Tom," the prospective mall developer resumed, "my personal history has been besieged with both risk and catastrophe. Nothing ventured; nothing gained has always been my personal motto. But Tom, do you want to hear something that's rather strange and inexplicable about this entire scenario?"

"What is that?" the bank president persuasively insisted.

"Lately, whenever I peer at these twelve flat black and white pictures, I feel as if the individuals' eyes are all staring at me from another indiscernible dimension," the mansion dweller declared. "I'm not ordinarily superstitious, but the entire phenomenal enigma is very eerie and uniquely arcane. And these two-dimensional likenesses situated upon this credenza weirdly project their mysterious eyes at least once a day as of late, and those stares seem to be penetrating right through me, as if the frightening, peculiar gapes are positively surreal; the horrendous, intimidating, alien X-ray eyes seem to be apparently originating from another world! And sometimes when I turn around quickly, the twenty-four eyes following me are surprisingly caught moving back to their initial positions."

"Well Jim," Thomas Monastra answered with general alarm and mental confusion, "it's often said that the eyes are the windows to the soul! But if you want my honest opinion about your uncanny *Twilight Zone* episodes, I think that your imagination coupled with your emotional anguish are together preventing you from evading your present state of imagination! I think that a few nights of good sleep will replenish your stability. Now then Jim, let's solidify the details of our next meeting on Saturday morning with your corporate CPA and your personal Stockbroker."

* * * * * * * * * * * *

Three days later on Saturday at 9 a.m. a trio of dependable financial gurus assembled upon the expansive curved driveway outside James Dante Carlino's palatial East First Road mansion. Prominent banker Thomas Monastra, reputable Stock and Bond Account Executive Richard Palmieri and reliable CPA William Tomasello were mutually gathered to intelligently finalize James Carlino's longtime aspiration of constructing a multimillion-dollar shopping center complex in pleasant Somers Point, just outside Ocean City, NJ.

"That's odd!" observed and exclaimed the somewhat worried visiting banker. "He's not responding to our doorbell rings. If anything, Mr. Carlino is usually prompt and punctual, especially ready to be available for such an important matter as his shopping center dream finally coming to fruition. Try ringing the doorbell again Richard! Perhaps our friend is finishing-up his morning coffee in the kitchen."

"Look through this side window!" the now-shocked stockbroker directed his companions. "I see a figure lying face-down on the floor underneath the side-wall drapes!"

"This is a very serious emergency! That's beyond a doubt Mr. Carlino lying there!" ascertained the alarmed-and-upset Certified Public Accountant. "My client has always been an ardent Elvis Presley fan! I would recognize those expensive imported blue suede shoes he's wearing anywhere!"

Nervous William Tomasello instinctively removed his cellphone from his left front pocket and swiftly dialed 911, and the AtlantiCare ambulance squad was instantaneously contacted through the town dispatcher to rush-out and promptly address the crisis. Led by blaring police car sirens, the on-a-mission rescue crew arrived upon the frenzied scene five minutes later. The two frenetic, under-duress on-duty cops violently impacted the dual front doors using a portable battering ram. Then, after several crucial minutes of futilely attempting to resuscitate the fallen victim, the certified EMT captain reluctantly pronounced the rich investor dead.

"James Carlino was undoubtedly one of the wealthiest men in Hammonton just a mere hour ago," CPA William Tomasello asserted and grimly confided, "but now like any other person who becomes deceased, the dead fellow isn't worth a plug nickel!"

* * * * * * * * * * * *

The other-dimension courtroom was gloomily dismal, dingy and obscure. The black-robed, apathetic two-dimensional Devil's Advocate stood before the elevated panel of twelve haunting phantoms, all pathetically gray-robed, similar-in-appearance, solemn-faced specters, and then the Frightful Figure serving as Chief Prosecutor began delivering his introductory announcement.

"I would like to expedite this trial of one James Dante Carlino by having each of you orally present an abbreviated statement about how *this* pernicious individual had diabolically harmed you, either physically or emotionally. Your mission is akin to how a Grand Jury presently operates in your former existence. I remind you that you are the twelve appointed prosecuting attorneys as well as being the twelve jurists who will ultimately pronounce a permanent sentence at the completion of this legal formality. In this well-defined procedure, there is no Defense Attorney for the Accused. And after your sagacious verdict has been rendered, I shall determine the precise punishment to be administered and exercised. Needless to say, the Defendant, or should I say 'Accused', will have no means of appeal after this case is evaluated and consequently disposed of. Let us commence this post-life inquisition with testimony from Mrs. Carmella Carlino."

"Thank you, Eminent Prosecutor for recognizing me first," prefaced deceased Carmella Carlino. "In July of 1969, my brother-in-law Mr. Pietro Carlino, who incidentally is still barely alive and on life support, now hardly breathing in a semi-conscious state, had five-hundred-thousand dollars hidden away inside a cheap metal 'quilt chest' in the rear of his master bedroom's walk-in cedar closet. Half of that cash money had been skimmed primarily from the family farm and should rightfully have belonged to my husband Lorenzo, Pietro Carlino's younger brother."

Gray-faced Jurist Carmella Carlino paused for a moment to gather and organize her abundant random thoughts. "My nefarious nephew James Carlino had certain Mafia and Cosa Nostra contacts throughout New Jersey. As one of the local syndicate's many crimes, four masked thugs broke into Pietro's house, tied-up his wife's hands behind her back and also viciously gagged her; then using another longer rope, the ruthless home invaders suspended my avaricious sister-in-law Angelina upside-down, hanging and dangling her from the upstairs bannister. While poor Angelina was being savagely assaulted, her husband Pietro had his head repeatedly held and dunked into the upstairs bathroom sink's basin that incidentally had been filled with scalding hot water. That terrible violence lasted until the beleaguered farmer finally told the molesters the three-digit combination to the master bedroom's cedar closet 'metallic quilt chest'. After purloining the stashed loot, the Mafia goons then quickly abandoned the crime scene with a half-million cold cash stuffed inside several laundry bags; yes, five thousand crisp, hundred-dollar bills had been vilely stolen. Evidently, my disgustingly greedy Mafia nephew James later used his share of the half-million bucks as seed money to start his own cold storage enterprises in Vineland. I conclude my testimony by stating that James had never expressed any particular remorse or contrition for his many wicked criminal misdeeds."

Bianca Carlino was the second jurist to prefer charges against the non-penitent 'Accused'. "My evil brother was the Carlino Farm treasurer, and over a ten-year period the despicable felon skimmed and siphoned over one and a half million dollars from the corporation. I never wanted to officially incriminate James because I feared the prospect of public scandal once the charges were published in local newspapers, which sometimes report news as tabloid-type information," Bianca confided and disclosed. "Also, the IRS would have rapidly gotten wind of the secret money withholding, and *that* sort of government investigation could have really exacerbated the whole problem. Fellow Jurists, I realize that I had an ugly mole-laden face during my earthly existence, but my brother James's egregious misconduct was indeed far uglier than my grotesque countenance ever was!"

"Thank you, Bianca for your valuable and insightful input," commended the assigned Devil's Advocate Prosecutor. "We'll now hear from Jurist Number Three, Lorenzo Carlino, Carmella Carlino's exploited husband."

"I despised my covetous nephew James with a wild hateful passion," Lorenzo began his strong indictment. "Besides constantly belittling and abusing me on the family farm in front of employees, my nephew was a crazed womanizer, a sexual predator who frequently abandoned marital fidelity in absurd escapades with at least two dozen whores, prostitutes and promiscuous females. Once I had taken my wife Carmella to a Broadway play and an overnight stay at a Manhattan hotel. After we arrived by taxi to the bustling Port Authority Bus Terminal, Carmella and I noticed James boarding a bus that would be heading to Atlantic City. My egotistical nephew was accompanied by a buxom blonde, who incidentally was not his often-ignored wife Lisa."

"Deplorable deportment indeed!" observed and acknowledged the drab, flat-as-a-billiard-table Devil's Advocate. "Let's now listen to damaging commentary from the specter of Lisa Nelson Carlino, the Accused Individual's first wife, our Jurist Number Four."

"Forget the provable fact that my heinous husband was a classic womanizer," Lisa Nelson Carlino defiantly stated to her judicial colleagues. "I was casually driving south on Pacific Highway 101 in a leased white Bentley when all of a sudden the right front wheel suspiciously separated from the brand-new car. My vehicle then careened and tumbled down a side ridge and soon caught fire with me inside. My body was severely burned and then deteriorated into an unidentifiable state. I hereby blame my husband James for maliciously causing my grievous death by auto," the former wife attested. "He wanted to dispose of me quickly, used his West Coast Mafia connections to rig my luxury vehicle for impending disaster, and then plotted to collect several hundred-thousand-dollars from a life insurance policy in the process. All of that diabolical California activity had occurred because I had threatened to report my husband's extra-marital affairs to the *Atlantic City Press* if James didn't stop cavorting around with porn stars and also immorally frequenting Atlantic City bordellos."

The fifth designated prosecutor on the Recently Deceased Court Docket was Eleanor Davidson of Edgewood, Maryland, a suburb of Baltimore. "James had offered to pay my hospital expenses for my debilitating ALS condition, but the craven liar never came through on his hollow promises. Instead, my demented cousin and his Mafia allies threatened my boss at the manufacturing plant where I had been employed, falsely claiming that I owed *him* a hundred thousand dollars' promissory note that never existed," Eleanor's apparition intrepidly testified. "The purpose of this illicit behavior on James's part was to recruit my husband Robert into the Baltimore mob syndicate to become a shakedown thug for citizens that had a hard time paying already owed extortion money. And since Rob stands a colossal six foot six in stature and weighs two-hundred and seventy-five pounds, my husband was a prime target for admission into the local Sicilian cartel."

Next on the crowded afterworld agenda happened to be Jurist Number Six, vociferous Franco Carlino, the younger brother and rival of James in the family hierarchy. "My older brother Jimmy was the epitome of harmful wrongdoing," Franco asserted to the other eleven attentive Jury Members and also to the Devil's Advocate Prosecutor. "I believe that James always possessed a distinct aversion to basic human decency. After I had been visited and physically assaulted by three of his Mafia chums, I had to pawn my diamond ring and my wife's jewelry just to make monthly extortion payments to the mob," Franco's shade audaciously stated. "Then I had to donate my fully-equipped late-model Lincoln Continental to the local Mafia so that its parts could go to selected junkyards and to Philly' chop shops for dismantlement and resale. I feared for my endangered life, and now I realize that my unexpected fatal plane crash had occurred because the engine had been spitefully tampered with and expertly sabotaged. Jimmy thought that our father Pietro was gradually liking me more than him, so my black-hearted brother surreptitiously organized my small craft plummet and violent crash into the Wharton State Forest, all happening upon my landing approach to Hammonton Municipal Airport."

"Apparition Number Seven, sister Barbara Carlino, you now have the floor to present a terse dissertation pertaining to the innumerable transgressions of your loathsome brother," the Devil's Advocate instructed. "I believe that your presentation will be the seventh panel recitation."

"Every time I recall my brother James's repulsive self-centered schemes," Barbara Carlino's shade recounted, "I think of the deceiving villain as being both the agony and the ecstasy. His obnoxious behaviors had agonizing consequences for me and for my family, but simultaneously, his misdeeds brought ecstasy to his selfish nature. My husband Steve and I were gaining satisfaction from churning some commendable profits while acquiring and then flipping houses in Palm Springs, California and later in South Padre Island, Texas. But when we set-up shop in Ft. Myers, Florida, my reprehensible older brother threatened us with arson. He effectively practiced extortion by predicting that his treacherous Mafia friends would burn-down our new South Florida home unless we participated in what amounted to a fraudulent Ponzi pyramid conspiracy," Barbara Carlino revealed. "After borrowing our credit cards' money to the limit, Steve and I invested seven-hundred-and-fifty thousand dollars in a real estate trust fund that was designed to pay us 20% interest every year. The first several years went smoothly until the unscrupulous ruse ran-out of newly-duped suckers to draw into the malignant plot. And the initial annual reports were handled by a team of corrupt accountants working for the mob," the taken-advantage-of sister denunciated. "The crooked accomplices' ruthless role was to make all suspect fraudulent records and correspondences appear to be legitimate! When I eventually died of breast cancer, I died broke, and I was in major financial debt!"

"We'll now hear from Prosecutor/Jurist Number Eight, Megyn Carlino Johnson, James Carlino's second cousin who had sacrificed plenty in her early life, growing-up in a destitute family having seven needy children," the Chief Prosecutor dressed in the large black robe carefully cited. "Make it brief so that I can speedily move to terminate this totally bureaucratic process!"

"I died penniless, thanks to the savage effects of being directly associated with my Satanic cousin James Carlino," Megyn Johnson commenced her questionable relative's character analysis. "After establishing a profitable guardrail installation company, Fred, my hard-working husband and I were ordered at gunpoint by James's iniquitous Mafia henchmen to contribute two hundred thousand dollars to be used to bribe three South Jersey mayors to allow for the acquisition and licensing of ten pizza parlors. The newly-created retail businesses were to be utilized for laundering and disguising mob money within the dynamic American capitalistic economic system. To accurately assess this dutiful exact moment in the hereafter," Megyn Johnson's spirit adamantly insisted, "I submit that I still fully resent my uncivilized cousin's destruction and ruination of my formerly happy life that had prevailed prior to me being stricken with full-blown leukemia."

"Thank you' Mrs. Johnson for offering your incisive testimony," the Chief Prosecutor praised. "Our mendacious Mr. James Dante Carlino definitely shows indications of being a prospective candidate for *Dante's Inferno*. Please forgive my flaccid attempt at humor," the slightly embarrassed Chief Prosecutor apologized, "but our subject-in-question shows behavioral propensities for being more of a pernicious *antagonist* than acting as a constructive *protagonist* in enacting his former life. With *that* rational illustration being elucidated, let's now listen to aggrieved Jurist Number Nine, deceased former middle school administrator, Gary Testa."

The school official, who had died from being painfully defeated by colon cancer, concisely complained that James Dante Carlino had been clandestinely involved in two major drug distribution networks, one in Paramus and the other located in Egg Harbor City, New Jersey. The Ninth Jurist discreetly charged that his underworld bowling buddy had gotten the school official hooked on meth and on crack cocaine. "I was leading a normal life until, who I considered to be my best pal, suddenly betrayed our friendship with drugs," the former educator affirmed. "Once I was addicted, my life went

74

downhill in a hurry. I simply can't forgive this foul menace named James Carlino for the harsh, malignant, deleterious effect his once-trusted acquaintance has had in dissolving the foundations of all my family relationships. I felt and still feel utter bitterness toward Jim, whom I still think and believe is a dyed-in-the-wool psychopath. True, I am partially to blame for my detrimental addiction," Gary Testa's gray ghost realized and stated, "but I warrant and swear that James Dante Carlino is the scoundrel principally responsible for my drug-related decline. I hereby insist that moral justice must be thoroughly implemented by this judicious panel."

Carol Sorrentino Carlino, James's second wife, also showed great enmity towards her "accused gangster former husband". The Tenth Jurist/Shade commenced her commentary by sternly reiterating first wife Lisa Nelson Carlino's boldly proclaimed main allegation. "In addition to being a dedicated womanizer," Carol's vengeful spirit stressed and grieved, "my deranged spouse promised that he would report my family's cold storage businesses to the IRS for owed taxes on siphoned-off money that had been advertently kept concealed from government scrutiny. The isolated Pocono Mountain lodge had been deeded in my name, so under unbelievable pressure exerted by James and his mob collaborators, I deemed it necessary to sell the property and swing the four-hundred-thousand-dollar cash settlement into financing my entrance into James's doomed Ponzi real estate pyramid scheme. And right after *that* implausible expense was made, I experienced the fatal ski accident near Camelback Mountain and consequently, lost my precious life. To sum-up *this* dramatic moment in eternity, I still attribute my painful death to James along with his association with the merciless mob in causing my demise to happen."

"Thank you for your salient and relevant discourse," the Devil's Advocate diplomatically remarked to the deceased second wife. "Now we'll listen to testimony from Mr. Benjamin Lucas, once regarded as a close confidante of Mr. James Dante Carlino. Please make your oration short and brief."

The Eleventh Witness/Jurist sat erect in his black two-dimensional chair and calmly addressed his peers and the gruesome-looking Devil's Advocate Prosecutor. "Certainly, when it boiled-down to human values, among them courtesy and fundamental morality, my dysfunctional second cousin regarded himself as being some sort of amoral iconoclast," Benjamin Lucas austerely declared and accused. "Jealous Jim chronically and voluntarily violated the essential premises provided in the Ten Commandments, the lesson taught in the Golden Rule 'Do unto Others', and also the teaching found in the marvelous precept 'Love Thy Neighbor as Thyself'. In my particular case, Mr. James Carlino both encouraged and fueled my gambling habit by perpetually bailing me out of accumulated arrears in order to make me more dependent on his manipulative control over me. My demonic cousin tried to make me quit my job as a recognized top-grade automobile mechanic and then illegally operate a mob chop-shop for stolen vehicles, the proposed scam located ten miles southeast of Hammonton in Hamilton Township. But to my credit," Benjamin Lucas clarified, "I refused to be affiliated with the local crime syndicate, but in the interim I became acutely paranoid and fearful that a mob hit squad would arrive at my home and either torture my wife Josephine or assassinate me for not cooperating with James's maniacal, egocentric out-of-control fanaticism. Esteemed Panel, I soon became excessively distraught and emotionally disheveled," Benjamin Lucas related to the biased jury. "I claim that the massive heart attack I had suffered was a direct result of the excruciating mental and emotional discomfort I then experienced, being subjected to periods of fatigue, depression, delirium, continuous apprehension and plenteous bouts of overwhelming hysteria; all because of James Dante Carlino!"

Finally, black-robed Justice/Prosecutor Number Twelve, Josephine Lucas, sat erect in her two-dimensional seat and began orating her personal connection to all-too-devious non-present soul. "I must validate the true testimonies of James's first and second wives, corroborating the fact that the guilty subject presently on trial was indeed a deceitful womanizer. Whenever my husband Ben was working at the auto' shop or rolling dice or playing poker in Atlantic City, this parasitic scoundrel Mr. James Carlino would visit our humble abode and soon attempt being aggressively amorous towards me. It reached a point where I would deliberately have my daughter Eileen staying at home by my side in order to deter the evil fiend from molesting me. But being used to getting what his twisted soul often desired," the aggrieved woman's specter alleged, "wily Mr. James Carlino persisted in his relentless pursuit of sadistic pleasure reflected in the form of sinful adultery."

"I thank all of the contributing Jurists for their convicting renditions relating to the fate and sentencing of absent Mr. James Dante Carlino's blemished soul, which certainly holds a redundancy of shameful misdeeds. Now then, if you believe that the aforementioned subject is guilty of committing a plethora of mortal and venial sins, I direct that you now raise over your heads the flat black placards located at your feet," the dark figure imperatively instructed. "Fine; I see that the panel is unanimous in its irreversible verdict. As you are well-aware, the stained non-in-attendance soul on trial has upon death both relinquished and surrendered its free will, so there is no legal objection or appeal to this court's supreme decision or authority. The 'Accused' had enacted multiple trespasses against this unified Jury of Twelve Plaintiffs, and his manifold sins were indeed most malevolent and exceedingly insidious. Therefore, I hereby remand the soul of James Dante Carlino to the custody of St. Peter, esteemed Keeper of the Eternal Gates. I herein rule and recommend that the Apostle's formidable angel guards will swiftly conduct Mr. Carlino's impure spirit to a dark, gravel-floored prison cell, and it will remain at *that* punitive destination for a duration of one thousand Earth years, specifically to undergo prescribed and required fire and lava purification. And then after the millennium period of solitary confinement has expired," the Devil's Advocate emphatically summarized, "the soul of Mr. Carlino will finally be exposed to Perpetual Light shining upon its formerly contaminated existence. This easily resolved trial now stands adjourned. The distinguished panel of qualified Jurists is now hereby dismissed."

"Sleep Paralysis"

In a required college literature class, I had diligently studied the profound essays of distinguished literary contributor Ralph Waldo Emerson and was also assigned to read the recognized classic book *Walden Pond,* authored by Henry David Thoreau. Both early nineteenth century writers/philosophers were devout advocates of "Transcendentalism", a rather remote and esoteric New England social movement that had its genesis in 1836.

The basic principle of the new "romantic treatise" was that Nature should "Transcend" objective reason and ought to be appreciated on a higher plane than either human art or mankind's contemporary science. In other words, "Pantheism" should trump logic when one evaluates himself or herself in relation to the remainder of humanity and when he or she assesses the wondrous external environment.

Transcendentalism was fundamentally a protesting of the rampant urban development that resulted from the rapid growth of the Industrial Revolution; hence, its agenda represented a rebellion against factories in city settings making employees into human robots completing redundant tasks in dismal and dank poorly ventilated working conditions. The infant Emersonian philosophy essentially maintained that Divinity (God represented in all green forests, lakes, fresh air and mountains) supersedes all human activity, especially where societal town and city living interfered with a citizen's need to privately live in harmony and "communion" with observable Nature.

A second important element of Transcendentalism espoused by Ralph Waldo Emerson and Henry David Thoreau maintained that responsible individual independence along with rugged self-sufficiency and self-reliance were necessary components of mortal happiness, of moral growth and of successful communion with Nature (the Divine; the physical environment). In fact, Thoreau abandoned New England society, and symbolically declaring his personal independence from laws and taxes on July 4th, the determined transcendentalist left clustered town life to rely on his own need to survive. The obstinate individualist constructed a modest cabin in the woods at Walden Pond. Hence, Thoreau happily lived separated (and on his own self-dependence) away from the mayhem and chaos associated with American society, which engendered interdependent co-existence and tax-hungry government dominance reigning supreme over the exploited individual in post-colonial Massachusetts civilization.

I believe that over the years my fact-minded psyche has been profoundly influenced by what I describe as "Reverse or Inverted Transcendentalism", a self-taught method where I practice both the art and science of Logic and Reason being deliberately elevated over "Emotional Reverence for Nature". My mental technique has organized my thinking acumen into a sophisticated behavioral equation. Since I've always regarded myself as a rational, independent, self-reliant person, I have a sharp contempt for people who constantly behave in an affectionate, emotional, doltish manner.

For the past three decades, I have experienced many unique episodes of Sleep Paralysis, a condition where the mind wakes-up from its deep REM slumber minutes before the lagging body has an opportunity to catch-up. During the average three-four-minute "twilight zone interval", I lay motionless in my bed with my non-blinking eyes wide open. I cannot move an arm or a leg, nor can I turn my hips in either direction and roll my body over, even though I'm fully aware of my physical limitations during *that* stressful period of "body freeze".

I've always theorized that there exists a definite connection between my secret practice of Inverted Transcendentalism and my propensity to sustain several moments of Sleep Paralysis at least once each and every month. 'Obviously, my body and mind are not progressing normally through the various phases of commonly waking-up,' I have often speculated. 'I don't at all think that my condition is a sign of psychological abnormality. But I've read in several influential research journals where Sleep Paralysis is a huge step forward for a subject to actually develop the capability of having consecutive out-of-body experiences.

Throughout the Middle Ages and the later Medieval Times, the general characteristics of sleep paralysis have been defined and affiliated with the undesired intrusion of "evil" beings and devious demons: wicked creatures that might today be similarly identified as alien space abductors. Virtually all cultures that have been academically analyzed by legitimate scholars (throughout ancient and modern history) have documented tales of formidable, nocturnal entities evilly terrorizing vulnerable humans waking-up from their deep sleep in the middle of the night. Adding an element of awe to these ongoing, mysterious sleep paralysis encounters that have been recorded over the ages, common victims have long sought plausible explanations to account for their later awareness of being frozen, disabled and terrified for several minutes

80

during incremental sleep stages. These nerve-racking "paralysis seizures" occur where the body is futilely attempting to speed-up and again synchronize with the already awake-but-petrified mind.

My rather revolutionary, abstract hypothesis is quite scrupulous, simple and compact. While my mortal being would be existing inside my immobile anatomy during my all-too-familiar state of "sleep paralysis", which I believed to be a certain aspect of suspended animation, my numbed mind would be able to generate an out-of-body *spiritual ejection* that could simultaneously energize a three-four minute period of wonderful time travel; for I conjectured that if I could temporarily escape the Newtonian constraints of physical space, then I could quickly thereafter also conquer the restrictions of time during my brief three-four minute sleep paralysis. I hypothesized that only a dedicated, laconic, pragmatic person (like myself) believing in Reverse Transcendentalism could ever begin to even contemplate performing such an extraordinary mind-body-space-time sleep experiment, being exercised in deliberate defiance of Einstein's mathematical Relativity.

* * * * * * * * * * * *

My sagacious plan for converting negative events that egregiously plagued my past life was rather elementary, if not rudimentary in scope and sequence. The "infallible formula" I had adopted for attaining remedy and relief from 2019 America might sound like it is totally naïve to the average person but in reality, my exceptional strategy was positively ingenious to say the least.

Before proceeding further with this relevant narrative, allow me to review in detail my excellent formula's exact, essential components: Objective Non-Emotion Transcendentalism + Fully Awake Sleep Paralysis + Out of Body Experience = Time Travel designed to alter my past failures and miseries, and I soberly had intended for the entire process to be accomplished within the brief three-four minute interval that my active mind and frozen body would be out of sync with each other.

I'm now seventy-seven years old, and my overall health has significantly deteriorated in the past decade. I attribute a great deal of this senior citizen demise to inhaling an abundance of cigarette nicotine and tar over the years, which I began addictively doing beginning at age fourteen and then having the behavioral scourge lasting-up until I reached twenty-eight. My parents in the 1940s and '50s were chronic smokers of tobacco brands Lucky Strike and Pall Mall, and when filter tip cigarettes became the vogue, mom and dad reluctantly switched their preferences to puffing-away on brands Winston and Salem, each of the obviously popular designations being named after the city of Winston-Salem, North Carolina.

Smoking during the golden ages of '50s and early '60s theater cinema and black and white TV shows was highly and effectively propagandized. Popular commercials featured "social modeling" where the detrimental habit of inhaling unhealthy nicotine and tar fumes was regarded as fashionable because movie stars like Humphrey Bogart, Lauren Bacall and Clark Gable along with television celebrities such as Dean Martin and Jackie Gleason set bad examples and smoked incessantly while performing their highly-promoted acting roles. The celebrity movie and TV stars dominating the spotlight were being conscientiously viewed all across the nation by the imitating American public.

* * * * * * * * * * * *

While anxiously preparing for my first adventure in initiating time travel to the past, each night I would seriously concentrate on a certain event and then my alert brain would relentlessly focus on the targeted situation initiating from the depths of my subconscious. This stark method I would utilize until my keen, acute awareness drifted-off to visit often-revered Mr. Sandman. While becoming increasingly drowsy, I did not dedicate my thoughts to a particular hour, day, week, month or year. Instead, I recollected a specific incident that my attention would hone-in upon; that is, after I would get all other competing clutter out of my specialized train of thought. Fortunately, to achieve my goal, at 3 a.m. on a cold February Sunday morning, a bout of temporary "Sleep Paralysis" set-in while my semi-hypnotized mind was ruminating about meeting my old Levittown, Pennsylvania buddy Tommy Gallagher at Mill Creek where the enslaved juvenile Marlboro smoker had introduced me in 1957 to one of his Marlboro "cancer sticks".

Every second during my precious three-minute time excursion back to 1957, which later was comparable to a vividly recalled mental newsreel, I skillfully took advantage of my fantastic psychic activity. While I had been immersed in my awakening paralysis state, I bluntly communicated to my fifteen-year-old pal, "No thanks Tommy. I prefer chewing gum. I'd rather have rotten teeth than contaminated lungs."

My modus operandi in speaking decisively to Tommy Gallagher during the "sci-fi" return visit to my youth was intended to later avoid developing a bad case of emphysema, which had deleteriously affected my breathing for two whole decades and which had greedily taken the lives of both my parents in the 1980s. I figured that by solving a formidable 2019 problem by preventively eliminating the difficulty in 1957, I could easily live longer under better and more favorable health conditions, and therefore be able to competently escape the pursuit of the Grim Reaper well into my nineties.

With my first three-minute time-travel mission enacted and completed, I felt my entire spirit being vacuumed back from the 1957 past and then sucked right into my 2019 body. It was a wild adrenalin rush that violently jolted me out of my captured state of sleep paralysis. I took twenty deep breaths to gradually readjust my chaotic mind and have my exhausted cerebrum slowly reunite with my semi-shocked, semi-anesthetized body. 'Yes, absolute success,' I remember evaluating. 'Yes, wonderful success! I had read on the Internet where Tommy Gallagher had died in 2011, but now I find great pleasure in knowing that I'll be an inhabitant of this Earth for many more years to come.'

For my second sleep-paralysis-time travel rendezvous with the changeable past, I was lying in bed in the middle of the night meditating about my 1960 senior high school year at Edgewood Regional, Tansboro, New Jersey. Although I was a stellar A student in English and Social Studies, I was conversely poor in mastering the challenging mechanics of Science and Math. Mr. Andrews was my Trigonometry instructor at Edgewood, and right from the outset, the no-nonsense teacher and I did not harmonize. In 2019, I now regret not astutely studying harder in learning the fundamentals and various complex functionalities of Sine, Cosine, Tangent, Cotangent, Secant and Cosecant; so consequently, I disgracefully failed the Edgewood High Trig class and was then required to take a Public Service bus for two entire summer months twenty-three miles west both to and from Collingswood High School for the expressed purpose of me gaining more proficiency and remediation in higher mathematics.

Since I had flunked a major core curriculum subject, I could not graduate on stage with my senior class. Student self-discipline along with high pupil expectations was much-more rigid back then before the mandates of fraudulent educational psychology and more liberal grading systems negatively poisoned public-school education. At any rate, in September of 1960 I returned to Edgewood High to receive my diploma, feeling guilty that I could not enter college for a full semester because of my former student dereliction of duty. The Edgewood principal informed me that I had to venture up to Mr.

Andrews classroom where a rerun of the pedagogue's final Trig Exam would be academically administered. Much to the austere math teacher's astonishment, I finished the rigorous math test in less than a half-hour and managed to get each and every item correct. I was directed by the Trig instructor to the Main Office where the also-surprised school principal handed me my coveted diploma.

'If I could think about being admitted into Mr. Andrews Trig class that first school day in September of 1959, I could mentally time-voyage to *that* date and change my combative personality to conform with the inflexible teacher's stringent classroom rules and regulations,' I shrewdly conjectured. 'I'll be the ideal academic learner, well-behaved and desiring to work both day and night on Trig equations in an assiduous manner. If I adequately apply myself with the appropriate effort, I'm sure that I'll become an A pupil and convincingly demonstrate to inflexible Mr. Andrews that I'm mature and competent in his coveted area of expertise.'

Incredibly, on the second Sunday in March of 2019 I momentarily time-journeyed back into Mr. Andrews' September 1960 educational math realm, smiled and won his confidence and friendship; and upon returning to March of 2019 three minutes later, I'm now absolutely certain (in the present time) that I had satisfactorily solved another major obstacle from my volatile youth that had harmfully prohibited me from having a smooth, uneventful transition from rebellious adolescence into adulthood.

My clever scheme was to intelligently address the origins of my 2019 problems in a precise chronological order, starting from 1957 and then advancing from my awkward formative years right up to the tumultuous present. Quite truthfully, I was becoming a degree overconfident and downright cocky regarding my recently discovered deft manipulation of the Transcendental-Sleep Paralysis-Out of Body-Space-Time Continuum.

My third grand problem-solving project demanded tremendous preparation on my part. I had been married to the former local beauty contestant Alice Palmieri for ten years between 1966 and '76, and soon after our disastrous honeymoon in San Diego, the domineering wench continuously berated me and later tried henpecking me around the spring of 1967. The only viable solution to my frustrating predicament with the Hammonton Peach Queen was to intentionally wander back to September of 1965 and cancel-out my engagement proposal that had been delivered inside the college senior's girl's dormitory.

'I believe that Alice must have been caustic Dame Van Winkle reincarnated,' I sarcastically mused as my about-to-slumber mind relaxed and lasered-in on that regrettable September 1965 college moment and place. 'I refuse to be a wimpy, gullible fool! But I only have a narrow time-window of three short minutes to destroy our flourishing romantic relationship. The upside is that I'll save two thousand dollars by returning the diamond engagement ring to the jeweler,' I imagined two hours before zooming-off that April morning into the past to participate in another out-of-body jaunt. All the while I fully realized that I had only three to four minutes to terminate our ongoing 1965 love affair.

"Alice, there's something urgent I have to tell you," my selfsame facsimile declared inside her disorganized dorm room. "I think I'm gay and have the hots for a guy going to graduate school at Villanova. For several years I've been surreptitiously covering-up this homosexual thing, but now I can't live with lying to you any longer. Goodbye Alice!" I feigned weeping as I wildly opened the dorm room door and then slammed it behind me just prior to my being swiftly transported by the "Powers That Be" back to my home's 2019 bed, again being a three-minute captive to the mercy of 'sleep paralysis'. After reuniting my traveling soul with my slow-awakening body, my gut instinct suggested to me that somehow my itinerant spirit had interfaced and then integrated with my 1965 body, complete its vital courier mandate and then magically zip back to my contemporary form still lying motionless in my bed.

In June of 1959 Mom and Dad had moved the family from Levittown, PA to Hammonton, NJ and my parents purchased and owned a small grocery store near the railroad tracks on Fairview Avenue. My folks had operated the business for fourteen years, and the respectable market was sold in the fall of '74 for several hundred thousand dollars. Within the next decade, my beloved parents had passed away, and my industrious folks had very generously left their only son an attractive two-story home and also a sizable cash and stock inheritance. Being quite glad that I could keep my new-found bonanzas all to myself, I searched for ways to supplement my meager income as a proletarian public-school English teacher.

A trustful faculty acquaintance introduced me to a certain slick entrepreneur who owned a total of six lucrative boardwalk pizza concessions on the Seaside Heights, Atlantic City, Wildwood and Ocean City, New Jersey boardwalks. "I'm going to sell my Wildwood pizza joints and use the money to expand my enterprises into boardwalk tee shirt stores and several amusement arcades," authoritarian Mr. Manny Schwartz related to me. "If you can come up with a few hundred thousand clams, I'll surrender the keys to my two Wildwood tomato pie operations. The thriving pizza stores will prove to be terrific cash cows that will more than triple your puny teaching salary! You can't go wrong, John."

As it turned-out, the "cash cow" pizza shops turned-out to be calamitous "money pits". I immediately took the alluring bait and made the huge investment, not knowing that Mr. Manny Schwartz was having arguments over delinquent rent payments with two different boardwalk landlords. In the final analysis, I quickly lost my inherited money when the ravenous beach landlords terminated the derelict leases; their actions coming soon after I had given *that* avaricious fat-cat pizza shop swindler a bona-fide check covering the entire two-hundred grand expense. However, thanks to the sublime time travel methodology I had brilliantly devised, my fourth journey back in time proved to be a most magnificent triumph.

'I can get the money back from *that* con-artist Schwartz,' I cunningly plotted in May of 2019. 'I'll just time travel back and outsmart *that* fast-talking conniver. I'll tell that carnival barker Mr. Manny Schwartz (the night before our big transaction would be finalized) that I'm reinvesting the alluded-to money in blue chip corporations listed on the New York Stock Exchange.' And so, formulating my infallible game plan, I calmly entered into my next sleep paralysis session and very scrupulously time traveled back to April of that formerly disastrous year. I decisively communicated via telephone to an enraged and disappointed Mr. Manny Schwartz that *our* prospective dead-in-the-water boardwalk pizza store deal was now officially "null and void".

After favorably retrieving my parents' inheritance money, I heard that many ordinary people like myself were making enormous capital gains intrepidly investing in startup penny stock technology companies. I earnestly conducted my preliminary research, so in 1988 I boldly purchased five million shares (at ten cents each) of a Colorado firm that promised to interconnect all existing types of computer systems and allow the separate entities to compatibly function together, effectively heralding-in a new dynamic industry. The amazing "black boxes" would both dispense and communicate information from one entity to every other computer company's machine. I had invested my life's savings into the novel penny stock enterprise, and I was thrilled owning five percent of a company destined to become a major Wall Street titan. As it turned out, in

1991 the Denver facility went bankrupt, making me an extremely despondent and distraught data-sharing investor.

In August of 2019, I felt embarrassed at being the victim of my own impetuous stupidity. I decided to aggressively rectify the very disturbing, adverse matter concerning the belly-up Denver computer firm by enthusiastically implementing the Transcendental-Sleep Paralysis-Out of Body-Time-Travel pattern. My distinct objective was to "reverse engineer" my totally catastrophic and preposterous penny stock investment. My rambunctious spirit again creatively left my physical form and ventured back to the year 1988. Inside my residence, I immediately preempted dialing the initial phone call I had made to my stockbroker about pumping the huge sum into the Colorado upstart and instead, I instructed my account executive to invest my hard-earned dollars into Apple and Microsoft stock certificates, which today in 2019 are worth many millions of authentic American bucks.

By September of 2019, I had proficiently trained my obedient brain to have on-demand out-of-body experiences along with subsequently initiating derivative time-travel adventures to modify negative past life episodes, which were now being efficaciously manifested as repeated successful demonstrations rather than being mere arcane, scientific experiments.

Ever since I had formulated and perfected my top-secret time travel knowledge, I've developed a truly selfish, sanctimonious, egotistical facet to my normally inflated sense of superiority. From 2010 to 2016, much to my chagrin, I had acquired a debilitating, self-destructive habit. I had succumbed to the vice of addictive gambling inside various Atlantic City casinos. I figured that I could cure my new-found bad habit by simply time traveling back to 2010. I did voyage back to August of *that* year and upon finding myself standing in my home kitchen, I opened the familiar rolltop desk, found a blank slip of paper, picked up a ballpoint pen conveniently located nearby and rapidly jotted-down the following note in my inimitable handwriting: "John: Don't dare begin playing poker, roulette, craps and slot machines in A.C. Don't sacrifice your mortal soul." Your alter ego, J.W.

While staring at the attractive oakwood table in the room's center, I decided to write my past self another longer message that pertained to a 2019 hip operation and eight inches of large intestine (excised in that same year) where a giant polyp had grown and needed to be surgically extracted. The second more lengthy 2010 missive read: "John: Have a colonoscopy done immediately to remove the big polyp forming in your large intestine. Also, stop being so frugal and hire a landscaping company to pick-up the fourteen thousand pine cones that will fall from the backyard dozen pine trees. If you don't, you'll soon need to also have a painful hip replacement operation, too." Your alter ego John.

The 2010 kitchen table reading notes evidently were a tremendous success because now landing back in bed in late September of 2019, I lucidly discerned that the dangerous, aching intestinal polyp no longer resided in my ascending colon and that my right hip showed no observable scar from any needed hospital operation. In another fortuitous venue, I just examined my online UBS stock account, and my lips smiled with delight upon me noticing that my blue-chip corporate holdings still were generating decent revenue and the sum remained at a handsome 3.5 million dollars.

* * * * * * * * * * * *

Sunday October 6th on the hanging kitchen wall calendar was my seventy-seventh birthday, which I later privately celebrated at the crowded Joe's Maplewood bar. "The World's Best Spaghetti" was as delectable as ever, the Italian dinner being topped-off with three tasty meatballs smeared with delectable hot tomato sauce. Two frosty mugs of Coors Light complemented my high-calorie "Sicilian pasta birthday meal".

I was feeling ecstatic sitting there upon the high stool at the bar with my merry mind contemplating the marvelous good health that I had been indulgently enjoying. 'Here's a salute to geniuses Ralph Waldo Emerson and Henry David Thoreau!' I silently imagined as I gratefully raised the second recently served cold mug of Coors Light. 'And here's to also honor the splendor of Transcendentalism, of Sleep Paralysis, of Out of Body Experiences and of marvelous Time Traveling, too,' I also reticently proposed.

On frigid Christmas Eve, I trudged over to the den's bookcase and grabbed off the shelf a dusty copy of Charles Dickens immortal masterpiece "A Christmas Carol." After thoroughly comprehending and appreciating each fantastic page that beautifully described the Ghost of Christmas Past, the Ghost of Christmas Present and the morbid Ghost of Christmas Future, I reveled in imbibing from a glass wholesome swigs of savory blackberry brandy. 'I've read this ingenious story at least fifty times starting in eighth grade as a motivated student and later for three-plus decades with my classes

88

while I was futilely laboring as a middle school English literature teacher,' I sincerely recalled and reminded myself.

The warmth emanating from the nearby red-brick fireplace plus me sipping my second glass of addictive blackberry brandy made my entire being feel a bit inebriated by the time I had fully completed my self-assigned Dickens reading task. 'This cold December night is now quite tolerable,' I concluded with a smile as the mantel clock hands approached midnight. 'I think I'll retire for the evening.'

I ambled upstairs to the master bedroom, removed my sweatshirt, pants and socks and casually tossed those items onto a side chair. Soon I lowered the bedspread and was snugly nestled under the clean sheets and cozy blankets. Before I could turn-on my tabletop flat-screen television from my horizontal bed position, instead, I felt an inclination to doze-off and initiate another astral journey back to the past to once again visit my Levittown, Pennsylvania teenage friend Tommy Gallagher, who had also introduced me to the use of alcohol besides the temptation of sampling Camel, Philip Morris and Chesterfield cigarettes.

At the stroke of midnight on the downstairs grandfather clock, my already-listless senses became cognizant that I had entered the standard Sleep Paralysis state where my muscles and appendages would ordinarily become numb and immobile. Without me ever blinking an eye, an uncanny form of telepathic communication was established by a very tall, grotesque-looking uninvited visitor, an awesome specter who somewhat resembled the macabre Ghost of Christmas Future.

'Hello John!' the gruesome-looking apparition very capably and mentally transmitted while standing above and beside me. 'Welcome to *my* gloomy, dark realm!'

'Are you my Guardian Angel?' my stunned mind telepathically answered in the form of an interrogative. 'Am I about to die just like Ebenezer Scrooge!'

'You *can* regard me as your Guardian Monitor,' the hideous-in-appearance creature's intelligence signaled. 'Congratulations John. You are one of the few rare humans who have learned the secret code typically associated with other-dimension out-of-body space-time mobility. However, your forbidden discovery has compelled me to arrive at your bedroom to inform that you've flagrantly violated a principal Universal Law. Your time traveling privileges are hereby revoked for abusing your allotted quota.'

'What?' my defiant brain foolishly challenged my omnipotent astral guest from my semi-comatose state. 'Why wasn't I warned?'

'Haven't you ever read the children's fable about the genie trapped in the bottle?' my uninvited visitor rhetorically asked. 'Humans are granted only three sacred wishes, but your arrogant ambition drove you to exceed the same glorious number that had also been allowed to feeble, parsimonious Ebenezer Scrooge. A second grievous offense committed by you occurred when you had written yourself two different notes upon your kitchen table in the year 2010, but in doing so, you had inadvertently exceeded the regular four-minute time limit period during your extended Sleep Paralysis roundabout. Sorry John, but after I depart your bedroom, your cosmic trip exploits into the past will then be permanently discontinued.'

'Am I going to die?' I fearfully thought and mentally transmitted. 'Please tell me I've not been selected for soul-migration into the afterlife. I don't want to die!'

'You will be allotted one full year to author your pedestrian autobiography,' the frightening Charon-like messenger related, 'and as your loyal Guardian Monitor, I must presently announce that you'll perish next Christmas Eve precisely when the downstairs clock strikes midnight. Now John,' the ghastly image imperatively stated, 'I strongly suggest that you get busy just as soon as you gently exit your current Sleep Paralysis spell.'

And after cerebrally delivering those drastic-and-dramatic words, the repulsive, enigmatic alien creature slowly-but-surely vanished into thin air.

"Rich Man, Poor Soul"

Sunday, July 27th to Wednesday, July 30th of 2014 my wife and I accompanied our grandson Dan and his eleven-year-old cousin Nick on a brief vacation excursion down to Ocean City, Maryland. The overall trip is rather scenic: Hammonton, New Jersey to the Garden State Parkway via the congested Atlantic City Expressway, and then motoring thirty-eight miles south to the Cape May-Lewes Ferry.

The hour and twenty-minute ride across tranquil Delaware Bay to Lewes was quite refreshing. And a short time-span later *that* nautical transit was followed by a pleasurable forty-five minute drive past Rehoboth Beach, Delaware and then short jaunts through Dewey Beach, picturesque Delaware Seashore Park, Bethany Beach, South Bethany and next Fenwick Island and amazingly, soon I was driving rather carefree into fabulous Ocean City, Maryland; a ten-mile commercial stretch comprised of fantastic restaurants, modern shopping centers, condominiums, bars, motels, hotels and abundant popular amusement areas.

The summer trip's destination was a rather sentimental and nostalgic one for me, for from 1967 to 1981, I had co-owned the Dealers Choice Amusement Arcade located under the Atlantic Hotel on the Ocean City Boardwalk. Joanne and I were excited to see what new businesses had been established in the general vicinity of our old summer haunts. We had booked reservations for connecting rooms on the second floor of the Quality Inn, 16th Street and the Boardwalk, twenty-one blocks north of my former place of commerce.

The first two days were spent with the four of us casually strolling along the crowded boardwalk, eating Thrashers French fries, consuming Dough Roller Pizza and also munching-on Candy Kitchen chocolates and Fishers Caramel Popcorn. Some random window shopping and buying seashore souvenirs were patiently accomplished in order to take home and distribute the purchased items to receptive family members. Of course, Dan and Nick enjoyed finding their way out of Trimpers Mirror Maze and later taking a seven-minute wooden carriage journey through the tourist-favorite, two-story Haunted House.

"Another arcade had occupied our former poker game store under the Atlantic," I reminded Joanne. "But now there's a retail sweatshirt and tee-shirt shop in the same location called 'Em Are Ducks'."

"Why such a silly name?" my wife logically asked.

"Because that's the way local hunters talk down here on the Delmarva Peninsula," I clarified. "Instead of the mallard shooters pronouncing 'Them Are Ducks', in a totally grammatically incorrect manner, they proudly say in local slang: 'Em Are Ducks'!"

After eating a hardy breakfast at the downstairs Quality Inn restaurant on our final day, the New Jersey vacationers checked-out of the hotel at ten-thirty a.m., and honoring an impulsive whim, I decided to visit nearby Berlin, Maryland before heading north to exhaust the remainder of the afternoon in peaceful Rehoboth Beach. On the main road leading into the town, my keen eyes spotted Ned's Nook, an oddball retail establishment that featured a wide variety of assorted junk, weird antiques and strange novelties dating back to the non-glorious Civil War era.   Remembering that I would occasionally visit Ned's Nook to escape the hustle and bustle of the O.C., Maryland Boardwalk in the 1970s, I slowly pulled my silver Nissan Maxima into the almost-empty gray-stone parking lot.

"This place looks like an indoor junkyard," complained grandson Dan from the back seat. "It has stuff that people back in Hammonton put-out for garbage collection. We could get most of this lousy junk for free at the Hammonton dump!"

"Let's go back to the boardwalk," Dan's cousin Nick stubbornly insisted. "I wanna' go through the Haunted House and the Mirror Maze again! In fact, I think that this creepy place is much scarier than the Haunted House could ever be!"

"I used to come here when I had the store in Ocean City, just to get away from all of the loud noise and honky-tonk activity," I diplomatically explained like a know-it-all adult. "Guys, I promise we'll be out of here in a half an hour. Then we'll drive up to Rehoboth Beach where I also had co-owned a beach and tee-shirt shop in the 1970s and early 80s. You two rascals can spend the entire afternoon eating hamburgers at Five Guys and playing arcade games at my expense. What do you two kids have to say about that?"

"It's a deal!" automatically agreed Dan. "I wanna' win a nice prize to take home. I hope they have some neat handcuffs like the ones that Nick won yesterday at Marty's Playland!"

"It's worth being bored at this dump!" Nick concluded and concurred. "Don't buy any rotten hamburgers in *there'* Uncle John! They'll probably be over a hundred years old! You might get food poisoning and have to have your stomach pumped!"

Inside the dark and dreary tin-roof building, I first cautiously admired an old RCA Radio cabinet, next a 1950s Muntz TV model followed by a rusty Kelvinator refrigerator, and then my wandering eyes scrutinized a large Flying-A Pegasus insignia along with several out-of-date greasy Esso and Sinclair gas station signs. While nonchalantly perusing the vast array of obsolete junk on display at Ned's Nook, my attention was instinctively drawn to a heavily dusty bookshelf where certain ancient-looking volumes were vertically exhibited. I reached-up my right hand and soon gingerly latched-onto an archaic-looking, tattered-but-impressive copy of 17th Century English poet John Milton's classic work *Paradise Lost,* and being highly bemused, I curiously read the faded print that was fairly evident upon the back cover.

"This epic poem contains over ten thousand lines of verse written *in medias res* with the essential story background being revealed later. The basic text entails an angelic war being fought over absolute control of Heaven, Adam and Eve's fateful adventures in the Garden of Eden, the rise of Satan as a potent evil force in human events, the allusion to a futuristic Son of God appearance upon the Earth, a description of God the Father, a profile of the Archangel Raphael, who had been swiftly dispatched to Eden to warn Adam and Eve of Lucifer's imminent encroachment, and finally, this book presents a graphic depiction of mighty Michael the Archangel, God's most trusty lieutenant who had seriously wounded pernicious Satan during the aforementioned prehistoric, supernatural Angelic Wars."

'I always wanted to read this remarkable book when I was a public-school teacher,' I honestly admitted to myself. 'But I was always too busy preparing specialized lessons on Twain, Poe, O. Henry, Jack London, Shakespeare, Washington Irving and Sir Arthur Conan Doyle to ever get around to reading *Paradise Lost* in my thirty-four-year English teacher career. Now that I'm retired from education, here's my chance to finally make-up for lost leisure time!'

I politely asked the elderly clerk standing behind the grimy counter the price of the antiquated piece of merchandise, and after momentarily examining the object, he specifically quoted, "Nine dollars and seventy-five cents."

Without any hesitation, and indeed recognizing the existence of a true bargain, I hastily reached into my pocket and handed the wrinkle-faced gent a crisp ten-dollar bill. The gray-bearded fellow shakily inserted the flimsy-looking book into a brown paper bag, gave me my quarter change, thanked me for my acquisition and then stepped five paces to his right to attend to the particular needs of another enraptured customer.

Being rather happy with my belated obtainment of *Paradise Lost*, my understanding wife and I benevolently escorted totally bored Dan and argumentative Nick back to the silver Maxima, and soon the dynamic entourage commenced our northern advance to placid Rehoboth Beach, Delaware, where we would relax and stay before eventually rendezvousing with the 4:30 Ferry from historic Lewes back to Victorian Cape May, New Jersey. Everything in the world seemed pleasantly normal up to then. My mind and heart were in complete harmony with the entire Universe. But I had no idea what John Milton's sensational masterpiece had in store for me.

* * * * * * * * * * * *

For thirty-four years I had been a dedicated New Jersey public school English teacher, and for sixteen of those same years an ambitious summertime businessman and an aspiring novelist and short story writer. I suspect that much truth exists in the speculated proposition that authors are indeed tortured souls, possibly either struggling with self-inflicted masochistic tendencies or with recurring sadistic impulses prevalent in their neurotic nature. I've often wished that I could live my adult life over again, using my accumulative knowledge and experience of the future to avoid certain mistakes and bad investments I had regrettably made in my earlier years.

On Saturday morning, August 1st I predictably awoke as usual at 5 a.m. and quietly exited the shadowy master bedroom. Joanne had been spending the weekend relaxing down the shore in a rented home in Ocean City, New Jersey. I slowly paced down the rose-carpeted hall and very deliberately entered the upstairs computer room, turned on the wall switch to the overhead light, carefully shut the door out of force of habit, opened my desk drawer and then warily removed the tarnished Ned's Nook copy of John Milton's *Paradise Lost*.

I perceptively noticed the dull-looking publisher's page, which explicitly featured the date of publication, April 24th, 1784, London, England. I prudently turned the book's first leaf, observing that the opposite side was blank. But then my fascinated pupils observed certain typed words suddenly appearing in beautiful italics, the stunning new language all being magically represented in the form of a rather incredibly bold announcement:

By Heaven's decree, your extraordinary wish shall be granted in order for you to achieve your individual Paradise Lost. Lie-down upon this room's spare sofa and fall fast asleep. When you wake-up, you'll be age eighteen again, living with your' family. You shall live your life over from August 1st 1960 to August 1st, 2014, changing important wrong decisions you had made into dramatic positive results. You will have this exceptional privilege once and once only, so optimistically avail yourself of this Divine opportunity.

Sincerely,

John Milton

Michael the Archangel

Astonishingly, the brief printed missive soon mystically vanished from the given space just as mysteriously as it had spectacularly appeared, leaving behind the formerly recognizable blank page. Being stunned and shocked from *that* most recent phenomenon, I meticulously placed the now-closed book back into the top desk drawer and anxiously pondered exactly what had just transpired.

Obeying the recently provided "blank page" instructions, I arose and promptly shut the overhead light switch, advanced my feet to the now-relevant side sofa, sat-down, reclined my body, put my addled head on the soft pillow, closed my eyes and then gradually dozed-off. When I awoke, much to my utter disbelief, I was again eighteen years old and living with my parents and younger sister and brother in the small stone house situated next to Pete's Farm Market, the newly purchased family business.

Initially it was an awkward, difficult adjustment for me, being a hormone-driven teenager again and having to abide by strict parental rules and regulations, but realizing that I had very special knowledge of future events, I immediately determined that I should make the most of my "most peculiar second chance predicament."

In April of 1959, my family had moved from Levittown, Pennsylvania to Elm, New Jersey, located in Camden County, just west of Hammonton in Atlantic County. In June of 1959, I had been invited to a Levittown birthday party given by a pretty girl I had once dated, Carol Zella. As I traveled *Route 206* south towards Hammonton after leaving my old flame's shindig, I saw that the two-lane highway was dark, quiet and deserted. I had mischievously buried the speedometer on Dad's '55 Chevy all the way from Atsion Lake to Hammonton, a distance of seven straight monotonous miles. Everything seemed copasetic until I had approached the traffic light at the intersection of *206* and *Route 30,* the *White Horse Pike.*

As I waited for the green light to appear, I noticed in the rearview mirror a large cloud of hot steam billowing-out from the Chevy's exhaust pipe. In my exuberance to experience intense speed, I had inadvertently broken the six cylinder's head gasket, and engine water had leaked into the crankcase, causing a dense jet of white steam to be emitted. I had recklessly cracked the motor block and had stupidly damaged the engine's camshaft. My wild joyride had resulted in a considerable unexpected expense for Pop, who did not savor the overall damage one iota.

Although Dad was not Robert Young, he often had to show me that *Father Knows Best.* Pop was a good judge of character, believed in punishment for misdeeds, and he also had me easily figured-out as if I had been a primary school simple addition problem. I was forbidden to drive his repaired '55 Chevy out of Hammonton for an entire year. But now, during my second time around as a teenager, I adroitly skirted conflict with my dad by dutifully honoring the 50 mile an hour *Route 206* speed limit all the distance from Atsion Lake to Hammonton.

Without a doubt during my *original* senior year in high school, I had neglectfully clowned-around and antagonized my self-righteous Trigonometry instructor, Mr. Andrews, who at the end of the term felt inclined to fail me, compelling me to attend summer school in a town seventeen or so miles east of Edgewood Regional High School. But on my second tour of duty as a high school senior, I suddenly became serious about obtaining a decent grade and so I became committed to conscientiously applying myself in learning the very complicated Sine, Cosine, Secant, Cosecant, Tangent and Cotangent Trigonometry functions. Much to my immense satisfaction, I had earned the respectable grade of B, and my genuine effort had skillfully evaded the necessity of attending the ever-dreaded summer school assignment.

Because I had then wisely passed Trigonometry, I could now be admitted into Glassboro State Teachers College. In my previous teen evolution, I had to stay out of higher education for an entire year, so after the family farm market closed in late October, my father had used his foreman's influence at his location of employment, Martin and Quade Company in Norristown, Pennsylvania, where against my obstinate will, I punctually became an apprentice welder of stainless

96

steel tube products, a job that I had formerly detested with a nasty passion. Fortunately, by showing emotional maturity and academic perseverance this fortuitous second time around, and by exerting myself and passing Trig, I no longer had wasted a full year of my life breathing-in toxic and obnoxious welding fumes.

On April 24th, 1966, Joanne and I were married at St. Joseph Church, Third Street, Hammonton, New Jersey. I was in my second year of teaching and my wife was about to graduate from Glassboro State College with an Elementary School teaching degree. I never had too much peace of mind working that first summer for my mercurial-tempered Sicilian father-in-law, who incidentally owned a reputable four hundred acre very successful peach and apple farm, so in my new alternate existence, I had intelligently traveled down to Ocean City, Maryland a year earlier than I had done the first time around, while giddily riding upon the ever-revolving Wheel of Life. A fellow teacher/friend needed a competent and trustworthy assistant manager to help him run Dealers Choice Arcade, so naturally I had perfectly and luckily fit the basic job description.

The following winter I had used my hard-earned savings and borrowed additional funds to invest in a partnership for Dealers Choice, an operation which consisted of thirty-poker machines, fifteen situated on either side of the store. A seated player would drop a dime into a side slot and five wheels would automatically rapidly rotate. Then the given player would press five red buttons on the machine's console and eventually develop a recognizable poker hand with actual playing cards indicated upon the five stopped wheels. Jacks or better would be worth ten cents towards prizes and merchandise, two pair twenty cents, three of a kind fifty cents, a straight seventy-five cents, a flush a dollar, four of a kind two dollars, a straight flush five dollars and finally, a royal flush would command Choice of the House, a totally noteworthy twenty-five dollar prize.

Around two hundred different gift items ranging from ten cents to twenty-five dollar stuffed animals, kitchen blenders, clock radios and cooking skillets were on shelf displays, and the interested clientele could accumulate coupons, add them together and upon finishing their boardwalk entertainment, trade the collected cash value tickets in for exhibited "plush" and "high-line" household appliances.

But several years later I quickly learned how the all-powerful Internal Revenue Service could absolutely crush an industrious boardwalk businessman's enthusiasm. Everything was functioning just fine until mid-July of 1976 when a pair of black-suited IRS agents sauntered into the Dealers Choice Arcade and stridently maintained that my thirty poker machines were "gaming devices" and not mere ordinary "amusement devices."

"These are not casino slot gaming machines with timers simultaneously halting the five wheels," I futilely argued. "They are common *amusement devices* approved by the State of Maryland, by the County and by the Town, which have all granted me licenses to legally operate. If they were *gaming devices* as you maintain, I would be violating my state, county and town *'game of skill'* licenses."

I next had my loyal manager demonstrate how he could use skill to register four aces and then a royal flush in spades on the five rectangular windows on one of the poker machine devices. The first unimpressed IRS agent declared, "He's a shill! The average person coming in here can't do that!"

The second IRS official then austerely stated, "You are hereby being assessed a hundred and fifty dollars per machine. How many years have you been in business here?"

"Ten years since 1967," I innocently and naively answered.

"Then your total fine liability will be in the neighborhood of forty-five thousand bucks," the first federal man cited with a broad grin, "and adding in associated interest and penalties of a decade-long non-compliance, your grand total owed Uncle Sam ought to be in the vicinity of seventy-five thousand smackers."

"And what if I don't pay you right away?" I shockingly asked. "What's the punishment under those circumstances?"

"Then we'll have to administer what we call 'a jeopardy seizure' of all your in-house machines and related property; we'll next padlock your doors and that drastic action will certainly make your landlord very unhappy with an empty closed store situated right in the middle of his busy block!"

In my second chance to redeem my former erratic economic life, thanks to the miraculous intercession of Mr. John Milton and the wondrous Archangel Michael, in the fall of 1975 my financially encumbered partner and I eagerly sold Dealers Choice to a Salisbury, Maryland amusement tycoon, and obviously the IRS investigation became *his* growing problem the following July. I then used half of the vital proceeds from the sale to invest in a very profitable boardwalk pretzel and lemonade concession, and the remainder of the sum was infused into a thriving hot dog and hamburger stand along with a majority stake in a well-patronized local bar, and soon I was making much more money with my new boardwalk enterprises in the altered version of 1976 than I had been earning before in 1976 when the rather distressful Dealers Choice "IRS federal government intrusion" had occurred.

During that same time period, I still operated my Rehoboth Beach boardwalk tee-shirt store where decals were heat-transferred by machines onto summer apparel, and so thanks to my cherished copy of *Paradise Lost,* I had deftly evaded financial disaster and was in the process of adroitly amassing an envious Merrill Lynch stock portfolio in the interim.

During the spring of 1979, in my first tour of duty, several of my former Dealers Choice managers and I had opened an amusement arcade on Missouri Avenue and the Boardwalk, Atlantic City, New Jersey. In the fall of 1981, we were notified by our mercenary landlords that our lease had been ruled null and void because the whole block had been recently sold to Caesar's World Incorporated for the construction of a magnificent boardwalk casino.

However, in my new second 1979 reality, I never invested in the prospective Atlantic City arcade enterprise, instead using the original seed money to purchase Oracle Corporation and Qualcomm stocks, which ultimately transformed into a terrific economic bonanza. My two partners and I also gambled our combined resources and acquired an old fleabag hotel on Pacific Avenue, which we gladly sold two years later to a huge casino syndicate for a considerable capital gain. That outstanding good fortune was soon parlayed into joint ownership of a prosperous Atlantic City Marina Bar, which effectively churned a handsome yearly dividend that subsequently allowed me in the 1990s to buy a rather decent amount of quality Google and Amazon.com stock. 'Making money is easy if one happens to know the future!' I reasoned.

In 1987, my loving grandmother had died, leaving me thirty-thousand dollars in her will. In my first mortal reality, I had foolishly invested the new-found money into an upstart computer company, which abruptly went bankrupt shortly thereafter. In my second chance at Wall Street redemption, I sagaciously utilized the windfall inheritance to obtain a handsome chunk of Comcast Cable stock, which to my personal satisfaction, then greatly appreciated in value over the course of the next economically volatile decade.

In 1993 I originally had made a forty-thousand-dollar gain in an upstart biotech company, but then brainlessly lost the easy-found dough that had been plowed into the stock of a suddenly defunct North Jersey appliance store distributor. In my second opportunity that had been beneficially granted me by *Paradise Lost,* the formerly dissipated money was healthily put to excellent advantage in my possession of more Apple and Google stock, which naturally over the past two decades has tremendously and marvelously enhanced my personal wealth.

And because of my superb knowledge of history, I cleverly sold all of my stock market acquisitions just prior to the "anticipated stock market crash of 2008", and a full year later, purchased fifty thousand shares of Ford Motor Company at three dollars apiece, which in 2013 were worth a staggering seventeen dollars each. In my substitute 2014 scenario, I had taken a mild risk and have invested half of my Ford proceeds into Yahoo and SoftBank Corporation, which together own fifty-one percent of a massive Chinese Internet juggernaut named Alibaba.

All the while during the lengthy enactment of my robust second series' financial escapades, I have been coyly using some of my sustained monetary resources to bolster my fledgling writing career, self-publishing various books in hardcover, in paperback and into familiar Kindle, Smashwords and Nook e-book formats. I'm hoping that this new minimum-risk entrepreneurial endeavor will sometime in the future translate into handsome inheritances for my devoted wife, my three sons and my four grandchildren.

Finally, looking back in retrospect, in 1968, during my alternate voyage through adulthood, I had diligently earned a Master's Degree in Guidance Counseling, so consequently, I engaged teenagers in one-to-one office conferences, and I didn't have to emotionally endure a thirty-four year teaching career being exposed to a plethora of defiant, insolent, undisciplined and recalcitrant public school "students" like I had encountered and suffered my first time around while wildly riding the extremely formidable and treacherous educational career carousel.

* * * * * * * * * * * *

During my second tenure on this stellar planet, I recollected having certain ankle and knee sprains accidentally sustained in 1997-'98, which I then discreetly eliminated from my human experiences. And in late February of 2014, I had had my first routine colonostomy done, which revealed a large polyp present in my ascending colon. On March 8th I had gotten the benign growth removed along with eight inches of large intestine at Virtua Hospital, but later on my second trip around, I had the first colonostomy completed in 2005, and as a result of my judicious judgment and insight, I had cunningly bypassed the painful surgery along with the accompanying uncomfortable 2014 four-day hospital recovery.

On Sunday, July 27th to Wednesday July 29th of 2014, I *again* drove Joanne, Dan and Nick down to Ocean City, Maryland via the Cape May-Lewes Ferry, just as I had done fifty-four years before. On Wednesday after breakfast at the Quality Inn we traveled to Ned's Nook in Berlin, Maryland. Inside the dilapidated store I immediately found the all-too-familiar dusty bookshelf, and my on-a-mission awareness instantly noticed that a copy of John Milton's *Paradise Lost* was not there occupying any physical space. Instead, I observed an ancient representation of *Dante's Inferno,* but feeling despicably craven at that oddly stark moment, I dared not even examine it.

On August 1st 2014, I awoke for the second time, more discerning and much wealthier than I had exited my slumber the first time around. Contrary to my previous mortal existence, my spouse now believes that I am a true stock market genius and that I'm not the pathetic loser that her gruff father had imagined me to be back in tumultuous 1965. Joanne and the rest of my merry family were safely away that particular Friday, vacationing at the splendid beach house I had purchased three years ago on 17th and the boardwalk, in pleasant Ocean City, New Jersey.

But my consciousness was aware that it was again August 1st. After fearfully and reluctantly stepping into my Hammonton home's upstairs computer room, I hesitated before opening the top desk drawer, which I recollected had contained the sensational copy *of Paradise Lost;* the wonderful book that I had intended to finally read and fully appreciate.

I nervously opened the archaic masterpiece, turned the initial leaf and next intensely glanced at the dull-looking publication page, which then instantly transformed into a full blank. Suddenly, much to my mounting consternation, a distinct other-world statement slowly appeared in medieval-style italics' script, and then several moments thereafter, the message eerily vanished into infinite oblivion. The incomparable dual synergies of the book's famous author along with the eternal talent of the omnipotent Archangel Michael were extraordinarily startling to say the least.

> *Well now, rich Jay Dubya, do the elementary math'*
> *and you'll arrive at the only possible conclusion. By*
> *Heaven's mandate, you had originally almost reached*

seventy-two years of age in 2014, and then your mediocre being was supernaturally transported back to 1960 to again live and rearrange your disheveled and haphazard financial and physical life. That unique opportunity has afforded you the expressed ability to make myriad shrewd business transactions. Now Sir, it is almost the appropriate time for your stained soul to finally make its necessary amends.

According to St. Peter's records, you are nearly seventy-two years old, and quite frankly, there isn't too much sand left inside your biological hourglass. In the final analysis, our accurate and infallible records clearly show that you will have to spend fifty-four monotonous Earth years quietly meditating your numerous faults languishing inside the vast confines of obscure Purgatory, the needed contemplations will be especially performed by your restive and secluded spirit. The specific punishment will be enacted for you to penitently atone for your nefarious propensity of blatantly and relentlessly practicing excessive and egotistical human greed.

May Almighty Merciful God save your poor lackluster soul,

John Milton

Archangel Michael

"Lost Identity"

My distraught mind's hollow memories gradually began coming together like myriad floating pieces converging into a lucid kaleidoscopic pattern. But despite my noble mental effort, I still was not remotely cognizant of either my first or my last name.

"Well now Patient X," Dr. Anthony Thornwell solemnly addressed me as I was worriedly lying prone in my hard-mattress hospital bed, "after very tedious and thorough research, the four professionals gathered here have finally figured-out your true identity."

"Well then, who am I?" I politely asked the stern-mannered-but-polite hospital physician. "I'm anxious to re-learn my name, even if it is simply John Doe."

"I believe *we* ought to gradually reveal that particular information to you as the delicate situation warrants," the truth-oriented doctor emphatically stated. "Let's first recap a few major items. The date today is Friday, February 22nd, 2013, and you're now resting comfortably in Room 207 of Mountain View Hospital, 3100 Tenaya Way, Las Vegas, Nevada. But before we get too involved in any actual detailed conversation," the medical man imperatively insisted, "let me briefly introduce you to these three other special people assembled inside your private room."

"Okay Doctor," I sincerely replied. "I'm sure that everyone present is here to help me discover who I am, or who I was. I hope I can remember everyone's name. My concentration is not one hundred percent valid at the moment!"

"This is Dr. Ivan Long to my immediate right," Dr. Thornwell calmly explained. "Dr. Long is a renowned psychiatrist with an international reputation and was instrumental in assisting us in painstakingly finding-out your identity. And to my left is Nurse Sierra Pierce, and standing next to her is Detective Thomas Manville of the Las Vegas Police Department."

"Was I the victim of a crime?" I promptly asked without any hesitation. "I think I remember being attacked and my head still aches! Yes, it all was very abrupt and violent!"

"We'll comprehensively summarize *that* specific aspect of your predicament in a few minutes," Dr. Thornwell promised with a forced grin. "But first Nurse Pierce will review from her notes several extraordinary remarks and phrases that you had made during your sleep periods extending over the past six days. In the interim, perhaps you can recall some germane situations and clarify a few remote issues for us. We've documented just about everything in our files and might need to consult the accumulative data to analyze future amnesia cases," the doctor elaborated, "and I trust that we can depend on your full and voluntary cooperation in constructively aiding our hospital study!"

"Yes, Doctor Thornwell," I then courteously answered, vertically nodding my head. "As long as I get to find-out my name, recall why I am in Las Vegas and fathom exactly what had happened to me, I'll gladly give you any information I can."

"Thank you!" eminent Dr. Ivan Long piped-up and stated as the conscientious psychiatrist jotted-down some supposedly relevant notes onto his hand-held pad. "As for *my* singular component in your case study, I've evaluated your individual circumstances and have concluded that the entire scope and sequence of vast time intervals happen to be most interesting, very intriguing to say the least."

The no-nonsense police officer next felt obligated to speak. "On Saturday afternoon, February 16th you were casually walking east in the direction of the Vegas Strip," Detective Thomas Manville contributed to the discussion, "but then you were wickedly assaulted from behind and knocked unconscious. An ambulance arrived and the paramedics administered immediate first responder assistance, eventually rendering your vital signs healthy enough to then transport you over here to the Mountain View Emergency Ward."

"What was the basic motivation for someone wanting to viciously clobber me?" I instantly asked. "Was the villain out to steal my wallet? Was it' adolescent mischief suddenly changed into malice? Do you know who had molested me?"

"Four young punks were swiftly following and targeting you without your knowledge," Detective Manville divulged. "Apparently three of them had convinced the fourth juvenile thug to play his version of the disturbing Knockout Game on you. After you were slugged on the right side of your skull," the officer informed, "you fell to the pavement, the second hard impact giving you a severe concussion. The four thrill-seeking creeps quickly realized that you had a wallet filled with cash and then the young rogues nefariously pilfered it. A moment later a senior citizen Good Samaritan was driving by and used his cell phone to call for help."

"Were the four irresponsible juvenile delinquents ever apprehended by the cops?" I wondered and verbally inquired. "I think I need to know *that* essential information so that I could have some much-needed closure to my current dilemma, having knowledge that justice is being served."

"Yes, but we'll provide you with *that* important background a little later," Detective Manville confided. "Now I'll defer to Nurse Pierce who will disclose what she had heard you mumbling and uttering during your bizarre deep sleep episodes."

"Your first sleep comments spoken on Sunday morning had to do with you toiling in a dimly lit salt mine, and your anxious voice was orally hoping that you could establish a better way of life somewhere else," Dr. Thornwell interrupted, asserting his ranking hospital authority and also austerely contributing to the dialogue while simultaneously trumping Nurse Sierra Pierce. "Now with the first stage salt mine scenario out of the way, I'll turn the remainder of the patient interview over to my competent Registered Nurse colleague."

Nurse Sierra Pierce then shared with her hospital room audience that I had been announcing from my sleep that I had been receiving Holy Communion in a strange foreign church with gruesome-looking three-dimensional figures of a crucified bleeding Christ being represented, the morbid-in-appearance spectacles being either statues or similar objects that were extending-out from the dark church's dull beige walls.

"I vaguely recollect those frightening images you've just vividly described," I verbally responded, all the while attempting to comprehend various hazy thoughts originating deep inside my nebulous mind. "The visions do dwell and haunt my subconscious, and truthfully, I find the shocking manifestations to be rather reprehensible!"

Sierra Pierce then resumed her rather perplexing monologue. "And then on Monday evening you had been having another traumatic experience, this time being engaged in fighting a wild forest fire that was terribly devastating a country lumber camp," the garrulous Registered Nurse stated. "And again, later on that same Monday night, you were frightfully depicting yourself' witnessing a horrible mass cemetery burial somewhere in a large city ghetto. And then on Tuesday afternoon while heavily snoozing," the talkative R.N. continued her prattle, "you were writhing-about in your bed, yelling that you were feeling nauseous, and then you almost began vomiting from claiming to be affected from a bout of terrible, overwhelming sea sickness!"

"Yes Nurse, I do vaguely recall those very disgusting events you've just communicated, but as to their precise time and place," I paused to reflect further on the elusive subject matter, "I can't clearly determine the exact times and specific places. I wish that my sense of remembering things could be more accurate."

"But on Tuesday evening after dozing-off," Nurse Pierce proceeded with her unusual narrative, "you were laboring hard in a brewery, rolling and stacking barrels inside the company warehouse. Again, the time setting and exact place of occupation were drastically missing from your fairly graphic verbal account."

"I wish I could be more helpful," I humbly apologized from my confined horizontal position upon the bed. "All that you're telling me now is somewhat meaningful in a small way, but precisely how it is significant to my life, well, that important aspect completely evades my general awareness!"

"And on Wednesday during an extended afternoon siesta," the garrulous hospital nurse continued her explicit recitation, "you were totally preoccupied in your sleep constructing a certain bridge spanning across a river, and in the meantime, having a stream of rifle bullets being shot at you as you speedily worked. And finally," Nurse Pierce summed-up her well-prepared report, "you kept repeating the strange words 'The Blue Heron', but being stymied, we couldn't decipher whether you were referring to a restaurant, to a bar, to a motel or perhaps to a golf course, any of which might be directly related to *that* specific phrase."

"I had found the Blue Heron allusion to be especially curious and fascinating," Dr. Ivan Long short-circuited the dedicated female nurse's speech. "In fact, those three words compelled me to develop a rather unique hypothesis, my evolving theory founded on the assumption that *you* had remarkably spoken about all of those eight aforementioned-but-disconnected events in an irregular-but-concise chronological order."

The reticent police official again felt a need to make a material comment. "But perhaps the biggest mystery of all Sir was your redundant reciting of the numbers 9783 over and over again," grim-faced Detective Manville declared. "At the outset, we were baffled and couldn't interpret whether the four digits pertained to a landline or cell phone number, to an obscure street address, or if they signified some enigmatic license plate, or whatever else. But in the end," the laconic Nevada police detective maintained, "those four muttered numbers 9783 became an absolutely vital clue in discovering who *you* really are and why *you* happened to be visiting Las Vegas."

* * * * * * * * * * * *

The pondering psychiatrist then honored his need to inject his exclusive observations into the hospital room conference. Dr. Ivan Long expressed that the assigned team had to mutually perform some "serious reverse engineering" in order to ascertain my given birth certificate appellations. The distinguished mind doctor disclosed that my mentioning of intensively working in a colossal salt mine immediately guided his mind to focus on an area of Southern Poland.

"It was sort of like me finding a Rosetta stone! I once visited the famous Wieliczka Salt Mines not too far from Krakow," the psyche examiner confidentially related. "Indeed, the incomparable mines had been constructed in the 13th Century and over the years had produced mainly common table salt. I had recently read in a geographic magazine where the massive underground facility had closed in 2007, but when they were still in operation, the famous mines featured a beautiful illuminated Cathedral Room along with three impressive side chapels and dozens of saint statues that had been carved out of salt."

Before I could mentally synchronize any elements of Dr. Long's lucid revelation (since my addled consciousness was encountering foggy memories and notions swirling around inside), Dr. Thornwell's sanctimonious voice filled the void as the egocentric staff surgeon pontificated about me dreaming of the foreign country church where the gruesome figures of an anguishing Christ were on exhibit.

"We believe that the alluded to church you had indicated in your sleep is named Ecce Homo, which is a popular shrine located in Calvaruso, Sicily; and the unique structure had been built four-hundred years ago," the chief medical doctor orally conveyed. "Your paternal grandfather had received his First Holy Communion there, and we immediately speculated that your recollection of the powerful family story you had probably heard many times in your youth had caused your subconscious mumbling about it."

"And then the four of us collaborated and collectively conjectured that the colossal forest fire you were imagining and subconsciously witnessing was also a tale from your fraternal Polish grandfather's side of the family," Nurse Sierra Pierce aptly vocalized. "Our speculative research found that your father had been born in Posen, just outside of Alpena, Michigan. Your grandfather, whom you had never known, had owned a logging camp, and ambitious Adalbert Wisniewski had leased hundreds of acres of forest land for timbering from the federal government. According to your younger brother's testimony over the phone," the R.N. elucidated, "in the early 1900s a huge conflagration had destroyed all of your grandfather's investment, and without owning any property insurance, your paternal ancestor had died a broken man a year later, and his remains are buried in a Posen, Michigan Cemetery."

My befuddled cerebrum was attempting to contemplate and organize into a logical pattern this temporarily concealed pertinent family history when loquacious Dr. Thornwell further added to my puzzlement. "And *your* graphic citing of a mass city burial was again connected with your father's side of the family, most of whom had moved from Michigan to Baltimore around 1910. Then in 1918, just toward the end of World War I, your Polish grandmother had died in East Baltimore, a poorer section of the city. An extremely contagious flu epidemic had broken-out all over East Coast America in general and also in that section of Maryland in particular. The deadly strain was called 'the Blue Death'. Over 3,000 Baltimore residents had become afflicted and had ultimately perished from the lethal outbreak. City undertakers were immensely overwhelmed with the excessive body count, and as a stark necessity, a morbid mass grave had been dug in a local cemetery to accommodate all of the stricken corpses. Your grandmother Hedwig Wisniewski was unfortunately among the deceased in the mass cemetery burial."

"I now see the three Polish links on my father's side represented between the salt mine, the forest fire and the mass city burial," I acknowledged, "and yes, I do recall visiting Baltimore relatives with my parents back in the '50s, some residing on Foster Avenue and others on Conklin. And I suppose that the Sicily shrine comes from my mother's side. Now I believe I remember something! My maternal grandfather had emigrated from Sicily to Ellis Island in 1910. Later he settled in Philadelphia where other uncles and cousins had been residing, and yes, my Italian grandfather served as an orderly at Walter Reed Hospital during World War I, and thereafter, later moved to New Jersey to open a fruit and produce farm market."

"Yes indeed," Dr. Long concurred with my precise descriptive commentary. "Your grandfather had gotten very sick on the rough cattle boat ride from Messina, Sicily to New York, and according to your wife's recent account over the telephone, Antonio Giacobbe never attempted to learn how to swim or even ever stepped into a lake, river or swimming pool after experiencing *that* negative, traumatic ocean crossing."

"And as a young man your father John once worked in a brewery in Baltimore, Maryland, which rapidly went bankrupt during the 1920s' Prohibition era," Dr. Thornwell enlightened my awakening memory. "Your original family surname was Wisniewski, but since Germans were better rooted in America in the early 1900s than were natives of Polish descent, your Aunt Marie had wisely changed your family name to...."

"To the German title Wiessner from the Polish surname Wisniewski!" I excitedly exclaimed. "Yes Dr., now I remember everything almost as clear as crystal! My father would often tell me that both he and I had been named after an old Baltimore Brewery, the John F. Wiessner Brewery on Gay St.! That's why my birth name is John Wiessner!"

"And your father was in the Army during World War II, serving in France, in Germany, in Luxembourg and in Holland," Dr. Thornwell embellished. "And your father...."

"Had been involved in constructing a vital pontoon bridge across the Rhine River," I recollected and enthusiastically uttered to my four visitors, "and the urgent construction project was being done because that vile monster Adolph Hitler had ordered all bridges across the strategic river to be destroyed in order to impede the advancement of American troops. Dad had often told me that snipers were firing shots at him and his brave soldier buddies as they hastily rushed to assemble the pontoons together."

"Yes," agreed Dr. Ivan Long with a smile quickly appearing upon his formerly stoic countenance. "Your actual name is indeed John Wiessner. It seems that your vulnerable amnesia-laden mind had been dealing with your identity loss in a rather vicarious way, bringing certain stories from your family's past to your mind's surface in an effort to finally recall who and what you have been and who and what you are! And the blue heron facet concerns..."

"Concerns a beautiful blue heron flying low across the Jersey highway near my home and then being clipped on the left wing by a speeding tractor trailer," I rightly answered, capably finishing the psychiatrist's statement. "The wounded bird managed to land upon the bank of a nearby pond, which had been its original destination. That perturbing incident happened the day before I had flown United Airways from Philadelphia to Las Vegas. My wife and I attempted to rescue the injured heron, but after several failed attempts, we called the county animal control, whose personnel came onto the scene right away and captured the hurt bird with a large net and then took the unfortunate creature away in their white county van for possible rehabilitation."

* * * * * * * * * * * *

Detective Thomas Manville believed it was his turn to offer valuable anecdotal details to supplement the eight separate clue components that had been rendered. The policeman soon shared his present law enforcement activity regarding the "most current Knockout Game assault case." Naturally, the plain-clothes officer's firm baritone voice methodically commanded everyone's attention.

"Mr. Wiessner, you had flown into McCarron International Airport on a direct United Airways flight from Philly', arriving in town at approximately noon on Saturday, February 16th. While here in Vegas, you were staying at your sister and brother-in-law's condo' located just several blocks from the Strip." The policeman then referred to his trusty notepad for clarification. "Their names are…."

"Stephen and Anne Hill," I said, finishing the stumped detective's declarative sentence. "And now I remember! The lock on the condo's door was much like one on a car entry, a combination of four numbers to be pressed on an outside hall wall pad, 9783."

"Do you remember why you were visiting Las Vegas?" Detective Manville interrogated. "I'm sure you do recollect if you think hard about it! And by the way, 'hard' does not mean 'hardly'!"

"My second son John Paul has a very stressful and sometimes excruciating hearing impairment," I sadly answered. "When he was nineteen, someone else at an outdoor party lit a fire-cracker that exploded several inches from his right ear. Since then, John Paul suffers from hyperacusis, which is a horrible condition far worse than tinnitus. Hyperacusis means that my son's ears are oversensitive to distinct noises and to high-frequency sounds like motorcycles, police car and ambulance sirens, and they're even hurt by small ice cubes plunking into a glass. The problem's far more debilitating than the more common ringing in the ears that's associated with tinnitus!"

"Okay John," plainclothesman Thomas Manville replied in a more personal manner, "but why were you in Vegas?"

"Well Sir, my sister and brother-in-law have made quite a decent living out of buying and flipping houses, especially ones located in warm climate resort areas like Vegas," I responded, inadvertently circumnavigating the fundamental question. "Of course, they've also

110

done house flipping in Phoenix, but first got started in Palm Springs and then later in South Padre Island, Texas. Now they're spending a week gallivanting around down in Cape Coral, Florida, eagerly exploring for a new business venture."

"But John," Detective Manville patiently reiterated, "tell us why you've come to Vegas without readily deviating and explaining why Anne and Stephen Hill have temporarily left Sin City for a week!"

"I came here searching for a small quiet-type business for my son John Paul, so I had been planning on attending the 2013 Franchise Exposition at the MGM Grand up on the Strip. The show was slated to happen for four days starting Sunday, February 17th! It seems that my good intentions have been rudely sabotaged by some young street hoods bent on playing the dreaded Knockout Game on me!"

Detective Manville next plausibly outlined how my sister and my wife were key principals in assisting the Vegas cops with the successful resolution of my legal case. Both ladies had endeavored many times to call me on my already stolen cell phone, but when no one answered by Wednesday, February 20th, both women became suspicious and intelligently notified the Las Vegas Police.

"And how did you manage to collar the punk teenagers?" I curiously asked. "The kid that knocked me onto Weird Street ought to take-up professional boxing! Maybe the local junior college offers a course in Assassination!"

"Well Mr. Wiessner, your wife and sister have verified and defined the eight peculiar stories you had been mumbling in your sleep," chimed-in Dr. Ivan Long. "Their valued input gave us a better perception of your general mental condition, both conscious and subconscious."

Detective Manville was ready with a feasible explanation about the young goons' fate. "The idiots that stole your wallet and cell phone tried using your VISA Card at a nearby Bank of America ATM, but the inept fools didn't realize that you had a debit card and not a credit card, so when the machine demanded the four-digit pin number, the four imbeciles panicked and ran away. Of course, their faces had been captured on the bank's exterior surveillance cameras."

"And what about my heisted cell phone and how about my pilfered wallet?" I requested knowing. "Have they been recovered? I had brought along a thousand bucks in gambling cash, you know!"

"Yes John, your wallet has been repossessed," the Las Vegas investigator communicated, "but your money stash has been spent by the brazen thieves on drugs and also on a 60-inch flat screen TV. As for your cell phone," Detective Manville indulgently laughed, "it's been recovered, fully intact. The dumb fools had answered your number after your wife and sister had given it to us. After calling them, we instantaneously knew the GPS coordinates of the punk robbers, who were soon arrested patronizing a local crack house."

A moment of silence was succeeded by me vociferating a random speculation that had popped into my mind. "Well now Folks, the Franchise Expo' is over, so I guess that my excursion out here to Vegas has evidently been a miserable failure!"

"Not exactly John!" Dr. Thornwell replied with a rare degree of emotion in his voice. "Here's my brother's business card! He's an ear doctor specializing in the treatment of hyperacusis. And his office is not too far from your New Jersey home, located right smack in the heart of downtown Manhattan! I'm confident that Dr. Mark Thornwell will be able to help your son John Paul with his truly unenviable ear malady!"

"Family Resentment"

Established back in 1935, the Bronson Family Vegetable Farm remotely situated on rustic rural Third Road in Hammonton, New Jersey was a brand name famous for quality produce in major food distribution centers along the East Coast from Baltimore to Boston. The business started-out during the Great Depression as a modest truck farm, hauling its freshly picked and packed vegetables to Dock Street commission houses in Philadelphia and to Hunts Point food centers in New York City's Bronx.

In 1960 old Joseph Bronson faced reality and handed-over the reins of the reputable operation to his two sons, Dennis and Ben, who specialized in raising asparagus, corn, green peppers, zucchini squash, cucumbers, eggplants and tomatoes. Over the past several decades the farm gradually expanded from the original hundred-fifty acres to a huge plantation of six hundred.

The industrious Bronson brothers missed-out on the post-*World War II* peach boom when the luscious, fuzzy fruit was the top producer in the Hammonton area where over eight thousand acres of the "Queen of Fruit" were annually grown and harvested. But then in the 1960s, blueberries began rivaling peaches as Hammonton's chief crop, and the eight-week short-season "blue fruit" eventually dominated the town's agriculture when the chain-store-favorite California O. Henry variety knocked New Jersey peaches out of popularity and virtually out of production.

But through the evolutionary transformation from peaches to blueberries (in the local Hammonton farming economy), the Bronson brothers still stuck to what they knew best, growing and harvesting vegetables, even though the Town of Hammonton (to this day) prides and promotes itself as "The Blueberry Capital of the World." Two shopping centers on *Route 30* attest to and verify the municipality's past and present agricultural glory: Peach Tree Plaza and Blueberry Crossing.

Like many working partnerships on various South Jersey farms, conflict between hard-headed owners often arise when one sibling desires to either be the dominant corporate authority in the daily operations or wants to create and develop a reputation as a successful independent grower on his own. The harmony that prevailed between Dennis and Ben Bronson in the early 1960s gradually disintegrated into distrust, discord and animosity by the year 2000. The formerly compatible owners decided to divide-up all their equipment, assets, irrigation lines, buildings and families into two separate entities on either side of Third Road: Dennis Bronson agreed to own and farm three hundred acres on the north-side of the two-lane county highway and Ben Bronson consented to owning and operating the remaining three hundred acres that existed on the south-side of Third Road.

Over the ensuing five years, the two brothers became resentful and envious of one another and their families didn't openly quarrel or feud but instead, virtually ignored each other, even at relatives' weddings, funerals, *Baptisms, Communions, Confirmations* and also at graduation parties. Cousins living on opposite sides of Third Road never acknowledged each other's passing on tractors or in pickup trucks, and the two competing clans pretended that "the other entity" wasn't of the same blood, sweat, tears and genetics.

In mid-January of 2005, Dennis Bronson really splurged and took his wife and family on an expensive two-month South Pacific vacation including stops and stays in exotic paradises Honolulu, Tahiti, New Zealand, Bali and Australia. The Dennis Bronson family returned from their sixty-day hiatus refreshed, renewed and ready to engage in the redundant annual activities known as spring planting, cultivating, irrigating, fertilizing, growing, harvesting, packing and selling their high-quality fancy vegetables. But unfortunately, memorable South Pacific leisure and pleasure soon turned into heartbreaking tragedy. On April 7, 2005 Dennis Bronson unexpectedly died of a massive heart attack after all desperate attempts at reviving him (by first his frantic delirious sons and then by Hammonton Rescue Squad paramedics) had failed.

On Monday evening, April 10th an open-casket viewing was held for sixty-seven-year-old Dennis Bronson at the spacious Marinella Funeral Home on North Third Street, and over five hundred local socialites including prominent Hammonton farmers, politicians, school board members and doctors and lawyers filed-past the casket and expressed their condolences to the grieving family. Everyone expected to attend was observed in the long line, but the family of Ben Bronson had been conspicuously absent. In fact, the south-side Third Road Bronsons weren't even mentioned in Dennis Bronson's extensive obituary appearing in the *Hammonton News*, in the *Hammonton Gazette* and in the *Atlantic City Press*.

And then on Tuesday morning, Ben Bronson, his wife and his sons and daughters did not have the decency or the courtesy to be present at Dennis Bronson's well-attended High Mass at St. Joseph Church and at his subsequent burial in a magnificent marble mausoleum in the First Road Greenmount Cemetery.

Dennis Bronson was indeed the more gregarious of the two feuding brothers. While sixty-two-year-old Ben was introverted and introspective, his older "sibling rival" Dennis was outgoing and more "public friendly." Dennis had belonged to service clubs like the Hammonton Lions and the Knights of Columbus, and Ben Bronson contemptuously resented his older brother's cordial nature, especially when the elder Bronson ran for Town Council on the Republican ticket and easily won a seat by campaigning vigorously, beating his Democratic rival in a landslide election.

Indeed, Dennis had been the more community-oriented and citizen-popular of the two. The likeable elder brother enjoyed public speaking, club leadership responsibilities and also working the grills and promoting good will at political banquets and at church barbecues. But the local politician further incurred *his* younger brother's jealousy when Dennis Bronson had used *his* political influence for what Ben and his envious family believed to be "excessive and decadent personal gain."

Back in 1995, the local Town Council had declared a building moratorium on all new house construction to abide by recently legislated strict New Jersey forest conservation laws. In the early 1980s, the New Jersey lawmakers in Trenton had established the creation of the Pinelands Commission, which had the expressed authority to regulate population growth in and around the environmentally sensitive Wharton State Forest.

According to careful definitions enforced by the new bureaucratic Commission, the "New Jersey Pinelands" extended from Absecon just west of Atlantic City to Atco seven miles west of Hammonton and from Vincentown seventeen miles north of the agricultural community to Vineland seventeen miles south. The "Pinelands" had Hammonton and its proud farmers located directly in the middle of the "core area" where building and population growth were both restricted and limited. New houses in the town's jurisdiction that weren't connected to water/sewer lines required approval of the "Almighty Pinelands Commission."

Hammonton farmers were deeply affected by the Pinelands and its governing Commission. Since *their* land value was now exclusively restricted to farm use property (that would ordinarily be worth a hundred thousand dollars an acre to an entrepreneurial real estate developer), it was now devalued to a meager five thousand dollars an acre because presently only area farmers would want to purchase the land from other farmers for agricultural purposes.

Consequently, because of very stringent Pinelands regulations, Hammonton fruit and vegetable growers had trouble borrowing money from banks and from farm credit bureaus to conduct their businesses, since *their* credit lines were determined by using their now devalued land assessments as "collateral." It cost most area vegetable growers like Dennis and Ben Bronson three hundred thousand dollars of "seed money" to get started each spring because big bucks had to be placed on the table to purchase the upcoming summer's fertilizers, sprays and special customized packages (with the farm's brand names printed on them) and payrolls before crops were ever picked, packed and shipped, along with myriad other miscellaneous accumulative spring expenses.

Farmers doing business in the Hammonton "highly governed and restricted Pinelands core area" were also limited in deciding *who* could build houses on their property. Their children were allowed to build new homes on three-acre tracts, and desperate farmers had to otherwise have their land divided into ten-acre zones if they wanted to sell those sub-divisions to non-family strangers (with a lot of money) desiring to erect dwellings on such sizable tracts.

Since the very autocratic New Jersey State Pinelands Commission required "core area residents" to hook-up to Hammonton city water lines and to town sewer lines, new growth was hampered by the State in the name of "natural environment preservation." And when the old, outdated Hammonton sewer plant began operating at full capacity, a restrictive building moratorium was adopted and enforced, and the Town Council (including at the time staunch Republican Dennis Bronson) had to abide by the State's inflexible land-use mandates.

The Hammonton area farmers along with peeved real estate developers boldly challenged the Pinelands Commission's authority in State courts, claiming that the new environmental laws were "Unconstitutional" and violated the farmers' rights to own and sell land at face value. The disgusted real estate moguls maintained that their "civil rights" to build and make profits were truly being abused. The costly litigations were aggressively pursued, but in the very end, the many challenges to State Authority were to no avail. The Pinelands Commission prevailed and won every legal wrangle intensively argued before sympathetic liberal judges, and the court decisions maintained that the "State's general good and welfare" were being upheld by the intelligently planned regional conserving and preserving of South Jersey forests, lakes and wildlife.

But the wily Hammonton farmers suspected that the real reason for the "stranglehold" Pinelands legislation (and its accompanying land restrictions) was more than mere discrimination against fruit and vegetable growers. Joseph Wharton of Philadelphia, founder of the prestigious *University of Pennsylvania* Wharton School of Business, once owned the South Jersey land today known as the Wharton State Forest. Wharton was a venture capitalist at heart whose ownership of the pineland forests (on either side of *Route 206* surrounding Atsion Lake and vicinity) had by coincidence seven trillion gallons of excellent pristine water reserves directly under the virgin forestland, and the attendant Pinelands were fed by the close-to-the-surface, freshwater Cohansey Aquifer. Philly' capitalist Joseph Wharton's grandiose scheme was to pump clean, pure water from the Wharton Forest Tract to the Philadelphia and New York metropolitan areas and economically profit from his diligent endeavor, but near the end of his life the nineteenth century investor changed his mind and heart and benevolently donated the beautiful acreage to the State of New Jersey.

The shrewd Hammonton farmers had suspected all along that the Pinelands building restrictions were not so much about protecting the pine trees as the State had asserted but about preserving the seven trillion gallons of pristine water lying beneath the forest trees as a reserve emergency water source for Philadelphia and New York.

* * * * * * * * * * * * *

In the late 1990's the colossal rift between the Bronson brothers became more intensified when the Town Council (of which Dennis Bronson was an influential member) passed a resolution to have a new sewage plant constructed (with Pinelands Commission approval) at local taxpayers' expense. When the Town's petition was studied and finally endorsed by the State, plans for new Hammonton sewage and water lines were quickly drawn-up. With the acceptance of the new high-capacity sewer system, some lucky farmers operating in the correct "building zones" could then sell one acre parcels to real estate developers at a hundred thousand dollars an acre because those properties could now link-up with city water and sewer usage and did not require sophisticated septic systems and water wells that were strictly regulated by the supreme New Jersey Pinelands Commission.

Dennis Bronson had been well-networked in the community and through his strong contacts with the City Zoning Board and with his noteworthy "political clout" on Town Council, the elder brother convinced other people in city government that (with the State approval of the new higher capacity sewage facility) it would be wise and judicious for the Town to have new water and sewer lines installed along the north side of Third Road that was more conveniently situated "closer to town." The town politicos supported Bronson's proposal and in 2002 the new water and sewer lines were installed to Dennis's benefit.

Ben Bronson and his jealous family despised what had transpired in what they labeled "Dennis's selfish and arrogant actions." The older brother's three hundred acres on the north side of Third Road were much more valuable than Ben's three hundred acres on the south side of the Atlantic County highway. By political savvy and by virtue of utilizing shrewd manipulation, Dennis's land was worth approximately 60 million dollars while Ben's property (under the jurisdiction of strict Pinelands' regulation) was valued at only 1.5 million at five thousand dollars an acre (when exclusively sold to another farmer interested in acquiring additional land). Needless to say, Ben Bronson and his family felt that they had become victims of Dennis Bronson's greed and cunning political maneuvering.

In March of 2003, Ben Bronson requested through his lawyer that the original six hundred acres be "re-divided equitably", but then the older brother, acting through *his* attorney's advice, bluntly refused the "flawed retroactive suggestion." Then six months later, Ben had requested through his accountant that his older brother purchase *his* land for five million dollars, but the older brother answered through a letter from *his* accountant that the price was estimated to be "three million dollars too much."

Finally, Ben ate humble pie and requested through his lawyer that Dennis lend him five hundred thousand dollars so that the younger sibling could avoid declaring bankruptcy and thus could continue the operation of *his* faltering vegetable farm, but the older brother declined to cooperate, citing that Ben's three-hundred acres were no longer considered part of the "family legacy." The mounting antipathy between the two Bronson families was rapidly reaching a crescendo. The Bronson brothers were no longer sibling adversaries; they were now bona fide, bitter sibling enemies.

* * * * * * * * * * * *

Police Chief Anthony Presti summoned Detective Mark Cirillo into his office (located in the police department basement of Town Hall on Central Avenue) for a private conference. The topic of discussion was the sudden unexpected death of prominent Hammontonian Dennis Bronson.

"You know Mark," the Chief prefaced, "Dennis Bronson and I were really close friends. In fact, confidentially, I own ten acres of ground on Chew Road between several large sections of the Bronson brothers' farms. I acquired the ground dirt-cheap after Denny clued me in about the probable lifting of the building moratorium and about the sewer and water lines goin' in on Third Road," the Chief elaborated. "I saw my pal's advice as an excellent opportunity to make a good quick capital gain on my recently acquired real estate property that incidentally Mark, has been changed from farm zoning to residential. That's one advantage of bein' a public official in this town," the Chief expressed to his loyal subordinate before lighting up his long fat *El Producto* cigar. "You kinda' know what's goin' to happen before it actually does happen, and a savvy inside person like myself can capitalize on the special knowledge before it becomes public."

"Well Chief, why did you call me in?" the sharp-minded young detective asked his superior. "Are ya' thinkin' about getting a real estate license or what?"

"Mark, I'm warnin' ya' to stop bein' so sarcastic and please kindly show me more respect. I'm a little suspicious about the circumstances surrounding Dennis Bronson's death," the Chief confided as he heavily puffed on his immense cigar. "I want to see if you can dig-up any information about possible foul play bein' involved. Your off-the-record investigation might be able to pin something tangible on that rotten skunk Ben, who didn't even have the common decency to pay his last respects to his brother. That's gratitude for ya'!"

The conscientious detective reflected deeply for a moment and then had several inspirations to share. "Well Chief," Detective Mark Cirillo began, "a couple years ago I understand that Ben had asked Dennis to re-divide their original six hundred acres so that each brother would have the same valued land assessments, but your good buddy Dennis nixed the idea when it was certain that the new Third Road sewer and water lines were to be laid down. Those combined factors would certainly give Ben a definite motive for wantin' to eliminate his brother."

"A motive does not actually constitute a crime," Chief Presti impressively articulated while remembering something salient he had learned in Law Enforcement 101. "And the exact cause of Dennis Bronson's death was officially determined to be a heart attack. Now Mark, I believe that something sinister might've triggered the coronary, but I can't prove it; it's just a suspicion; a wild hunch without any substantial evidence. And the Atlantic County coroner's office's autopsy found no signs of poison or drugs present in Dennis's body. But I still have an inkling that there's more to his sudden death than meets the eye."

"Well then Chief, it's rumored all over town in every barber shop and beauty salon that Dennis refused to buy his financially strapped brother out for five million smackers, but your friend declined and rejected Ben's humble solicitation. And then Dennis again denied Ben's request for a $500,000.00 loan according to coffee shop conversations. All of these facts could easily provide Ben with a good motive to eliminate Dennis, but like you said Chief, motives don't constitute crimes."

"Look Mark," the Chief expounded on his hypothesis, "we know that Dennis's property is valued at over sixty million with the re-zoning of Third Road and with the heavy-duty north-side sewer and water lines bein' operational. We also know that Ben feels dejected and cheated because his three hundred acres is only worth 1.5 million if sold to another farmer because of the lousy Pinelands' regulations. There's still another viable motive, but like we already know, motives...."

"Do not constitute actual crimes!" Detective Cirillo robotically answered. "So, what do you want me to do Chief? Watch some old Peter Falk *Columbo* or Joe Friday *Dragnet* stories on cable TV and develop some brilliant fictional idea?"

"Stop actin' so juvenile and bein' so damned cynical!" the Chief admonished his favorite detective on the force. "I want you to figure-out some new angle that somehow implicates Ben Bronson in his brother's untimely death. I hate the no-good scoundrel with a passion and would like to see the callow-minded punk put behind bars, maybe not for murder, but for some less egregious offense. It could even be trespassin' or spittin' on the sidewalk or loiterin', as far as I'm concerned. Now get on that secret detail and find me something relevant!"

Detective Mark Cirillo left Chief Anthony Presti's downstairs office with a resolute mind to excavate some heretofore unknown significant facts within the community that were relative to Dennis

Bronson's much-grieved departure from this Earth. The investigator did not employ the conventional direct approach, that is, using interviews and interrogations. Instead the alert plainclothes cop kept his eyes and ears open and closely listened to community gossip. 'If some skullduggery were involved in Dennis Bronson's death that had not been indicated in the coroner's bland report,' Mark Cirillo conjectured, 'then surely someone in Ben Bronson's family would eventually slip-up and make a boastful comment to a close friend or to a casual acquaintance at a bar or at a *Confirmation* party.'

Two weeks later a very exuberant Detective Cirillo entered Chief Presti's downstairs office all out of breath. The Chief cavalierly glanced-up from reading the front-page headlines of the *Atlantic City Press* to precisely discern what *his* principal informant had to eagerly divulge.

"Mark, what is it?" the Chief rhetorically asked. "Did your ridiculous girlfriend propose to you again or what?"

"No Chief, it's something more vital and important than that!" Detective Cirillo replied without realizing exactly what his mentor had asked. "There's something pretty essential swirling in the wind concerning Dennis Bronson's death that wasn't chronicled in his obituary and wasn't identified and cited in the coroner's autopsy report."

"Well Sherlock Holmes, gather your breath and collect your senses and please tell me!" the usually skeptical Chief-of-Police characteristically chided. "Get to the point, even though I believe that points are for pinheads!"

"Well, I just contacted the *EPA* and the New Jersey Pinelands Commission on the phone and discovered that a week before Dennis Bronson's unexpected death his three hundred acres of choice real estate had failed the State's harsh standards for property development," the Detective revealed to his highly focused boss. "It seems that the farm ground north of Third Road was saturated with *DDT*, a banned toxic chemical pesticide that had been popular among local farmers in the 1950s. His entire farm is contaminated. The ground has been condemned!"

"Were soil tests performed in the past?" the now-concerned Chief Cop wanted to know. "The EPA and the Pinelands officials are very dedicated to conductin' soil tests on area farms."

"Yes, four years ago while the building moratorium was in effect Dennis Bronson's farm had passed the environmental tests with flying colors," Detective Cirillo stated. "It's my theory that while Dennis and his family were vacationing in Hawaii and Tahiti for two solid months that Ben Bronson and his sons mutually conspired and poisoned the north side Third Road three hundred acres with an abundance of illegal *DDT*. But I believe we need additional evidence to substantiate my findings and build a case against that dastardly hermit Ben and his ornery, jealous sons."

"Mark, *DDT* shouldn't be too hard to trace because the lethal chemical is both obsolete and forbidden to be used," Chief Presti assumed and related. "We might not be able to indict and prove murder, but we might be capable of sending Ben Bronson to the county clinker for a couple years on direct charges of maliciously polluting the environment, of trespassing, of vandalism and of crop devastation. Now I got a stellar idea that might help us in arrestin' and convictin' that slippery weasel Ben Bronson. I truly now believe Mark that Dennis had suffered his lethal heart attack wonderin' how his ground had gotten poisoned with an obsolete chemical and then theorizing who would have the unmitigated audacity to commit such a cruel misdeed."

"What's your instruction?" the young detective respectfully demanded. "Give me your corroborative evidence so that we can conduct a collaborative investigation," Detective Cirillo reflexively laughed as the police subordinate thoroughly appreciated his slightly-clever play-on-words.

"Mark, while you were yappin' away, I've just made a brilliant deduction," the egocentric Chief commended himself as was his bad habit. "As you know, I own a fairly large parcel of ground on Chew Road situated directly between sections of the Bronson brothers' farms. Now if Ben and his sons drove their tractors and sprayers across my land to get to Dennis's back acres while the older brother and his entire family were celebratin' their prospective sixty million dollar bonanza in the South Pacific," the Chief objectively pontificated, "then some of the poisonous chemical would've leaked-out of their sprayers' tanks and left an invisible toxic trail clear across my ten acres. That'll be all the corroborative evidence necessary to launch charges against that yellow-bellied rogue Ben Bronson. I order you to get in touch with some soil testing experts right away and have sand, dirt and gravel samples taken from the main dirt roads runnin' through my property and then have the potential evidence fully analyzed. Like they say Mark," Chief Presti elucidated, "there's more than one way to skin a cat, whatever the hell that means!"

"Yes Sir, even though Ben probably caused his brother's death, if we can't get the culprit for murder," the quick-learning detective insisted to his vindictive superior, "then we'll gladly throw him in the Mays Landing county slammer for committing other less horrendous violations."

"Now you're talkin' my language," commended the impressed Chief-of-Police. "Really Mark, if ya' keep developin' your law enforcement thinkin' skills, you might someday become a future Hammonton Police Chief!"

"Growing Young"

December 7th, 2014 had become my own personal self-inflicted *Pearl Harbor Day.* I recollect that *that* particular Sunday morning started-out quite routine and nondescript. After waking-up early, shaving, dressing, and then hastily drinking a tall glass of orange juice, I promptly left my Hammonton, New Jersey Pleasant Street humble ranch home, entered my green *2012 Subaru Outback* and mechanically drove four blocks to St. Mary of Mt. Carmel Church on Third and French Street to attend 9 a.m. Mass, where each and every Sunday I predictably sit isolated and self-exiled in the next-to-last right-side pew nearest the center aisle.

After the perfunctory religious service was finished, I silently departed the all-too-familiar building, re-entered my *Outback* in the church parking lot and drove my dependable automobile twelve miles west on Route 30 toward Berlin to peacefully enjoy a delicious breakfast in complete anonymity. Being introverted as is my shy demeanor, I impatiently sat alone among the singular patrons at the Berlin Diner's counter and soon ordered a Belgian waffle topped with bananas, walnuts and an abundance of whipped cream.

"Where ya' from Stranger?" the middle-aged brunette waitress asked, cheerfully initiating a casual conversation. "You're new in here! Ya' don't live in Berlin, I do believe."

"You're right about *that* observation!" I all-too-politely answered. "I'm from Hammonton."

"What's wrong with the Silver Coin Diner?" the chatty waitress quickly asked. "They have great food there too, ya' know. My sister-in-law is a hostess at that diner and says the tips are terrific."

"Well," I uncomfortably replied, shifting my level position upon my elevated seat, "I felt I needed a change in venue this morning so I'm exploring a little bit out of my regular territory. Confidentially, I have to buy some new heater filters over at the local *Home Depot.* My habit is to change the buggers six times a year; three times for spring and summer air-conditioning and then three times for the fall and winter heating system when our nemesis Old Man Winter invades South Jersey on the yearly calendar. It's quite an annual ritual for me!"

"That's right!" the attractive waitress verified with a forced smile. "You don't have a *Home Depot* over in Hammonton. Your town only has a smaller-type *Wal*Mart* store. The huge Berlin box-store you're gonna' patronize certainly has a much better selection of hardware and home products! But be careful Mr.! It's December 7th,

Pearl Harbor Day. Don't be jinxed and have to survive your own private 'Day of Infamy'!"

"I promise not to buy any Japanese heater filters!" I quipped.

The nosy customer seated just two stools down had been eavesdropping on *our* courteous, non-flirtatious dialogue. Hearing the flash-point words "Pearl Harbor," the old geezer felt obligated to contribute what he valued as being somewhat significant to the general diner verbal exchange.

"After Pearl Harbor," the elderly codger awkwardly interrupted, "my pop was drafted into the Army at age thirty-six, since there was a basic shortage of manpower to go up against Hitler and his evil minions. Pop served in France, Germany, Luxembourg, Holland and Belgium before returning back to the States. My ears got me interested in *your* discussion when you had mentioned Belgian waffle. It made me think of my pop stationed in Belgium."

"Did your dad bring home any special trophies or interesting souvenirs from *World War II?*" I inquired, attempting to exhibit a degree of social decorum and interest. "A French or Dutch wife perhaps! Maybe some very delicious Brussels sprouts!" I innocently joked, contrary to my usual introspective nature.

"Yes," the elderly fellow remarked, ignoring my feeble attempt at humor before taking another sip of hot coffee. "Pop found a nifty bombshell casing and had it engraved with the names of all the cities, towns, villages and countries he had visited on his three-year European tour of duty. The finished mortar shell was a beautiful metallic piece that Mom used as a flower vase in the family den."

After consuming my delectable Belgian waffle, side-of-bacon and coffee breakfast, I deposited a three dollar tip on the diner's front serving counter, quietly said "Goodbye" to both the 'affable waitress' and the garrulous 'old curmudgeon', paid my breakfast bill at the cashier and then exited the then semi-crowded Berlin Diner. I ambled to the back lot, climbed into my green *Subaru,* fired-up the engine and headed west on *Route 30* in the direction of the Berlin Shopping Center and the popular *Home Depot* store.

'This superficial task should only take about fifteen minutes,' I reckoned as my left foot stepped upon and released the car's emergency brake. 'In another hour I'll be home replacing the 16 x 25 x 1-inch gas heater filter down in my cellar. But I gotta' remember to buy a large *Snickers* candy bar on my way out!'

After locking the doors of my *Outback,* I sauntered into the Berlin *Home Depot,* quickly located the appropriate exact-size air filters in a side aisle, and when I bent-down to grab the two sought-

126

after items, a heavy cardboard merchandise box fell from the top overhead shelf. The dangerous object grazed the right side of my scalp and ear and then violently crashed into my right arm and chest; the simultaneous impacts immediately knocking me to the tiled floor in an unconscious state.

In retrospect, it was *that* specific event that placed my long-kept longevity secret in jeopardy of having public disclosure and scrutiny. The next thing I could remember, I was lying in a hospital bed experiencing heightened agony and discomfort, and next a pleasant blonde-haired nurse was informing me that the actual date was Monday, December 29th and then disclosing that I had been surviving in a deep coma for over a three-week period. But truthfully, at that moment I was absolutely glad to be alive!

* * * * * * * * * * * *

That late December Monday afternoon I had fully awoken from my three-week-long unconscious state and my drowsy pupils immediately noticed the distinguishable presence of a vertical I-V stand and a side catheter/urine bag. Instantly I was aware that I had been occupying a hospital bed.

"Where am I? Who are you? What the heck happened?" I neurotically asked the nurse and doctor peering-down at me while standing next to my bed.

"I'm Dr. Stephen Arena and this is Nurse Linda Rizzotte," the physician professionally introduced himself and his assistant. "I'm the surgeon who had operated on you. You had quite a near-death experience at the Berlin *Home Depot,* I must admit. If that enormous box had hit you squarely on the head, I don't think we'd be having this informal conversation right now!"

"What hospital is this?" I requested knowing. "It looks pretty modern and new."

"You're in Room 311 at Virtua Hospital, Route 73 in Voorhees," Nurse Rizzotte related with a somber expression displayed upon her face. "The Berlin Rescue Squad transported you here soon after your near-tragic *Home Depot* accident."

Everything seemed fuzzy and nebulous at that exact moment, so my new medical companions decided to prattle about the harsh weather, about the *Philadelphia Eagles* football team and about the impending winter snowstorm before returning to their review of my identity and my improving condition. The pair suggested that they were happy to note that I apparently was not suffering from either amnesia or any severe memory loss.

"You were fairly easy to identify from your New Jersey driver's license and from your wallet's credit cards," stern-faced Dr. Arena indicated. "But one aspect of the entire matter seriously concerns me. Your license amazingly shows that your birthdate was July 2nd, 1899. Is that a misprint that needs to be changed and rectified? The date seems to defy basic reality!"

"That would make you approximately 115 years old!" Nurse Linda Rizzotte exclaimed and then disbelievingly shook her head from side-to-side. "The oldest man still living in the United States is...."

"Reportedly 112 years old," Dr. Stephen Arena finished and objectively reported, "and that aged fellow happens to be residing in New York City. As a matter of fact, I had read a fascinating magazine article about him last week. The guy was born in Spain and then later emigrated to the U.S."

"And not that it's so important, but we've also noticed that you've never donated blood to the American Red Cross," Nurse Rizzotte stated. "Is there something especially wrong with your blood? For example, do you have a history of Hepatitis C antibodies or any other irregularity like that?"

Those startling perceptive commentaries had made me become rather anxious and nervous. I feared that my coveted long-held secret might be harmfully revealed and exposed. I worried that my former orderly human existence was suddenly becoming unraveled and disheveled, all because of the unfortunate *Home Depot* incident I had experienced. Momentarily, I had become lost for words. Then after careful neurotic deliberation, I uttered what constituted a boldface lie which I orally conveyed in a depressed state of mind. "I've always had a fear of needles. Yes, fear of needles has kept me from giving blood over the years!"

"As you probably know," the medical doctor diplomatically explained, sensing that I had been clumsily prevaricating, "your blood type is O Positive. O negative is often referred to as 'the Universal Donor'. Because of the complicated operations we had to perform on you," Dr. Arena hesitated and then resumed his incisive narrative, "we had to administer four units of RH O Positive blood during the lengthy six-hour O.R. procedures, all due to your critical loss of plasma."

"Over the years," I shakily declared from my sitting semi-erect hospital bed position, "I've become an unrecognized authority on blood," I almost guiltily confessed. "I probably know more about the composition and properties of blood than anyone working in your sophisticated hospital labs."

I continued delivering my comprehensive explanation by citing that blood is manufactured in a person's bone marrow and that the vital body substance can be broken-down into erythrocytes, or red blood cells, leukocytes, or white blood cells, platelets, which allow for clotting and coagulating, plasma, hemoglobin and finally, into essential proteins. "Too many leukocytes, which are part of the body's immune system, could lead to leukemia, and having not enough platelets could drastically mean developing hemophilia. A healthy human body depends on just the right ratio of these indispensable and fantastically interrelated blood elements."

"Granted, you do understand plenty about the chemistry and functionality of blood," Dr. Arena complimented my conceited expertise. "Whatever caused you to be so academically enamored and intrigued about *that* highly specialized subject?"

"I suppose it all started with me seeing the 1931 black and white movie *Dracula* at the Hippodrome Theater in downtown Baltimore," I recalled and declared to my astonished listeners. "It was an impressive vampire movie, and over the decades I too have evolved into a sort of contemporary vampire myself," I im*patient*ly mentioned, obviously confusing the wits of my two-member audience. "In the original classic film starring Bela Lugosi, Dr. Van Helsing had performed blood transfusions on a patient named Lucy Weston, and that's precisely when I had organized my eccentric blood immortality theory."

"Yes, I've read Bram Stoker's novel at least a half-dozen times since high school," Nurse Linda Rizzotte contributed, "but your Lucy Weston appearing in the film version was really named Lucy Westenra in the famous *Dracula* novel."

"Wait a minute now!" a slightly irritated Dr. Arena insisted. "You're losing me by your weird account, evidently leaving-out some pertinent details. We've conducted a meticulous background check on you and I must acknowledge that we've discovered that your unique driver's license is incredibly accurate. You were indeed born in Posen, Michigan just outside of Alpena on July 2nd, 1899. Your family then moved to Baltimore around 1907. And so, remarkably," Dr. Arena cleared his throat and continued his precisely on-target commentary, "your claim about seeing the movie *Dracula* at the Hippodrome Theater in 1931 seems to jibe with our intensive background research done on you. Now for the sake of logic and sanity," the skilled surgeon suavely qualified, "please reveal how you've managed to age to a ripe 115 and still look like a rejuvenated man of fifty years. You don't have any dark age marks on your hands or any expected wrinkles on your neck and face!"

"That's totally correct!" Nurse Rizzotte concurred with her immediate superior. "Have you discovered the Fountain of Youth that Ponce de Leon had been futilely seeking?"

"Well," I reluctantly answered in response, "the New Jersey Department of Motor Vehicles has for a long time been mighty suspicious about my recorded chronological age," I verbally shared. "I have to take a new written test every two years along with a thorough-and-redundant behind-the-wheel test, too. The Motor Vehicle inspectors are flabbergasted about my phenomenal mental acumen along with my extraordinary physical dexterity. As you've both already learned," I deliberately hesitated and paused to gauge the doctor and the nurse's overt reactions to my seemingly peculiar statements, "I'm now probably the oldest man currently living in the United States!"

"This is one oddball story that most definitely must be published in the American Medical Association Journal," amazed Dr. Arena instinctively determined. "Sir, you must reveal how you've managed to achieve the age of 115 without ever exhibiting any signs of being affected by the common and debilitating aging process!"

At that most critical juncture of our rather unorthodox hospital room conference, my mind and body suddenly felt weak and fatigued. Much to the frustration and consternation of Dr. Arena and Nurse Rizzotte, my weary eyes slowly shut, and next my encumbered consciousness was soon drifting-off into a rather disturbed-and-stressful dream slumber.

* * * * * * * * * * * *

On Tuesday morning at 9:30 Dr. Stephen Arena and Nurse Linda Rizzotte escorted two black-business-suit and tie gentlemen into Virtua Hospital Room 311. Earlier that morning I had been disconnected from the bothersome catheter and accompanying urine bag, and my regenerated spirit possessed a degree more energy because I had finally eaten solid food for breakfast two hours before.

"These two federal government men have a distinct interest in *investigating,* or should I more discreetly say 'interviewing' you about your rather bizarre age situation," Dr. Arena candidly greeted. "May I now introduce Mr. Frank Mitchell of the Social Service

130

Agency and Mr. Lawrence Delaney, who is representing the Internal Revenue Service."

"Have I committed any major felony while I was hibernating in the coma?" I defensively replied. "I hope I'm not being interrogated without any lawyer being present to protect my First Amendment civil rights!"

"We promise that we won't prosecute you in any way," Mr. Mitchell pledged with a grin. "Mr. Delaney and I are only interested in ascertaining how you've successfully defeated the aging process. We hope that you'll be cooperative in answering our basic questions. Just be a little patriotic, that's all we ask. Uncle Sam is relying on your honesty, you know!"

"Well Gentlemen," I skeptically declared to my new-found federal acquaintances, "the U.S. Social Security System was set-up to compensate workers that paid into it upon reaching their retirements. But obviously," I boldly and bravely clarified, "people living back in the 1940s had a life expectancy of only around fifty-six years. The government was betting that few public and private sector employees would ever reach age 62 to collect their monthly entitlement checks."

"Very sagacious observation," Inspector Delaney answered. "Our Washington records reveal that in *your* working lifetime you were once a prosperous grocery store owner, a prominent fruit and produce broker and distributor, and also a partner for sixteen years in various boardwalk businesses in New Jersey, Delaware and Maryland. Isn't *that* information all true?"

"Yes," I suspiciously affirmed. "Now please tell me what your relevant concerns are in relation to me."

"Mr. Frank Mitchell and Mr. Lawrence Delaney only would like to learn how you've conquered aging in order to live to be 115," Nurse Rizzotte expressed, hoping to ease the general tension that quite ostensibly dominated the room's cold atmosphere. "They've already stated with Dr. Arena and me as their witnesses that you'll suffer no federal consequences from truthfully conferring with us."

"Yes," piped-up Dr. Arena. "From the government's perspective, if all citizens lived to be 115, the Social Security Trust System along with the entire U.S. Treasury would go bankrupt within the next fifty years. I truly hope that you now fathom the government's curious examination of your incomparable longevity from 1899 up to the present. It's all quite innocuous, you see!"

"Why don't you begin where you had left off yesterday," constructively recommended Nurse Rizzotte. "You can start with your captivation with the 1931 movie *Dracula* and with your strange interest in blood transfusions."

"This ought to prove to be a rather 'sanguine' story," jested Mr. Frank Mitchell in an effort to allay my obvious apprehension. "Already Sir, Mr. Delaney and I feel like we're your blood brothers," Mitchell joshed.

I inhaled several deep breaths and cautiously collected my random memories and thoughts. I then steadfastly stated that from the movie *Dracula* I had considered all facets of the art and science of blood transfusions. I had conjectured the prospect of 'What if I were to have a doctor remove my blood at certain intervals over the span of a month and then give me back my younger drained blood five years later so that the technique could be repeated every half decade?' I then concluded my sensational exposition by saying, "I had hypothesized that the fresh old blood from my body would favorably replenish my vital organs like my lungs, liver, pancreas and spleen and therefore, the younger five-year-old injected blood would allow me to effectively stifle the dreaded aging process?" I directly divulged to my four avid listeners.

"Astounding to say the least!" evaluated and articulated Dr. Arena. "In certain Transylvanian legends, vampires live for centuries acquiring blood samples to drink from selected victims. In *your* case, you are kind of imitating a vampire by inserting your younger blood back into your body and substituting it for your tired blood every five years or so. And that's probably why you still look like you're a young and fit sixty-year-old male specimen, even though you are way beyond being a deteriorating centenarian!"

"Brilliant idea!" agreed Nurse Rizzotte while addressing me as I was sitting almost vertical in my elevated hospital bed. "But you could only have adopted *this* exceptional self-transfusion practice of yours forty or forty-five years ago!"

"Why is that?" curiously asked the now-bewildered Social Security official. "Why is it only forty or forty-five years ago?"

"Because Mr. Mitchell," Dr. Arena plausibly explained, "blood can only be preserved over time by freezing it at a very low temperature, and *that* complex technology has only been recently perfected within the past half century. It's quite elementary to understand. Blood must be stored at a minus 85 degrees after being initially frozen at a minus 122 degrees."

"How many pints' of precious blood does the average human have in his body?" wondered and asked Mr. Lawrence Delaney. "I think I remember from a high school science class that it's about six quarts, which I presume is equivalent to around…"

"Twelve pints," I estimated and voluntarily offered. "Each pint is called a 'unit', and the average male has around twelve pints constantly flowing inside his arteries, veins and capillaries, with each separate pint or unit weighing precisely 16.7 ounces."

Dr. Arena then pontificated about how donated blood is normally distributed for hospital use, and next the veteran surgeon emphasized that the dark red fluid is usually broken-down into plasma, hemoglobin, red blood cells, white blood cells, proteins and platelets for necessary individual medical and O.R. requirements.

"So *you* say that over the course of the past fifty years, you've gotten blood specialists to administer your own whole blood that had been drained from your veins five years prior, and now you maintain that this frozen older blood stimulates your immune system and revitalizes your principal vital organs too!" assessed and marveled Mr. Delaney. "That's so preposterously simple! Why hadn't anyone in the scientific or medical communities ever considered that sort of revolutionary-yet-rudimentary experiment? I mean, why is blood ordinarily only donated to give to other people?"

"Yes Sir," I frankly confided to the perplexed IRS Treasury Man. "I have to pay a blood expert ten thousand dollars to remove my twelve pints of blood over a month's time and then provide another ten thousand bucks to replace my blood with the new/old blood five years later. But truthfully, most of my life's savings have been spent on the very costly and illicit underground economy frozen blood storage fees," I genuinely elaborated. "The entire enterprise can be quite expensive as you can well-imagine, but in stark reality, 'virtual immortality' does have its price! That's why this former multimillionaire must now live in a modest ranch home over in Hammonton. I've traded my wealth for longevity!"

"This whole confidential matter is entirely preposterous!" claimed and exclaimed Social Security Inspector Frank Mitchell. "Yet conversely, it's not a colossal hoax at all! Your prodigious 115 years upon this Earth verify your seemingly ludicrous assertions! According to indisputable government records, you actually *were* born in 1899! Government documents also show that *you* had been married in 1942 in Elkton, Maryland and that your wife had died in 1974. Yes, you *were* born in Michigan in 1899!" florid-faced Mr. Mitchell uncharacteristically bellowed. "That's totally unbelievable! Why that's even before Queen Victoria had died over in England!

Historically speaking, it's remarkably eighteen whole years before America's involvement in World War I!"

"Exactly Mr. Mitchell!" I enthusiastically acceded, automatically nodding my still-aching head up and down. "Now I hope that you two eminent Gentlemen will accept and appreciate the legitimacy of my former blood-transfusion secret. But I can't guarantee that the explicit method I've just described will satisfactorily work for all other human beings! In summary, older blood cells get tired and worn-out, eventually not being able to perfectly duplicate themselves as thawed-out five-year younger cells can more easily do."

"And to my knowledge," Dr. Stephen Arena pertinently stressed, "no other humans except *you* had ever imaginatively had twelve pints of their own *whole blood* frozen and sinisterly held in the underground black market, and then systematically transfused back into their own bodies every five years or so."

"Have you had any fears living all these years guarding this miraculous knowledge you've just shared with us?" sincerely asked exasperated Treasury Department employee Mr. Lawrence Delaney. "The emotional pressure must've been quite extreme!"

"Yes," I soberly replied. "Even though I could retain my youthful vitality and appearance, I always worried about how I could avoid any accidental death in, let's say for example, an auto' collision, or perhaps drowning. In fact, I haven't gone swimming in the ocean, in a lake or in a pool ever since I began receiving my essential blood transfusions beginning back around 1968. And that's the honest-to-God truth!"

"And you almost were permanently eliminated at the Berlin *Home Depot* with that heavy large box descending upon you," astutely noted Nurse Linda Rizzotte. "That near-disaster was a close call which almost sent you directly to the cemetery."

I had little opportunity to express my deepest gratitude to Dr. Arena, to Nurse Rizzotte and to the absent Berlin Rescue Squad paramedics.

"Sir, you don't have to worry about going to a federal penitentiary for committing any red-blooded felony," Inspector Frank Mitchell told me with his absurd statement being followed by a mild chuckle. "And we won't implicate and investigate any of your black-market co-conspirators either! The main reason for Mr. Delaney and me being here today is to save our country's fragile Social Security System from entering imminent insolvency," the very high-ranking Washington agent austerely announced. "Now here's my proposal agreement. For obvious reasons, it's both

134

mandatory and imperative for the five of us to take an official oath to never divulge the essence of this esoteric blood-rejuvenating secret that has been discussed and described today in this New Jersey hospital room. Is this matter perfectly clear?"

"Yes!" we all chanted in unison before ever repeating and reciting our dutiful allegiance to the United States of America. "Yes!" we all coincidentally reiterated.

"Excellent then!" exclaimed a very relieved Mr. Frank Mitchell. "Now please raise your right hands and patriotically repeat after me, "I hereby solemnly swear that...."

"Corporal Teleportation"

Many fascinating science-fiction tales elaborately explore the theme of Time Travel, but the incredible true story I'm about to relate lucidly describes the reality of my own personal "Space Travel", which I presently refer to as "Inexplicable Contemporary Teleportation". Forget about the common utilization of literary techniques known as flashback and fore-shadowing. The authentic account that I'm about to recollect and share will be delivered in an accurate, chronological pattern from beginning to end. My Sicilian next-door neighbor Howard Graziano can testify to some of my tale's undeniable veracity.

Howard and I live on Pratt Street in Hammonton, NJ, which is parallel to French Street on the east. These two roads are important to our town because in between them lies the normally empty Carnival Grounds, where nearby St. Joseph Catholic Church (and its affiliated Mt. Carmel Society) annually celebrate the religious feast of Our Lady of Mt. Carmel the week of the 16th of July. Over twenty-thousand people (mostly religious pilgrims) visit the town on *that* special date, which is almost double the number of actual Hammonton daily inhabitants.

Howard is a burly retired town policeman who belongs to the Mt. Carmel Society, which has a building and beer garden that borders the Carnival Grounds on Tilton Street, which runs east-west between Pratt and French. Conversely, I am a retired plumber and have long been a proud card-carrying member of The Sons of Italy, Garibaldi Lodge 1658, historically located on *North Third Street,* which is a main town thoroughfare that also features St. Joseph Church running parallel to Tilton on the *south side* between Pratt and French. The four-street configuration (Pratt, French, Third and Tilton) makes the gravel Carnival Grounds form a large, rectangular town landmark.

Howard is a devout family man living with his wife Jean, since the couple's three grown children are married and living in other parts of South Jersey. In my case, I'm a confirmed bachelor living happy and alone in a cozy yellow brick bungalow. At age seventy-six, I still occasionally date several women who are widowed, but for the most part, I prefer an independent lifestyle devoid of marital stress along with complicated family responsibilities.

My brawny friend and neighbor Howard Graziano is quite reliable and sometimes indispensable, and *we* often perform favors for one another: I'll change and replace his hot water heater or install a new kitchen faucet for Howie, and he'll assist me in trimming my bushes in early autumn or laying-down mulch around my shrubs and lawn trees in the spring.

In May of 2019, two months before the popular Amusements of America traveling carnival pulled-into "the Grounds", I had ordered a thirty-nine-inch television set that had been prominently listed on eBay. The following Tuesday, the heavy device arrived at my residence, and it required two muscular FedEx delivery employees to carry the newly acquired entertainment device onto my front porch. I already had two TVs in my home: one in the den and one in my master bedroom, but I had figured that I would have a third monitor strategically situated atop the spare bedroom's ancient bureau to accommodate my corpulent cousin Mario, who would annually visit Hammonton to commemorate "the Catholic Feast" and march in the traditional procession of saint statues through town. Naturally, Howard Graziano was conveniently available to especially assist me in transporting the heavy cardboard carton from the front porch into my cherished, humble abode.

"John, what did this monster cost?" Howie asked as I used a sharp blade box-cutter to fragment the flat-screen's exterior box. "It must weigh almost as much as you do!"

"Three hundred and fifty dollars," I bragged and answered. "I think I got quite a bargain on eBay. If you take the time to shop online," I continued prattling, "plenty of good deals can be made. Say Howie: There doesn't seem to be any ordinary brand name or company logo on this TV!"

My very capable assistant then carefully examined the impressive-looking item more in detail. "This is really quite peculiar, John. There doesn't seem to be any serial identification number, either," marveled and replied my Good Samaritan neighbor before we lifted the heavy mechanism onto the spare bedroom bureau. "I hope you haven't naively purchased contraband merchandise!" Howie joked. "Well anyway, good luck with your eBay acquisition," Graziano expressed before using his handkerchief to wipe-away a quantity of recently produced sweat from his forehead. "Don't worry; I'm retired and I won't arrest you!"

"I'll call my Internet service provider later this afternoon and arrange to have it hooked-up to my desktop computer line," I confidently stated. "This baby should add a few premium bucks to my already expensive cable bill, but when a guy's a bachelor," I egotistically commented with a broad smile, "he'll watch a surplus of sports, comedy shows and pay-per-view movies. That's just the nature of the animal."

"Well good luck with it, John," Howie wished and casually remarked. "I hope this baby lasts as long as the LG in my living room and the Samsung in my bedroom. Now where's that cold bottle of beer that you promised me before we heisted this cumbersome machine onto your bureau. I'll have a nice Coors Light or Budweiser if you don't mind."

Comcast Xfinity arrived on the premises late Friday afternoon, May 21st, 2019 to connect the new brandless unit to my regular house service. All was fine and dandy when the new TV showed a female commentator standing outside Chicago's Wrigley Field and interviewing several exuberant Windy City fans entering the park to watch an upcoming evening baseball game between the Cubs and the visiting Phillies. Feeling satisfied that the TV was working, I thanked the courteous Comcast installation technician for his expertise and upon his departure, I shut the object off.

'I just have enough time to mow the lawn and eat a quick, delicious ham, lettuce and tomato sandwich before game time,' I mentally concluded while checking my wristwatch. 'I'll sit in the spare room's red armchair and officially christen my new TV. What better way to enjoy my nameless apparatus other than me viewing an exciting Phillies baseball game at Wrigley Field? Let's see how much sliced ham I have in the 'fridge.'

That May 21st 2019 evening, when I nonchalantly grabbed the spare room TV's remote control and flicked-on the device, a rather strange screen appeared that oddly read: "Channel 6: Welcome to Cosmos Television Network." No sooner had those extraordinary words vanished, well, so did I. To my total astonishment, my mind and body were magically transported into a seat in the left field stands of Chicago's Wrigley Field where for six fantastic minutes I was witnessing the Cubs' Javier Baez batting and stubbornly fouling-off pitches in the bottom of the Ninth Inning. Then, much to my overall dissatisfaction, pinch-hitter Baez came through in the clutch and smashed a climactic single to seal a Cubs 3-2 victory over the lackluster Phillies.

'This is impossible!' I instantly thought as the jubilant Cubs fans surrounding me eagerly began evacuating the stadium. 'I've always wanted to see a game here at Wrigley,' I remember assessing my bizarre predicament and then admiring the famous ivy growing on the outfield brick walls, 'but how the heck did I ever get over a thousand miles west of Hammonton in a matter of seconds to see the ending of a night game here in Illinois?' I wondered and worried.

'This entire arcane scenario is horribly uncanny! I dare not tell Howie or the guys over at the Sons of Italy one word of it!'

Before my heart and emotions could calm-down, my body was abruptly and swiftly teleported back to my Pratt Street residence's spare room. After my form had reappeared in the red armchair, my awed mind instinctively glanced at my watch to verify the time and place of my new-found reality. 'I was away for a brief six-minute baseball fan adventure,' I logically considered. 'And coincidentally, the unique TV was set on Channel 6 to view the Phillies-Cubs game,' I nervously determined in what amounted to a bewildered and addled state of mind. 'Is there some sort of crazy correlation between the amazing six-minute time interval and the TV setting Channel 6?' my perplexed brain incredulously contemplated. 'I'll do some more curious experimenting tomorrow after I gain enough courage to activate the TV again!'

At noon on Saturday, May 22^{nd,} I felt audacious enough to again sit in the spare bedroom's red armchair and see if I could cleverly duplicate my uncanny "space teleportation" experience. I used the TV's remote control to commence the system and was encouraged upon observing a screen showing a black background with distinctive white letters indicating: "Welcome Back to the Cosmos Network." Feeling adventurous, I methodically punched-in "Channel 7" upon the remote in an attempt to notice exactly what kind of new episode would materialize besides the mind-boggling six-minute Wrigley Field phenomenon produced on Channel 6.

Before I finished thinking 'Whatever happened to NBC, CBS, ABC, Fox News, CNN C-NBC, PBS and MS-NBC', the cursory introductory message disappeared and an attractive brunette female reporter came into focus on Channel 7. The woman was standing in front of the enormous landmark Deno Ferris Wheel, which is only found near the boardwalk in Coney Island.

"I'm here in the Coney Island section of Brooklyn to describe the many rides and tourist attractions that are a crucial part of this world-famous resort," the lady TV journalist declared. "We'll start our scenic tour with a glimpse of the giant Deno Ferris Wheel, which has been a mainstay of Coney Island ever since the roaring 1920s."

As the comely woman continued her scripted monologue, my mind's memory flashed back to August of 1960. I was seventeen and had been working for my grandparents at Square Deal Farm Market on the White Horse Pike in Hammonton. I was a friend of Anthony "Tatar" Bertino, a five-foot-ten-inch kid who weighed two hundred and forty pounds of raw, brute strength. Bertino had acquired the nickname "Tatar" because his father was an established South Jersey sweet potato farmer. That particular Sunday morning *we* had received permission from our folks for Tatar and me to drive one-hundred-twenty miles up the New Jersey Turnpike and then through the Lincoln Tunnel in my father's white Chevy Impala. Our mutual fantasy goal was to check-out the many exciting activities going-on in Coney Island.

After parking my dad's car in a lot near Times Square around 11 a.m., Tatar and I descended into a subway station and bought tokens to be transported by the Q Train across the Brooklyn Bridge on the way to the famous honky-tonk boardwalk. At an elevated platform stop in Brooklyn, a kid wearing a black leather jacket boarded our car and immediately, Tatar grabbed the surprised punk by the collar and hurled the junior hoodlum right through the still-open carriage doors onto the cement waiting platform. The doors closed, leaving the bruised-up kid lying motionless upon the concrete stop as the Q train sped off.

I looked around at the few remaining passengers randomly seated as if they were pathetic zombies. Two riders were sleeping, another guy appeared to be intoxicated and two women (who I believed had witnessed the brief altercation) pretended not to be staring at ferocious and mercurial Tatar and me.

"What did you do that for!" I yelled at Bertino. "That kid did nothing to you!"

"I didn't like the way the wise ass was looking at me!" my formidable cross-eyed companion replied. "He was cruisin' for a bruisin' and I gave it to him before he could mouth-off!"

"But that kid probably belongs to a local street gang," I surmised and stated. "He'll gather together ten of his delinquent friends and they'll come after us with chains, switchblades and crowbars at Coney Island."

"I don't care!" Tatar angrily retorted. "Let them come! You fight one of them and I'll beat the crap out of the other nine!"

Tatar and I departed the Q Train at Stillwell Avenue and followed the swift-moving crowd to Surf Ave. where we ravenously downed two hot dogs apiece at Nathan's, and as we quickened our pace in the direction of the boardwalk, we were amazed to see and hear legendary Fats Domino performing at an open-air bar singing the early rock and roll classic "Ain't That A Shame".

"Black entertainers need small jobs like this one just to make ends meet," I objectively explained to "Tate". "White artists like Pat Boone do cover versions of original black recordings like 'Ain't

That A Shame', and the white renditions are promoted on the radio by mostly white DJs."

After reflecting on my one and only 1960 visit to Coney Island with inimitable Anthony Tatar Bertino, I bravely pressed the remote numeral "7" again and almost instantly, I found myself walking slowly on the boardwalk in front of the colossal Deno Ferris Wheel. Mentally comparing my Brooklyn space-excursion with my first Cosmos TV jaunt to Wrigley Field, I reckoned that I had only '7 minutes of time' to make my visual notetaking. 'There's the Cyclone Roller Coaster, and the familiar Parachute Jump Tower over there, but George Tilyou's Steeplechase Park Horse Race Ride that I remember from 1960 is no longer here,' I shockingly recognized as I looked-around in both directions to gain a better perception of the total physical environment. 'But this place over on the right now called Luna Park did not exist when Tatar and I were here back in 1960, and the Cyclone is now a major part of Luna Park. And the original wood-structured Thunderbolt Roller Coaster is nowhere in sight and has been replaced by a modern steel-constructed one bearing the same name,' my still-stunned eyes noticed as they glanced to the south. 'This could only mean that I'm really strolling around Coney Island in 2019 and not 1960!'

My short seven-minute surreal time allotment had apparently expired and next my consciousness suddenly felt my body and mind being whisked back a hundred and twenty miles south to my red armchair in the spare room on Pratt Street. 'Tatar wasn't with me this time to Coney Island,' I sadly evaluated before taking ten deep breaths. 'I've seen him send at least five kids in ambulances to hospitals when he was playing defensive guard for St. Joseph High. Those other opposing high school offensive linemen didn't stand a chance. It's too bad that Tatar passed-away in 2010. I really miss the guy's zaniness tremendously, along with his awesome bodyguard protection. Nobody in their right mind ever messed with Tatar.'

On Monday, May 24th I felt both inspired and motivated to initiate my third totally indecipherable "Space Travel" safari. 'If I switch to Channel 3 on the Cosmos Network,' I presumed and speculated, 'I should wind-up in a fairly neat place for only three minutes. I'm beginning to really like this most interesting eBay TV. I no longer fear the mysterious mechanism or question the weird science behind it, but I want to learn more about its functioning.'

I pressed "3" on the remote and in several seconds saw and heard a male commentator speaking about a new abstract art exhibit at the Palm Spring, California Art Museum. In a matter of three seconds, I was no longer seated in my red armchair but instead, found myself in front of the Sonny Bono statue in downtown Palm Springs. A thermometer on a store façade registered "98 Degrees". Numerous restaurants and retail shops dotted the road, where an overhead street sign read "Palm Canyon Drive" with another sign pointing in the opposite direction revealing: "To Indian Canyon Drive". A group of garrulous tourists were chatting incessantly about their desires to visit nearby Cathedral City, Rancho Mirage and Palm Desert, but before I could converse with any of the talkative strangers, evidently my short three minute tenure had terminated and before I could utter a syllable, after enduring precisely three minutes in the hot desert temperature, my human form was promptly transported back to my spare room and red armchair in my cozy Pratt Street bungalow.

'This time I had traveled nearly three thousand miles west to beautiful Palm Springs,' I comprehended. 'I was never there before and always wanted to vacation in the famous resort. This 'space teleportation' stuff is rather exhilarating. I think I'll take another impromptu detour from Hammonton and see where the arcane television will take me. I'm not a Time Traveler,' I then realized. 'I'm a Space Traveler.'

Feeling in complete command of the incomprehensible "cosmic" process, I haughtily pushed the 4 Button on the remote and soon my pupils viewed a camera crew industriously setting-up equipment to film a celebrity interview in front of a classic Miami Beach, Florida hotel. 'Wow!' I reactively noticed and thought. 'I'd recognize that curved building anywhere. It's the magnificent Fontainbleau, used as a majestic background scene in the movie thriller 'Goldfinger', starring Sean Connery as James Bond, Agent 007. The resplendent architectural wonder is right next to the Eden Roc luxury palace, and it's also a mile or so up the coast from the famous art deco hotels dotting the shore in semi-tropical South Miami Beach. I love palm trees swaying in the breeze and smelling the fresh, salty ocean air,' I remember appreciating as my delightful four-minute excursion smoothly ended and I was soon again seated in a baffled state of mind inside my bungalow's very mediocre spare bedroom.

The second Wednesday in July of 2019, I had just returned from exhaustive grocery shopping at the local ShopRite supermarket and after unpacking my purchases and placing the items into the refrigerator, the pantry cupboard and the nearby Lazy-Susan, my persistent, lethargic mood was fully dominated by extreme boredom. Throwing caution to the wind, I decided to try dialing-up Channel 5 on the incomparable Cosmos Network Television System and see what unpredictable euphoria awaited me.

After seeing and listening to a suave Baltimore, Maryland news anchor describing the exotic seafood selections available at the city's fabled Inner Harbor, I felt my body's presence being escorted by inexplicable Cosmos Network technology to *that* alluring marine location. Immediately, I fathomed the exact surroundings of my most recent destination, and before I could saunter along the exquisite waterfront or sample some delectable spicy shrimp served at Phillips Seafood, I turned and viewed the Aquarium on the opposite side of the tranquil harbor. 'The unique Channel Number 5 definitely corresponds to a 5-minute interval,' I associated and concluded. 'I don't even remember flying over the Delaware River or zooming past the Twin Delaware Memorial Bridges to arrive here! Oh well, I suppose it's now time to again rendezvous with my red armchair.'

No matter whether I had journeyed three-thousand-miles west to fabulous Palm Springs, California, or ventured a mere one hundred miles south to Baltimore, Maryland, the teleportation space travel time metric in both cases seemed to be identical in duration.

* * * * * * * * * * * *

September of 2019 arrived on the kitchen wall calendar, with the Labor Day weekend marking the unofficial end of summer for nearby Atlantic City, Ocean City and Wildwood beach resorts. My greedy mind facetiously entertained the quixotic notion of selling abbreviated travel excursions to wealthy patrons for exorbitant money sums, but then surrendering my unfeasible ambitions to hard practicality, I soberly weighed the possibility of someone getting injured between channel destinations and then suing me an enormous amount for some unforeseen liability occurring. 'And who can I ever trust with sharing the stellar knowledge of this most singular Cosmos Network TV?' I seriously wondered. 'I have no choice. I must keep this great secret to myself!'

On Tuesday, September 10th, I again felt a compulsive need to "Space Travel", so I impatiently sat in the red armchair and deliberately pressed Number 7 on the remote control, recollecting that my mind would soon enter a mesmerized state after landing somewhere else more interesting in the world than commonplace Hammonton, New Jersey. A public service network television panel was seated at a round table introducing a video travelogue pertaining to "a popular Mediterranean cruise ship port."

'I only have seven minutes to tour this terrific place,' I reckoned as my disheveled mind adjusted to my new whereabouts. 'That public television program I've just seen I've viewed several times before. This city park is absolutely gorgeous. I must be standing in the Palace Square in Monaco because I see tourists entering the Casino Monte-Carlo over there,' my eyes interpreted. 'And yes, over there near the sea is the Oceanographic Marine Museum dedicated to the inventor of SCUBA oxygen tanks, Jacques Cousteau. I know from watching ordinary television that there's a changing of the guard at the Prince's Palace that happens around noon, but since I'm short on time, I'll search around to see if I can locate the cathedral where Princess Grace and Prince Rainier are buried. If I recall, Grace Kelly was a glamorous 50's movie star and also a Broadway stage actress from Philadelphia.' But before I had the opportunity to locate St. Nicholas Cathedral located somewhere in the vicinity of the superb and exotic Monaco Square, the grains of sand in my trip hourglass had ceased falling and before I could discern anything else, I was speeding body and soul back to 347 Pratt Street.

* * * * * * * * * * * *

After enjoying a few beers over at the Sons of Italy with my affable neighbor Howard Graziano, at approximately 5 p.m. on Thursday, September 12th I calmly decided to escape the redundant monotony of Pratt Street and see what geographic surprise Channel 8 would entail. I index-fingered the remote's "Numero Ocho" and instantly thereafter observed a newscast rerun of President Donald Trump on Air Force One landing in Taormina, Sicily for an important economic conference with the leaders of other G-7 countries. I hastily realized that my unscheduled voyage to the glorious Italian island would represent my second consecutive international European teleportation.

'Moments later, I found myself witnessing new arrivals entering the eye-appealing lobby of the Hotel Villa Schuler. Instinctively, I turned around and noticed in the distance powerful Mt. Etna spewing volcanic smoke into the clear-blue sky from its snow-laden crest. I entered the fine, small hotel establishment, paced through the lobby and then stepped through a spectacular tropical garden featuring colorful indigenous plants and flowers.

Soon my random exploration came to marble steps, which I meticulously ascended and counted to be twenty-two before reaching Umberto Street, a narrow, slated pedestrian walkway which afforded to spend-happy tourists a variety of pizza shops, picturesque outdoor dining accommodations, gelato and cannoli vendors and sundry tee-shirt emporiums to sample. Just as I was approaching the steps leading-up to the memorable restaurant that had been featured in the "Godfather" movie, I became aware that my eight-minute pleasure journey was about to end. In a matter of seconds, my total being was predictably hurtling through *space* back to nondescript Hammonton, New Jersey.

On Thursday morning, September 19th, I was reading the front-page articles in the Atlantic City Press, which I had purchased at the Hammonton News and Tobacco Store up on the White Horse Pike. Naturally, as is my habit, I stopped at the nearby Dunkin Donuts and bought two double-chocolate delights along with a cup of delicious coffee to wash-down and help digest the myriad calories that would be dropping-down into my stomach.

'The Phillies are playing the Braves tonight in Atlanta,' I pondered with my mind imprisoned in a temporary doldrum. 'In the meantime, I think I'll have a little Cosmos Network space-travel adventure to generate some much-needed energy. I'm anxious to see what Channel 9 has in store for me. I hope it's as excellent as Channel 8 with me wandering-around in Taormina had been.'

On the new TV venue, a history professor was standing in front of a handsome summer mansion and announcing that the impressive residence was where "Michigan governors often stayed" for their summer hiatuses. Before I could say "Lower Peninsula" three times, I found myself conscientiously trekking along the all-too-busy ferry docks on scenic Mackinac Island. I soon understood that no automobiles, buses or trucks were allowed to traffic the streets and that tourists had to hire horse-drawn carriages and taxis to have mobility to anywhere.

Numerous fudge shops and other tourist traps seemed to be magnetically attracting spendthrift, gullible customers who were rambunctiously seeking to part with their vacation dollars, and up on a hill my eager eyes studied the illustrious Victorian-styled Grand Hotel, where several classic motion pictures had been filmed. 'Horses are used here for everything ranging from people transportation to freight movement,' I immediately comprehended. 'This whole place is designed to appear and operate exactly as it had existed before Henry Ford made Model Ts affordable to the average

American family.' But before I could scrutinize Main Street on Michigan's time-frozen Mackinac Island any further, I was cognizant of myself being swiftly conveyed back to my tidy bungalow near the gravel-based Our Lady of Mt. Carmel Carnival Grounds in Hammonton.

By the end of September, I had abandoned most aspects of humility, modesty and inordinate self-deprecation that had previously been prime characteristics of my former plumber bashful personality. Now my general behavior and attitude could be more accurately described as being ego-driven and coarsely smattered with a trifle of arrogance thrown-in to boot. Feeling genuinely emboldened and obstinate, I overconfidently sat in the red armchair and using my nimble left thumb, I forcefully pushed the digits 1 and 0 upon the mystical-but-taken-for-granted channel selector pad.

The thirty-nine-inch flat-screen resting upon the spare bedroom bureau faithfully displayed a prominent Republican candidate being interviewed and questioned by a bevy of aggressive cable and media news reporters. Simultaneous to itinerant me witnessing the know-it-all politician speaking, I was soon briskly transported to the top steps of the United States Capitol Building. I looked-out to the west and viewed the white granite Washington Monument and the prodigious, gleaming Lincoln Memorial aligned in a straight like. Being and feeling like a seasoned veteran of contemporary Space Travel Teleportation, I rather foolishly and irresponsibly ignored any potentially negative federal government encounters that might henceforth ensue. Possessing a self-assurance that bordered on pure impudence, and not placing any credence in "primitive superstition", I carelessly submitted to a detrimental instinct and expeditiously pressed Numbers 1 and 3 onto the out-of-this-world remote before returning to the safety of Hammonton. My experimental intent was that I wanted to brazenly see what lucky or unlucky situation might confront my intrusive appearance in esteemed Washington, D.C.

'Hey, what's wrong?' I remember thinking. 'No TV reporter holding a microphone is introducing the next Cosmos Network scene. And there's nothing discernible happening except a flurry of blinking and fluttering horizontal and vertical lines interfering with any vivid picture being transmitted!'

Then my active brain reviewed the current set of circumstances more astutely. 'No one around ever seems to witness either my coming or going. I hope I can spend thirteen minutes in Monaco or in Taormina,' I thought just before my spirit and form were being propelled and thrust out of my spare room red armchair to Number 13's geographic location.

Upon landing in a semi-tropical paradise, my pupils scanned the northern horizon and detected a dark mountain protruding into the sea, which I directly recognized from countless TV shows and movies as Diamondhead. 'Great bunions! I do believe I'll be investigating a fantastic floral environment along with gorgeous palm trees while spending thirteen minutes in Honolulu, Hawaii walking near Waikiki Beach. Holy cow!' I mentally marveled. 'My own eyes and brain do not deceive me! Right this precious minute I'm ambling around for the first time ever on the beautiful island of Oahu. Thirteen minutes doesn't give me nearly enough time to get a taxi ride over to visit the historic Pearl Harbor Memorial.'

As I was casually passing by a crowded shopping mall, a loud thud followed by a palpable boom (that resembled a distant dynamite blast) was suddenly detected by my ears. A human herd of around fifty terrified people wildly stampeded and scrambled out of the retail center's main entrance glass doors, their forward blitz roughly knocking me down to the pavement. Several of the alarmed sprinters trampled over my prone anatomy, and the pain from their hysterical panic confirmed that this Hawaiian manifestation of mine was indeed more reality than imagined fantasy.

After the mad rush had finished, an EMT squad pulled-up to the curb and attended to several cuts on my forehead and other accompanying bruises that were evident on both my wrists. "What happened?" I gasped while enduring my agony.

"A building collapsed behind the mall and we think the crowd, or should I say 'boisterous mob' that was inside the shopping area thought an explosion had occurred, or perhaps an insane terrorist was on the loose after making a loud detonation," the principal attending EMT officer related. 'Your minor injuries are a result of their panic charge."

"Yes Sir," the second rescue squad member attested. "We're living in very precarious times indeed!"

A full half-hour had elapsed since I had been teleported to Honolulu by unlucky Number 13, but there was no indication that I was going to be imminently transported back to Hammonton. At the island's international airport, I exhausted the available balance on my wallet's credit card, arranging to fly from Hawaii to San Francisco, and I felt extremely embarrassed calling my buddy Howard Graziano to wire me four-hundred-dollars to fly Delta airlines from California back to Philadelphia.

'Wow!' I thought just as the streamlined jet was touching-down onto the 'Philly runway. 'If I had been teleported to Monaco or Taormina, I wouldn't have my passport with me and I would've been detained indefinitely before leaving. Thank goodness I only needed my New Jersey driver's license to get out of Hawaii.'

My loyal and dependable next-door neighbor picked me up in his red Toyota Avalon after I had self-consciously exited Terminal D without carrying any suitcase. "How did you ever wind-up in San Francisco when you were roaming around downtown Hammonton just yesterday?" Howard asked his fatigued passenger as my good friend drove his brand-new Avalon across the Walt Whitman Bridge back into Southern Jersey.

"It's a long story Howie," I maintained, refusing to attempt explaining to him San Francisco let alone Hawaii. "Someday I'll be able to tell you the whole thing from beginning to end. Right now, all that I require is plenty of rest and relaxation," I insisted. "Maybe after downing four or five frosted mugs of cold beer over at the Sons of Italy, I'll be able to reveal to you the entire nutcase saga!"

"Say John, if you ever want to sell that neat TV you recently got from eBay, let me know!" Graziano uttered as my jaw nearly fell out of my mouth. "I really like that baby!"

"No Howie," I replied, feigning being majorly disconsolate. "That TV is a real bummer with a weak picture showing faded colors. I wouldn't stick you with *that* lemon for one second."

"What do you intend to do with it?" my inquisitive Sicilian pal asked. "It cost you a pretty penny."

"I'll list the thing back on eBay with a price tag of two hundred dollars," I most honestly answered. "I'm sure that some unfortunate frugal sucker looking for an outstanding bargain will buy the unreliable thing without exhibiting any hesitation!"

"A Ride Through the Wharton Forest"

The first Wednesday of every glorious September, the retired middle school teachers of Hammonton, New Jersey congregate at a local eatery or tavern to celebrate the fact that the aged pedagogues no longer have to enter a school building and instruct rebellious, undisciplined teenagers. The surviving pensioners meet at a variety of restaurants, including Illiano's on Twelfth Street, Marcello's on Bellevue Avenue and Horton Street, Rocco's Town House on North Third Street, the Red Barn on Highway 206, Andy's on Route 54, Joe's Italian Maplewood Inn on Route 30, and DiDonato's Family Fun Center, also on Route 30, the White Horse Pike. For their September 4th, 2019 conclave, the chosen venue was the popular West End Bar and Grill, on Twelfth Street and West End Avenue.

While conversing and commiserating about eye-cataract removals, knee and hip replacement operations, open heart surgeries and minor breathing problems, the sixteen assembled male and female former teachers were anything but despondent about not having to enter a classroom on the first Wednesday after Labor Day and confronting certain all-too-challenging behavioral problems associated with defiant male and female juveniles going through the difficult throes of early pubescence. Jack Butler and Mack Vaughn were two of the annual participants in the "thank goodness we're not involved in formal public-school education any longer" get-togethers.

After the jovial hour and a half of socializing, reminiscing and general camaraderie had terminated, Mack and Jack exited the side steps of the West End Bar and Grill in very good spirits. The taller fellow (Jack), an amiable Social Security-age former science teacher, and the latter (Mack), a knowledgeable English instructor had been fine friends and deer hunting buddies for over thirty years. Both distinguished gentlemen belonged to the legendary Boot Hill Gun Club that maintained an old dilapidated cabin (on private farm land) bordering the Wharton State Forest on State Highway 206.

"Say Mack," retired science teacher Jack Butler merrily began speaking as the two men crossed West End Avenue to the restaurant's parking lot. "It's a pleasant Wednesday afternoon with temperatures ascending to around eighty. What do ya' say we spend some time scouting-out a new site for our 2019 deer-hunting-stand. I've already ordered a bin of sweet potatoes from Joe Donio to lure the big bucks over to our next elevated platform; that is, after *we* construct it!"

"That's right Jack," Mack Vaughn concurred. "Drive your Jeep over to my place in about an hour. I think you still remember where Walnut Street is," the good-natured English language authority jokingly remarked. "Deer season is only two months away, and before we'll know it, Thanksgiving will be over. Then it's that magical first week of December when the Boot Hill guys forget their family and business troubles and assemble for a happy week to engage in genuine male bonding."

"Okay Mack," Jack Butler predictably agreed. "Last year, old Tony Maccarella had a few too many shots of Jim Beam at the cabin and told me he remembered when McKinley was president. Ha, ha, ha; that exaggeration would make old Tony about a hundred and fifty years old! Ha, ha, ha!" the Jeep driver laughed. "And after a full week of chowing-down venison and boozing at Boot Hill, old inebriated Tony looks sort of like that ancient cowboy actor Gabby Hays, and likewise, at the end of deer week we'll be looking like those bearded Smith Brothers featured on the 1960s cough drop boxes. See ya' Mack in an hour or so!"

At 2:15 p.m. Jack Butler picked-up Mack Vaughn in his four-wheel drive vehicle and took Walnut Street to Old Forks Road, which is better known to elderly Hammonton folks as "Cemetery Avenue". A left at the light opposite Hammonton High School and after passing Oak Road, Jack made a right turn onto Walker Road, and then the vintage black Jeep was soon speeding past what had formerly been peach and apple orchards, which were now mostly blueberry and blackberry fields. The dependable Jeep stopped at a dangerous rural intersection, and next crossed Union Road, taking the dusty, dirt trail through a small patch of woods, and in short time the vehicle was cutting across impressively expansive Tuckahoe Turf Farm.

"I recall when this ground was mostly peach and apple orchards along with occasional tomato and pepper fields located back here," passenger Mack Vaughn recollected. "Now it's just open ground good for growing sod. Just about every new housing development in South Jersey gets their instant lawns from Tuckahoe Turf. But one good thing about the turf farm is that the owners allow soccer tournaments to take place on their multiple grass fields. Excited kids and their families come from as far away as New York State and Connecticut to compete here."

"And directly ahead is the miniature pine tree area where my dad used to take me to cut-down our living-room Christmas tree," Jack

Butler sentimentally added. "Beyond the short pines is *our* favorite secret entrance into Wharton State Forest."

"Wasn't *that* named after Joseph Wharton, the guy who once owned all of this pristine forest?" the passenger asked.

"Right Mack," Jack Butler verified. "Mr. Wharton figured he would use the trillions of gallons of fresh water sitting under the enormous pine forest to pump the 'agua' west across the Delaware into Philadelphia and then also north across the Hudson into New York City. After huge reservoirs were built above New York and on the Delaware above Philly, Joe Wharton felt compelled to abandon his grand water distribution scheme."

"Isn't the Wharton School of Economics at the University of Pennsylvania named after that rich guy Joseph Wharton?" Mack Vaughn inquired. "I believe that that's the school President Donald Trump often brags he had attended!"

"You're right!" Jack Butler confirmed as the avid deer-hunter adroitly piloted his very capable Jeep over several nasty bumps. "I guarantee that you won't see Donald Trump in these woods, but maybe we'll run into Forrest Gump! Ha, ha, ha!"

'There's our secret entrance into the Wharton tract directly up ahead," Mack observed and noted. "Did you know that the town of Hammonton includes about seven miles of the Wharton tract going almost all the way up 206 to Atsion Lake?"

"Right," Jack Butler confirmed. "I think that area-wise, Vineland is the largest municipality in New Jersey and Hammonton is perhaps the second. Both towns were designed and mapped by a fella' named Charles K. Landis."

"Wow Jack!" Maurice "Mack" Vaughn realized and exclaimed. "That explains why the main drag in Vineland is called Landis Avenue. And even the main street over in Sea Isle City is also named Landis Ave. Say Jack, do you think you're gonna' again win the Lions Club November Turkey Shoot."

"I'm a lead pipe cinch to easily win that event thanks to my grandpop's Old Betsy," Butler proudly predicted. "That's the finest shootin' long-gun anywhere in South Jersey!"

* * * * * * * * * * * *

That Wednesday afternoon Jack Butler's wife Jessica and Mack Vaughn's spouse Jennifer were shopping together browsing the stores at the still very prosperous Cherry Hill Mall. As the reliable black Jeep entered the outer fringe of the Pine Barrens, it soon penetrated into the denser coniferous forest trail that exhibited clusters of deciduous trees beginning to show their autumnal hues. Almost instantly, the men's casual conversation morphed into other much more serious subjects besides their genial reviewing of local history and geography.

"Ya' know Mack," Jack Butler candidly said to his rider, "times are sure changin'. My neighbors across the street avoid the fancy shoppin' malls and buy most everything online. Just yesterday," the retired science teacher lectured, "they had a U.S. Post Office truck, a FedEx truck and a brown UPS truck inside their U-shaped driveway all deliverin' packages at the same time."

"Suburban shopping malls will soon become extinct just like the dinosaurs, the Philadelphia Athletics and primitive Neanderthals," amenable Jeep passenger Mack Vaughn elaborated. "By the way, Jennifer promised to call me at four-thirty to inform *us* that she and your wife have arrived home safe and sound from Cherry Hill."

"Jessica loves to use the cell phone too," Jack Butler courteously answered. "We're thinkin' about abandoning our three landline phones and just goin' a hundred percent cellular. That's the way to go with this new 5G technology comin' into play."

The topic of discussion soon abruptly switched to national politics as Jack Butler deftly maneuvered his trusty Jeep around a perilous, narrow Wharton Tract bend. The loyal friends were both of the conservative persuasion and in the past, *their* more rigid philosophy often deviated from the liberal views of their union-oriented academic colleagues, many of whom vehemently disapproved of hunting deer and even shooting rabbits in the area woods.

"Taxes are positively drivin' many senior citizens out of Jersey," driver Jack Butler emphasized as his bouncing passenger further adjusted *his* seat belt. "They're movin' down south to the Carolinas in droves where the cost of livin' is much cheaper. That includes real estate taxes and house and car insurances. Soon *we* won't be able to live comfortably in Jersey either!"

"Correct!" retired English teacher Maurice "Mack" Vaughn replied as Jack "John" Butler navigated his Jeep along the familiar trail. "I've read where New Jersey is even considerin' taxin' the pensions of retired teachers livin' in other states. Next to California, New York and Illinois, Jersey is the absolute pits when it comes to parasitic government expenses! Also, Jack," Mack resumed his narrative, "there's even a New Jersey capital gains tax of two-percent if any Jersey resident sells his or her house and decides to

154

move to another more tax-friendly state," the now-mentally-stimulated passenger angrily conveyed. "And these climate-change fanatics are completely off the rails," the language arts mentor further commented. "The Earth is over four billion years old, and these nutcase ignoramuses think it's destined to end in twelve years! Give me a freakin' break!"

The retired middle school science instructor was not to be denied his inflexible opinion. "And Mack, the left-wing Socialists in our federal Congress never want to give us humble taxpayers a break," Jack Butler affirmed as the driver gradually slowed-down to ramble over a large tree branch that had been lying across the pine-needle-laden trail. "Our naïve liberal teaching colleagues never understood that the local, the state and the federal government own half of their annual salaries. Unless you're an accomplished crook or swindler successfully operatin' in the huge underground economy," Jack Butler loudly indicated, "the government is your lifelong partner. No state or country is worth ownin' half of my life's labor. It's plain and simple logic, Mack. The more taxes we pay, the less freedom we have for our families to enjoy better food, nicer houses and finer, more expensive summer vacations. Instead of flying to the Virgin Islands or to Hawaii," Butler adamantly insisted to his like-thinking amigo, "Jessica and the kids always had to settle for summer hiatuses in Atlantic City and Wildwood."

"Excellent point!" Mack verbally responded, reflexively nodding his head. "Last night I researched on the Internet where New Jersey pays over twelve billion dollars for its Medicaid obligations. That's why our state teacher pension fund is in jeopardy of goin' bankrupt. The state caters to welfare recipients and to illegal aliens!" the Jeep passenger asserted. "The Governor is robbin' Peter to pay Paul, but Peter's runnin' out of cash something fierce!" Butler sternly vociferated and ranted to his preoccupied audience of one. "And the left-wingers are tearin' down Civil War statues and rewritin' and revisin' our true history. Not even our Founding Fathers are safe from the radicals' brutal treachery. They're even tryin' to besmirch George Washington, Thomas Jefferson, Abe Lincoln and Andrew Jackson, not to mention destroyin' and cursin' the good name of Christopher Columbus! I mean, Jack, ten years ago Hammonton was fifty-nine percent Italian! Now it's only forty-seven percent! Columbus is still revered in town by the older, more traditional Sicilians, but all that's changin' now with all of the Mexicans invadin' our little community!"

After identifying how the "young Socialist militants" on the left are merely "antagonistic extremists who bitterly hate America", and how "the young college punks are taught lunatic ideas by their Vietnam-era ultra-liberal-arts university professors", who were anti-authority and anti-war late 1960s Chicago Democratic Convention demonstrators, a moment of silence reigned within the Jeep. After again sharing a series of nasty road bumps, Mack and Jack recommenced their standard anti-left rhetoric.

"Too many blood-suckin' leeches are totally ruinin' this once great country," the aggravated driver pontificated. "Phony elitist pseudo-intellectuals, that's what they are! Ya' know Maurice," Jack Butler uttered the formal appellation with a smile, "these left-wing radicals want to control every aspect of our lives from womb to tomb. The moronic fools stupidly are planning for *us* to go the way of Cuba and Venezuela. Red China has publicly announced that by the year 2035, the Communist regime will surpass the U.S. both economically and militarily," Butler emphatically described as he gripped the Jeep's steering wheel more tightly. "And the crazy liberal hypocrites want us to go entirely with solar and wind energy and completely drop the use of fossil fuels. Really Mack, the demented and failed Socialist philosophy has also infected most of the press and TV media and as we both well-know, the bulk of public-school education, too. Ya' wanna' know something Mack," Jack Butler continued his graphic and biased diatribe, "get ready to start singin' 'Yankee Doodle' again. This country is headin' for the Second American Revolution with the same basic theme as the first: Taxation without representation!"

The tirade of alternating generalizations between the two "avowed junior capitalists" continued unabated. "Jack, you're perfectly on target good buddy!" Mack Vaughn aptly articulated his harangue while still occasionally bouncing up and down in his bucket seat. "Conservatives are the children of the American Revolution, and I maintain that liberals are the chaotic offspring of the violent-but-failed French Revolution that led to Robespierre and the tumultuous Reign of Terror. Honestly Jack, I do believe that Socialists and Communists are the true agents of anarchy within this great country and throughout the whole-wide world! Say Good Buddy," Vaughn continued after thrice clearing his throat, "what's with this new trail up on our left! I've never seen that one before! It looks like it's just been recently plowed through the woods!"

"Just like Christopher Columbus, I'm always one for new-found adventure and discovery," John Charles Butler boldly enunciated to his very observant passenger. "Ya' never know what peculiar events will turn-up when explorin' this deep into these isolated South Jersey Pine Barrens."

* * * * * * * * * * * *

Following the newly plowed path for a mile and a half to the northwest, Jack Butler drove his mud-covered black Jeep deeper into a denser section of the shadowy Pine Barrens Forest. While warily encroaching into dark uncharted territory, the apprehensive passenger suggested that the braver man behind the wheel make a U-turn at the next clearing.

"I've never been in this part of the woods before, either," Jack Butler stated. "Deer could easily hide in these thick tree clusters. Ya' know Mack, I've seen bucks crawl through the brushes on their knees to evade and escape hunters," the driver related. "The doe know that it isn't huntin' season for them yet, so in December, the expectant females act as decoys to protect the wary bucks. Deer are plenty smarter than the average citizen gives them credit for. In January, after the fawns are delivered, then both bucks and the already-mated doe lie low."

"What's *that* up ahead," Mack Vaughn declared while nervously pointing with his left index finger. "Two armed guys standin' there are wearin' camouflage military uniforms that are jungle variety, but the sentinels are not New Jersey National Guard soldiers. The fellas' look like they do plenty of shoppin' at the bargain Army & Navy Store on the Pike over in Berlin."

The pair of para-military lookouts mutually raised their assault rifles upon seeing and hearing the noisy approach of the oncoming Jeep. Jack Butler's all-terrain vehicle came to a sudden halt at what appeared to be an improvised entrance gate. Burly Guard Number One quickly initiated an austere interrogation.

"Where you men headin'? You two wanderers must be lost just like that mythical continent Atlantis!"

"We're just deer hunters out cruisin' the forest. We both live in Hammonton," Jack informed his stern-looking questioner, speaking in a normal tone through the driver's-side rolled-down window. "We accidentally came across a trail that we've never seen before; then we followed it until my hunting partner and I wound-up introducin' ourselves to you guys."

"You've been trespassin' onto private property belonging to Colonel William Saunders, commander of the local chapter of the

Winslow Township People's Militia," the Second Guard imperatively related from outside Mack Vaughn's open passenger-side window. "Now as a matter of fact, there are only two ways onto these remote premises. The first is a dirt trail off of Chew Road that goes in a straight line between 206 and Route 30. The second more remote access is by means of the sandy trail that you two nimrods by chance discovered and followed."

"We apologize for our intrusion," the Jeep driver stated. "We thought that we were still ridin' inside the Wharton State Forest. Mack and I hope we haven't inconvenienced anybody," the driver politely added. "It was just a simple, idiotic mistake committed on our part; no harm or grief intended. We were just out scoutin' for a place to locate this December's deer platform."

"We're sorry Gentlemen, but we gotta' take you itinerant boys into temporary custody," the First Militia Watchman grimly commanded. "You'll remain here and be our honored hostages for at least seven hours. You'll be back in Hammonton before the TV baseball playoffs begin later this evenin'."

"First things first; you fellas' gotta' hand-over your cell phones so that we can turn-them off," the second property guardsman demanded. "Then you two strangers can accompany us into the militia's lodge situated right over there where the smoke is risin' from the chimney. At least you'll be warm and cozy inside if the weather turns chilly after dusk."

After disarming the separate pocket cell phone devices, the on-a-mission militia guards and their pair of designated captives held a brief conversation about *their* contemporary liberal-conservative Garden State and federal policies. The verbal exchanges covered the political spectrum including liberal judges, illegal immigration, excessive taxation, welfare-gone-amok and finally, government control of individual rights that have been specifically defined by the First Ten Amendments of the United States Constitution. The militia sentries were somewhat impressed that Mack and Jack's political views were compatible with and apparently coincided with their own.

"If you fellas' are interested in joinin' our active militia, Fred here and I could sponsor you boys into the fraternity," the narrow-minded First Guard proposed. "We're lookin' for new members with similar ideas. Think it over."

"Well Jim," the second pretend New World Order soldier-wannabe' eagerly stated, "we could contact Colonel Saunders about installin' these Hammonton recruits into the militia, even though our

158

guests live a few towns over. What do ya' say about joinin' our exclusive club?"

"What's so important that you have to keep us here for seven hours?" objected Jack Butler. "Are you havin' some kind of strategic meeting this evening?"

"Well, if ya' really wanna' know, our vital mission should be completed in a matter of seven hours," Guard Fred confidentially shared. "Our group, along with several others in South Jersey are gonna' soon conduct joint exercises that are bound to make the newspapers' front pages, if ever revealed. Our militia's exact instructions are to kidnap four liberal Winslow Township and Waterford Township municipal judges and then hold the traitors for ransom," the deep woods piney further expressed. "We already have one of them in the cabin bound and shackled to a chair and gagged, so we don't have to listen to his nonsensical screamin' protests."

"And we believe that the two townships' cowardly politicians will gladly cough-up the ransom money for the judges' release because they're afraid of bad press publicity that'll also be reported in the other media outlets," Guard Jim orally supplemented. "Our ace card in the hole is that we'll discharge our hostages a week at a time so that we don't receive our cache of cash from the gutless politicians all at once."

"And if someone spills the beans," Guard Fred stubbornly interrupted his mammoth-sized confederate, "then the politicos involved will be systematically assassinated one by one. Once the local bureaucrats understand what the dire consequences are, I'm sure they'll remain silent after the requested payoffs are made."

"I'm sorry," Jack Butler prefaced his responding statement. "Even though Mack and I have parallel political views to yours, we can't advocate either violence or unlawful extortion. I suppose you'll have to take us both into custody for non-cooperation to your militant rules. I admit; I'm a conservative patriot, and so is Mack, but in the end, we both believe in the rule of law along with the peaceful resolution of differences of political opinion," the Jeep driver declared. "Maybe twenty years from now, if the country's path becomes much worse than it presently is, we would join your campaign. But right now, we can't commit to endorsin' your radical plot to overthrow the government."

"Okay fellas'," Guard Fred uttered while deliberately waving the barrel of his AK-47 at the Jeep's obstinate occupants. "Don't say we never gave you men the opportunity to become a part of our well-trained militia," Sentinel Number Two remarked, seemingly quite frustrated and disappointed at experiencing rejection. "Park your Jeep in yonder space and then shut-off your engine. You're both now bein' kept under temporary house arrest. Hope you Hammonton outsiders don't mind being tied to chairs and nicely gagged for the next seven hours."

"Just remember," Guard Jim boisterously contributed and ranted, "the population of the U.S. is now three hundred and thirty million. A hundred and thirty million parasites are already existin' on some form of welfare. All four of *us* so-called citizens are forced by Washington to subsidize this growin' illegal alien fiasco with our hard-earned tax dollars!"

* * * * * * * * * * * *

The two Hammonton trespassers were given "lavatory privileges" and then separately tethered to their individual chairs, which were sitting opposite that of a prominent Winslow Township municipal court judge, who already had been bound and gagged for three hours after being maliciously abducted from the driveway of his posh residence. After being routinely gagged by their chatty captors, disgruntled and distraught Mack Vaughn and Jack Butler had no choice other than to listen to a lengthy litany of local militia propaganda being exchanged by brainwashed uniformed vigilantes Fred and Jim.

"I think this diversity in America chaos all began in 1964 with the insane Celler Act under Lyndon Baines Johnson," Militiaman Fred adamantly opined. "Before 1964, nine out of ten immigrants had originated from Europe. Those newcomers were mostly Caucasians, mostly Christians and were mostly products of Western Civilization that could easily assimilate into the USA. After the passage of the Democrat-sponsored Celler Act," the husky Sentinel continued his talking-points' prattle, "the entire immigration system then became inverted with only one out of ten new arrivals to America coming from Europe while the other nine-tenths have entered our country from Africa, from the Middle East, from Asia and from Central and South America. As you can plainly see Jim," backwoods Militiaman Fred strongly clarified, "the entire demographics of our once great nation have lousily grown over the course of the last fifty-five years into the cancerous ethnic mess that we now experience in 2019."

The wholly indoctrinated piney Guards continued with their memorized, discriminating talking agenda. "And the radical left has

160

this preposterous, fake romance with Climate Change, which used to be falsely called Global Warming," Militiaman Jim coyly claimed and lectured to his like-minded comrade. "The ugly idea of the enemy Socialists is to destroy America by reducing the vital production and the use of fossil fuels down to nothing. Such insanity will give Communist China a tremendous economic advantage over the then crippled United States. Just consider this fact Fred," Vigilante Jim remarked before inhaling a deep drag from his cigarette. "China, India and Russia are the biggest polluters of the atmosphere in the whole world. China and India have over a thousand coal power plants apiece while the United States has only fifteen. But the phony media wants the American public to believe that the USA is the biggest culprit in releasing carbon emissions into the air. It's all an elaborate international hoax Fred," Guard Jim strenuously argued. "The radical Democrat-Socialists want a world government functionin' under the jurisdiction of the U.N., and *that* tragedy-in-progress only means that our sacred Constitution will be subordinated to the mandates of the United Nations Charter. We have to nip this disastrous Communist plot in the bud!"

At 6:15 p.m., the totally biased conversation occurring within the cabin was rudely interrupted as two tear gas cannisters were shot through the secluded lodge's main room window panes. Shattered glass shards were sent flying in all directions as clouds of pungent tear gas permeated the air, irritating the eyes of all five occupants. The front cabin door was savagely smashed open, and in seconds, six frightful members of the Camden County SWAT Team burst into the under-siege building.

Immediately, incapacitated Militiamen Fred and Jim were clubbed on their heads and knocked silly by the oxygen-masked assault squad members. The encumbered, kidnapped township judge, the two coughing Hammonton deer hunters and the pair of desperado anti-government militiamen were next swiftly escorted out of the fume-infested cabin. While surprised sentry hicks Fred and Jim were taken into custody by New Jersey State Policemen (that had also been dispatched to take part in the raid), Captain Robert Ingemi professionally explained to deep-breathing Mack Vaughn and Jack Butler precisely how the entire raid scenario had developed.

"This was perhaps the most fascinating State Police operation that I've ever participated in," the Captain framed his explanation. "Two hours ago, your wives became worried that you two forest roamers hadn't answered their urgent cell phone calls. The alarmed ladies, Jessica and Jennifer I believe, contacted the local police in

Hammonton, who then forwarded the missing persons' bulletin to the State Police and to all area police departments including Winslow Township, Waterford Township and Camden County. Our combined units then collaborated with the Camden County SWAT Team, and that's how fifty dedicated law enforcement personnel converged on this remote cabin to make these very crucial arrests. But it all started with *your* concerned wives!"

"But Captain Ingemi," Mack Vaughn wondered and critically asked, "there's a massive plot happening right now to kidnap three more area judges and then precariously hold them for ransom under the threat of imminent assassination!"

"Don't be rambunctiously jumping to conclusions without knowing all of the details!" answered the knowledgeable State Police official. "We've had this notorious Winslow Township villain Colonel William Saunders under surveillance for over a year now, but we've never had sufficient evidence to put him in the slammer. Confidentially, we've just arrested this thug Saunders and three of his henchmen entering the Old White Horse Pike, a half-mile or so from the Chew Road main entrance to this cabin. Three other response units out on patrol are in the process of putting the cuffs on fifteen other militia rebels, all associated participants in this illicit plot of intimidating appointed and elected area judges," the State Police Commander related. "Mr. Saunders had hoped that his extreme transgressions and extortion plots here on the Wharton Forest fringe would cause similar Second Amendment militia groups to stage other similar rebellious insurrections in various states throughout the country. These rebel militia punks we're now arresting aren't patriots! They're just as extreme on the right as Antifa is on the left!"

"But Captain, our cell phones were turned-off by the two Militia Guards just after we approached the cabin's back gate in my Jeep!" Jack Butler exclaimed. "How did you ever find us under those impossible circumstances?"

"Here's something that the average American is unaware of," Captain Ingemi aptly replied with a wide grin displayed upon his countenance. "When any ordinary cell phone is turned-off, it'll cease communicating with all nearby cell towers, but each inactive phone can be traced to its exact last GPS location where it had been powered-down. The NSA in Washington has the ability to track cell phones even when they're turned-off. That special service is one truly magnificent blessing that's been bestowed on grateful law enforcement by modern telephone technology."

162

"Contemporary Illuminati"

My father had four older sisters when he had been growing-up in Baltimore, Maryland in the early 1900s. Born in Posen, Michigan in 1908, a small village around twenty miles northwest of Alpena on the Lower Peninsula near Lake Huron, dad's family had been engaged in the very difficult logging business; renting timberland acres from the government and harvesting trees to be sent to thriving sawmills to then be converted into lumber.

In 1912 a raging forest fire completely devastated my Polish grandfather Adalbert's timber camp and also his home, and without insurance coverage, being mentally and emotionally depressed, the paternal patriarch succumbed to pneumonia and soon died a year later. Out of financial necessity, Adalbert's wife Hedwig then moved her five children to East Baltimore, Maryland, traveling by steam train to live with relatives who had coincidentally settled in the growing metropolis. But in the fall of 1918, a horrific influenza epidemic had descended upon major East Coast cities, and my grandmother (whom I had also never known) perished in 1918 at age fifty-three, and the enormous pandemic was so severe that Hedwig had to be buried in a hastily excavated, flu-victim mass grave.

Aunt Genevieve was my father's eldest sister who instinctively assumed the responsibility of raising her four younger siblings. As far as I can recollect, everyone casually called her "Aunt Jenny", but when the very strict woman was in *my* presence, she was always very formally and courteously addressed and referred to as "Aunt Genevieve". Born in 1897, my father's revered sister was quite fastidious indeed in her complex mannerisms, for I recall from the early 1950s that the family matriarch would never allow children (including me) to sit in her living room inside her handsomely-furnished upscale home located on Taylor Avenue, located just above the tranquil Overlea section of North Baltimore.

Austere Aunt Jenny was married to Uncle Henry Curtis, a very successful, reputable construction engineer in the 1930s and '40s. My aunt accompanied "Uncle Hank" on his various business adventures to Egypt and Saudi Arabia where her ambitious husband was involved in important building projects in regard to erecting profitable manufacturing and oil refining facilities. But much to their mutual dismay, Aunt Jenny and Uncle Hank never had any children during their many years of marital bliss.

Aunt Elsie was my father's second oldest sister. She had married Uncle James Miller (a bread delivery man), and the middle-class pair had one son Milton, who had been a bombardier on a B-29 in the WWII Pacific Theater. Unfortunately, my neurotic Cousin Milton had encountered a mental breakdown from his gruesome war experience and died in 1955 from debilitating brain cancer. Suffering from grief at losing his only child, Uncle Jimmy died three years afterwards, and in 1960, Aunt Elsie married vociferous Uncle Al Albert, who was a likeable Jewish entrepreneur that owned two prominent fur stores that catered to wealthy women on Grace Street in Richmond, Virginia.

My father's next sister in line was Aunt Lillian, and she was a beautiful lady who had married Uncle Philip Sawyer, an affable postmaster in North Baltimore. Worrisome Aunt Lillian suffered from heightened depression when Uncle Phil was away serving as an Army Lieutenant in Germany during WWII, and she sadly died as a patient in a Maryland mental institution in 1953. Uncle Phil and Aunt Lillian had one daughter, my favorite cousin Carol, who died of multiple sclerosis in 1988. Soon thereafter, plagued with grief and despair, my dear Uncle Phil passed away in 1989.

Aunt Veronica, my father's fourth sister, had married Uncle Lester Wilson, an East Baltimore police sergeant in the mid-1930s. The twosome had four children: David, Stephen, Mildred and Catherine. Uncle Lester and Aunt Veronica lived in a modest row home on Fleet Street, just south of Eastern Avenue. All four Wilson children married, but both Mildred and Catherine passed-on in the early 1980s; the former from a heart attack and the latter from breast cancer. My cousin David married but never had children, but Cousin Stephen had a very industrious son named Frank. Regrettably, humble Aunt Veronica and convivial Uncle Lester dually died in Virginia in 1969 when a vehicle approaching in the opposite direction on a two-lane highway impacted their automobile while the couple was on their way to visit Uncle Al Albert and Aunt Elsie at their resplendent summer home, which was situated near the confluence of the Potomac River and the Chesapeake Bay.

Aunt Genevieve had revealed to my mother on several occasions that I had been her favorite nephew, and so I always believed that I was in competition for a massive inheritance with my adversarial cousins David and Stephen Wilson, who both perceptibly appeared to be artificially cordial towards me at venerable Aunt Jenny's Baltimore wake and funeral that had been held in early May of 1992.

A full month later, I received a legal letter from Otto Hernandez, Esquire, informing me that I was to attend a meeting for the purpose of the "Disposition of Mrs. Genevieve Curtis's Will", and the family conference was scheduled to occur in downtown Baltimore at 11 a.m. sharp on Wednesday, July 1st. Naturally, from previous conversations with my mother, I was quite excited about the prospect of being the principal heir to Aunt Genevieve's rather lucrative estate.

* * * * * * * * * * * *

I had stayed the night of June 30th at a motor lodge just off I-95 in Edgewood, Maryland, which is a placid town that was about a thirty-five-minute drive south to center city Baltimore. After enjoying a hardy bacon, eggs and home-fries breakfast at an area diner, I nervously navigated my red Nissan Murano through the Harbor Tunnel, remembering that the Patapsco River above flowed west near Ellicott City, where Aunt Genevieve and Uncle Henry Curtis had lived after moving-out of their Taylor Avenue abode. The well-to-do relatives had purchased a large ranch home in an exclusive, high-end estates' development just off of Route 40, west of Baltimore City. I anxiously stepped on my SUV's accelerator in anticipation of learning all of the essential, favorable details pertaining to prospective provisions included in Aunt Jenny's will.

Attorney Otto Hernandez's law office was on the third floor of the downtown Transamerica Building, 100 Light Street, so after parking my car in a high-rise garage, I took the appropriate elevator down to ground level and proceeded ambling two blocks to my prescribed destination. In the lobby I entered the 'UP' elevator and after three other visitors shuffled inside the crowded cubicle, I ascended to and exited onto the third level. I confidently introduced myself and my reason for being there to a general receptionist, so then the seated-and-polite blonde-hair woman directed me to advance down the hall to Mrs. Caroline Straus, Barrister Hernandez's private secretary, who then professionally escorted me into the lawyer's attractive, walnut-paneled bailiwick.

At exactly 11 a.m., I was immediately greeted by Mr. Hernandez, and then my presence was instantly recognized by my first cousins David and Stephen Wilson, who each eagerly shook my right hand. Steve's only son Frank was also in attendance, so I automatically presumed that the fledgling Army First Lieutenant would be another beneficiary that had been announced and identified in Aunt Genevieve's will.

"This proceeding should be relatively brief since there are only you four recipients mentioned in Mrs. Curtis's last will and testament," Lawyer Hernandez formally indicated before imbibing a sip from his bottled water. "I trust that the four of you understand this common circumstance for assembling in my office and that you are willing to commence with me enunciating the simple details and the accurate dispensing of assets and properties; all of which have been specifically outlined in your deceased aunt's final intentions. Are there any questions thus far?"

David, Stephen and Frank Wilson along with myself all concurred with loquacious Attorney Otto Hernandez's preliminary assessment by simultaneously nodding our heads in agreement. I sat comfortably in my red leather chair as the by-the-book lawyer reviewed the particulars, which were carefully stipulated upon the paper from which he was reading.

"To David Wilson, you are to receive the sum of five-hundred-thousand dollars represented in a certificate of deposit at the main office of Bank of America, 100 Charles Street, Baltimore; and to nephew Stephen Wilson, your money inheritance is quite identical in nature to that of your brother David: you are to receive five-hundred thousand dollars in a facsimile account established in your name at the same banking institution."

Both David and Stephen smiled in reaction to hearing the very favorable oral deliverance. "And to Stephen Wilson's son Francis, better known as Frank," Barrister Hernandez emphatically stated and then paused, "your very generous Aunt Genevieve lovingly leaves to you her Ellicott City home located on Clearwater Drive in an estates development just off Route 40 west of Baltimore City. And Francis, all of your beloved aunt's furniture, appliances, garage equipment, jewelry and wall fixtures are also included in the finalization of your most propitious inheritance."

Cousins Stephen and Frank seemed to be exceptionally receptive and compatible with the ultimate disposition of Aunt Genevieve's home, but First Cousin David gave the impression of being more-than-slightly disappointed, avaricious and jealous, judging by the grim, wrinkled expression being shown upon his face.

"And now for the fourth element of Genevieve Curtis's rather elementary will," Otto Hernandez articulated before consuming several additional ounces of semi-cold water from his plastic bottle. "I'll have to now stand and walk over to my personal closet."

The lawyer next opened the louvered-brown-door and removed a five-foot-high, antique-looking, standing lamp from inside the dark enclosure, which he then gracefully carried with both hands over to his huge mahogany desk. "This Sir is what your deceased Aunt

166

Genevieve wishes for you to have," the suave-but-encumbered estates' lawyer quite diplomatically and almost-apologetically communicated. "Mrs. Curtis declares and directs in her last will and testament that *you* should amply admire and appreciate this marvelous, extraordinary lamp of Egyptian design; especially the unique brass head of Queen Nerfertiti that's now conspicuously ornamenting the lamp's exquisite canopy."

I momentarily glanced to my left and incidentally observed that my three cousin companions were alternately snickering and chuckling at my rather peculiar inheritance, and even Mr. Otto Hernandez seemed quite out-of-character, being amused at my unexpected gift that I had traveled 110 miles from Hammonton, New Jersey to gratefully acquire. The lamp itself was exceptionally ornate, and I recalled from my youth that the singular "conversation piece" had remained stationary while always situated in a remote corner (and adjacent to the bar) of Uncle Henry and Aunt Jenny's fabulous Taylor Avenue club basement.

Ten minutes later, feeling more-than-moderately embarrassed and humiliated, I quietly left the premises carrying the decorative lamp, and all the time thinking that childless Aunt Genevieve had promised my mother that I had always been her favorite nephew. However, at *that* awkward ten-minute interval, I felt extremely stupid and excessively mortified as I clumsily transported the unusually odd, heavy item down the busy central Baltimore thoroughfare as seemingly myriad fellow pedestrians stared at me carrying my most bizarre and eccentric recently obtained possession.

'This Egyptian lamp must have been purchased when Uncle Henry was conducting official business while being corporately assigned in Egypt,' I defensively surmised. 'Although the lampstand has an electric cord, the object is almost entirely covered with green patina, and I guess that the artifact must have experienced progressive oxidation while evolving over many decades,' I further theorized. 'This' precise visual observation leads me to suspect that the 'Nerfertiti Lamp' that's now securely and horizontally positioned inside the rear compartment of my Nissan Murano had been meticulously manufactured by Egyptian craftsmen several centuries prior to Thomas Edison and Nikola Tesla ever experimenting in their respective laboratories with DC and AC electric currents. Knowing Aunt Genevieve's flair for stellar curios,' I surmised, 'my new-found special lamp must engender some other esoteric or arcane function besides basically only furnishing normal living room or club basement illumination,' I wishfully speculated.

As I drove east across the Delaware Memorial Bridge into New Jersey, I further ruminated, 'I'm rather certain that this exotic ancient lamp had been skillfully modified and altered, perhaps a century ago; and then through modern science, the metallic thing had been eventually transformed into an operating electrical device!' I imaginatively conjectured. 'The lamp itself seems to have some inexplicable, mystical quality about it!' I hopefully concluded as my mind negatively recalled my three narcissistic cousins being lustily entertained when Attorney Otto Hernandez had announced the object's physical existence and presented its final transfer to me. 'Oh well! It's now back to good old Hammonton and the implausible explanation of all of this strange inheritance to my always-skeptical wife! And if I ever were intrepid enough to tell my spouse the entire day's story, Barbara would proceed to have me evaluated for swift admission into nearby Ancora State Mental Hospital.'

* * * * * * * * * * * *

Arriving home at 4 p.m. on July 1st, and according to a phone conversation with my wife the night before when I had been staying at the Edgewood, Maryland motel, I remembered that Barbara would be away at choir practice at St. Joseph Church on North 3rd Street in downtown Hammonton. Her coincidental absence allowed me sufficient time to cautiously remove the inherited Egyptian lamp from the rear of my red Murano and deftly station the estate relic in the corner opposite the two-story colonial house's entrance, positioning "Nerfertiti" directly above an armchair in my home's living room. A curved bay window separated the aforementioned red and light brown striped chair from its duplicate counterpart. A sofa with small, red diamond patterned fabric was beneath the living room's north side wall and situated below a large oval mirror, and a stand-up piano along with a tan Queen Anne chair and an accompanying vertical glass and wooden curio finished-off the room's physical appearance.

Much to my immediate delight, I plugged the lamp's cord into a convenient electrical socket, and the circular bulb inside the black shade instantly emitted a rather powerful illumination. As I closely peered at the intense stream of bright light, I soon heard the right-side garage door raising, meaning that Barbara was arriving home from her church chorus rehearsal. I quickly turned-off the lamp.

"Hi Barb," I greeted as the woman-of-the-house entered the laundry room from the two-car garage. After applying a huge hug

168

with my arms around my spouse's svelte waist, I facetiously asked, "Was your friend Alice Mazzagatti present playing the organ this afternoon?" I foolishly joked, deliberately referring to the fact that Hammonton, New Jersey is often regarded as the U.S. town with the highest percentage of Italian population.

"No Hubby," Barbara matter-of-factly answered with a forced grin. "Alice was asked to play for a Baptism at St. Nicholas Church over in Egg Harbor, so Rosalie Pinizotto was her reliable substitute and I must tell you, she performed quite admirably."

"Well then, were your soprano friends Marie Costa, Roberta Franchetti, Anita Perna, Josephine Marinella, Antoinette Penza and Millicent Colasurdo present and singing on-key?"

"Yes," my wife affirmed, realizing that I was still making a weak attempt at verbalizing ethnic humor. "And altos Anna DeMarco, Laura Giacobbe, Angelina Mortellite, Sophia Battaglia, Roseann Fitipaldi, Rita DiFilippo and Monica Berenato were also in attendance, and we all were harmonizing together beautifully. And after practice," my wife further elaborated, "Father Pete treated us all to a surprise social in the church basement featuring chocolate cake, tasty homemade cookies, delectable cannolis filled with ricotta cheese along with delicious fresh-brewed coffee!" the former Barbara Francine Curreri replied.

"Well Barb, my mother was Sicilian, so I suppose I'm eligible and qualified to join the infamous Sons of Italy Garibaldi Lodge; that is, if an audacious member has the necessary courage to ever sponsor me into that notorious club!"

"Tell me, how did things go down in Baltimore? Did you receive your mammoth inheritance that Aunt Genevieve had promised your mother you would get? How was your long-awaited rendezvous with your cousins?"

Feeling remarkably chided, I suddenly resented Barbara's cavalier, condescending attitude as immensely represented in her contentious preface. Waving my right hand, I half-heartedly led my wife into the commonplace den, up a step to the familiar kitchen and then down the short hall to the living room where the Egyptian lampstand existed with royal Nerfertiti seemingly guarding-over the formal red and light brown striped comfortable chair.

"What's *that* atrocious eyesore!" my soul-mate boisterously exclaimed. "How come there's all that hideous green corrosion over most of it?"

"That's called patina!" I calmly-and-patiently educated. "It's a natural oxidation of brass or copper that occurs over time; sometimes over centuries. You'll see the same brown-to-green coating process on outdoor statues all over Washington D.C. and even evident on the Statue of Liberty."

"I think I should sit down in order to listen and fully comprehend your fantastic story concerning this oddball lamp!" Barbara exaggerated, feigning mild dizziness. "Yes, I think I need a sedative or a powerful tranquilizer tablet right about now!"

My marital partner slowly sat in the striped chair next to the bay window and then concealing my excitement, I nonchalantly flicked the rotator switch underneath the pitch-black shade to the "on" position. Being satisfied that the Nerfertiti lamp was still excellently working, I reluctantly resumed my nondescript narrative.

"Barb, the image here at the top is that of an ancient Egyptian Queen; her name is, or should I say 'was' Nerfertiti," I academically began my preposterous monologue. "The figure depicted is rather famous and often imitated in various art forms!"

"Yes, I know," my wife austerely responded. "I've seen *that* unique image in mall gift shops and also being sold in several specialty retail stores in Atlantic City casinos. I was familiar with the portrayal but not acquainted with the ancient woman's name."

Then something totally weird occurred that incredibly defied all aspects of human scientific logic. During the moment of silence that had ensued, my wife's voice and words were somehow telepathically transmitted in my direction without her lips ever moving. I hypothesized that the light originating from the oval bulb above her head was capturing and interpreting her secret thoughts and then incredulously beaming them to my receptive mind, all of that phenomenon transpiring in some magical activity that I could not even remotely fathom.

'John, you're either a silly dunce or a complete dolt, absurdly thinking that Aunt Genevieve had favored you over your Baltimore cousins,' Barbara mentally signaled. 'You would occasionally visit and see her maybe once a year; I'll bet that David and Stephen were filibustering and lobbying for her favors almost daily.'

"Barbara, I know you believe that I'm naïve and gullible in regard to this unique Egyptian lamp; I mean, me driving all the way to downtown Baltimore to get this really neat memento," I self-consciously admitted. "I recall Aunt Jenny once revealing that this outlandish-looking lamp had been purchased from a curio shop in Alexandria, Egypt."

'Could have been cheaply bought at a shabby pawn shop in Alexandria, Virginia for what this tin-piece of garbage is actually worth in real dollars and cents! It's a true hunk of junk that belongs on a rubbish heap,' Barbara's mind caustically criticized. 'The Goodwill Store would probably sell it for scrap metal,' sarcastically thought and challenged my wife's all-too-fierce readable mind. "Now John," my suspicious female soulmate orally continued her contrary train of thought, "what did your competing three cousins genuinely inherit?"

"Well, David and Stephen each had gotten terrific bank certificates of five-hundred-thousand dollars each, and Steve's son Frank, my fortunate second cousin, inherited Aunt Jenny's Ellicott City mini-mansion, which is valued at a half-a-million also!"

'You are without a doubt a stupid, quixotic idiot!' Barbara's cynical brain broadcasted in my direction via the priceless lamp's prodigious supernatural wizardry. 'You are beyond a shadow of a doubt an undisciplined John Foolery; Tom's mentally deficient twin brother! Your three cousins have always been especially greedy, and now they've seriously taken advantage of you; probably by maliciously changing your aunt's will!'

Soon I again heard my better-half's contrived, sanctimonious, real voice. "Well John," my lady partner's unimpressed natural tone uttered, "you can turn-off this hot lightbulb that's burning a little too-intensely over my head. It's almost as annoying as your melancholy inheritance story. Perhaps tomorrow we can take this deplorable white elephant over to the antique dealer on 12th Street and be lucky enough to have it appraised for maybe five measly dollars."

"Okay Honey. I'll consider your noteworthy suggestion the next time majestic Halley's Comet decides to encounter and harass our precious Earth!" I defiantly countered.

The first Saturday in August I received a surprise visit from obnoxious Cousin David Wilson, who claimed to be stopping by on his way to a gigantic merchandising exhibit show occurring at the newly refurbished Atlantic City Boardwalk Convention Hall. After egotistically divulging to me that Stephen, Frank and he were perfectly thrilled at the revelation of their abundant inheritances from Aunt Genevieve's seemingly biased will, I shrewdly turned-on the sublime Nerfertiti lamp, thus activating the magnificent "psychic bulb" and then convincingly asked all-too-talkative David to sit-down in the fancy striped chair.

"Where's Barbara?" my inquisitive relative asked. "I missed her at Aunt Jenny's viewing. I believe your wife also missed Aunt Elsie's wake, too!"

"Her sister came down with a mild summer cold, so my wife's now over in Waterford making Eileen a bowl of hot chicken soup," I all-too-sincerely explained.

"Tell me John, what do you think about this crusty-old, lackluster Egyptian lamp?" my rude, covetous cousin superficially stated. "I felt pretty darn bad witnessing and then hearing about your paltry inheritance at the downtown Baltimore attorney's office. I'll make you a gentleman's proposition you can't refuse. I'm willing to take the less-than-mediocre monstrosity off your hands by giving you a reasonable consolation of ten thousand dollars from my inheritance if you're willing to graciously accept my offer!"

"No thanks Dave," I solemnly declined. "I truly love this outstanding lamp and respect its historic legacy tremendously. I believe that I'll honorably treasure my nice Nerfertiti keepsake for as long as I shall live."

Suddenly, my perceptive mind detected Cousin David's distinctive voice being arcanely delivered by means of some uncanny brainwave communication. 'You pathetic, moronic imbecile. I just only came to your house to see and relish great envy in your eyes. And now I realize that you're even much dumber and more impractically knuckleheaded than I had ever reckoned you would be. No wonder why Aunt Genevieve treated you just like the pitiful numbskull that you actually are in her last will and testament!'

"Er John," haughty David Wilson neurotically spoke in order to interrupt the apparent void of extended silence, "if my memory is correct, this strange-looking lamp behind me had once occupied a corner of Uncle Henry's club basement out on Taylor Avenue that now I distinctly remember ever since I was a kid."

"Yes Dave, our beloved Aunt Jenny told me back in the early 1960s that Uncle Hank had purchased the novelty from a back-alley curio shop in Alexandria, Egypt. You must confess; the intriguing item does possess a degree of charm and dignity."

"It sure does John," my all-too-devious cousin falsely attested. "How about if I up the ante and offer to buy the crusty thing from you for twenty thousand? Honestly, I'm willing and happy to share a small portion of my recent fortune with you!"

"No thanks Dave," I stubbornly answered. "I'm rather euphoric about owning something special that Aunt Jenny always took pride in having. I want you to know that this vintage Egyptian lamp is much more than a mere fascinating souvenir to me! It has tremendous sentimental value!"

'Asinine ignoramus! Dopey blockhead!' my conscientious wit adroitly intercepted in a series of harsh brainwaves being beamed from my cousin's corrupt cerebrum. "Say John, can you please turn-off this rusty, dilapidated lamp? It's wickedly burning a crater right into the bald spot on top of my skull!"

On Labor Day weekend, to my chagrin, I was unexpectedly visited by my insufferable and arrogant first cousin, Stephen Wilson. "Where's Barbara?" the stealthy, self-centered rogue inquired as I answered the front doorbell. "I missed her at Aunt Jenny's wake. And at Aunt Elsie's viewing, too!"

"You just missed her again right here," I confirmed. "She's out grocery shopping at Wal*Mart and then going to ShopRite!"

During our initial dialogue, David Wilson's junior brother was not at all modest, monotonously bragging about his colossal half-million-dollar bonanza. Just like *his* all-too-conceited older sibling, 'unbearable Steve' disclosed that he intended to use his new-found wealth to buy two spectacular vacation condos: one on the bay in Ocean City, Maryland and the other in sunny Vero Beach, Florida.

Sitting beneath the regal Nerfertiti lamp, Stephen selfishly boasted, "And John, my son Frank has just been promoted to Army Captain. The energetic kid's going to go far in military life; right to the ceiling! Just look at how successful my dynamic boy is already!" Then my reprehensible and repulsive cousin nastily thought, 'And you John remained a lowly school teacher these past thirty or so years. No wonder why Aunt Jenny loathed and disfavored you so.'

"Where are you heading?" I peevishly inquired, fully realizing that our fragile discussion had reached a massive impasse. "Are you en-route to the tourist-trap A.C. casinos?"

"No John. I'm on my way to Manhattan for a joyful New York University class reunion. I haven't seen my zany college roommate and my obnoxious fraternity brothers for at least a decade. Cousin John, can you please turn-off this terrible lamp that's making me perspire like a squeezed sponge? I feel like my delicate scalp is about to ignite!"

"Your wish is my command," I frivolously replied, pretending to be the fabled genie of Aladdin's astonishing lamp. "I'm most pleased to be your grateful servant!"

'Ha, ha Johnny Boy! You empty-headed ridiculous cretin! You're a motley, simpleton clown!' my despicable, ruthless Maryland cousin diabolically contemplated and unknowingly transmitted. 'You truly deserve owning this wholly disgusting, obsolete, green-corroded piece-of-junk lamp!'

The Wednesday evening after Labor Day Barbara was out of the house diligently and faithfully attending her bi-weekly Women's Civic Club meeting over on Valley Avenue. The night before, my mercurial-behaving wife had been complaining about hearing a mouse aggressively doing some scratching above the hall closet ceiling, so being a valiant, loyal husband, I furtively plotted the creature's demise by smearing peanut butter as bait and then creatively setting the designated trap underneath the dignified Nerfertiti lamp, which ideally had four short brass legs; each one elevated three inches above the living room's hardwood floor.

After carefully setting the brand-new trap, I cleverly determined that I should conduct an impromptu experiment by switching-on the Egyptian lamp and next sitting in the red and light-brown striped chair beneath it, just to see and ascertain what the sinister effect might be and feel like. After assuming my position in the chair, to my frustration, three seconds later the magical light shockingly extinguished. Being perplexed, I immediately rose from my seat, frenetically unscrewed the oval lightbulb and then thoroughly examined it.

'There aren't any markings on it whatsoever,' I astutely observed. 'Not even any watt number or descriptive language I.D. I suppose that as of now good old Nerfertiti has permanently lost her astounding psychic communication ability!'

After school on Thursday afternoon, I eagerly brought the expired lightbulb to the town's largest lighting distribution warehouse, but the knowledgeable proprietor firmly insisted that he had never before ever seen such an unusual bulb. I returned home in a disconsolate frame of mind, so then, out of pure curiosity, with both hands I gently lifted the Nerfertiti lamp to notice whether or not I had successfully caught the persistent rodent that had been mischievously disturbing and bothering my wife.

'Barb's still doing her secretary thing over at her boss's real estate office, so let's see if I've outsmarted the pesky rascal with this new mouse-trap I had set in the center of the lamp's four brass legs.'

Much to my satisfaction, my flawless strategy had sagely caught the feisty pest, but before I could adequately celebrate my major accomplishment, I observed that the furry nuisance was still alive with its right leg and tail ensnared under the spring-triggered hinge as the small mammal frantically attempted to escape its painful predicament. Then, when I had inadvertently elevated the lampstand to inspect my frightened capture, my alert ears had heard a subtle, low rattle-sound originating from inside the lamp's base.

I gingerly lifted the trap from the living room floor as the doomed rodent rotated and scrambled about, endeavoring to emancipate itself from its agonizing incarceration. Feeling a sense of urgency, I quickly carried my wounded, foul quarry to the downstairs powder room and then tossed the trap face-down into the toilet bowl with the expressed intention of drowning the furiously wriggling mouse.

I hastily sauntered back through the den, the kitchen and the short hall and next paced to the living room to comprehensively investigate the mysterious low-rattling noise that my keen ears had discerned. Lifting the lamp in a very deliberate fashion, I laid the cherished object horizontally upon the arms of the nearby red and light-brown striped chair and in the process, again detected the internal rattle coming from inside the lamp's base, which my peering eyes instantly perceived as a faded, colored scene of the incomparable desert Sphinx shown with three dull, illustrated pyramids along with several caravan camels in the background.

Being motivated by my ongoing discovery, I speedily rushed into the laundry room to remove a screwdriver from the wall cabinet. After finding the useful tool inside a plastic container, I again darted into the adjacent powder room.

The obstinate-and-exhausted home intruder was still alive and amazingly had managed to partially ascend the wet and slippery side of the white porcelain bowel; desperately squirming and dragging the trap with it. Gaining new respect for the mouse's desire to live, I impulsively grabbed the trap, stepped to the mudroom's side door and employed the utilitarian screwdriver to mercifully liberate the struggling rodent from its precarious entrapment. The tiny, maligned animal slowly maneuvered its fearful path to freedom, scurrying between a large rhododendron bush and the home's external red chimney bricks.

My next task was to inspect the enchanted lamp's base by using the ordinary screwdriver to remove the eight rusted screws that had fastened the faded Sphinx/pyramid/camel-caravan illustration to the mystical lamp's interior frame. Much to my bewilderment, a square-shaped second lightbulb (loosely held to the lamp's underframe) was soon coincidentally discovered. 'So that's what was causing the rattling sound to occur!' I inferred and assessed. 'This second bulb was probably knocked loose when the mousetrap had been sprung and consequently snapped and flew upwards with the weight of the attached rodent providing more upward force. The accidental impact caused this square lightbulb to become slightly separated from his bracket mounting; the jolt had jarred the second bulb a trifle loose; just enough to make it weakly rattle inside its tethering bracket.'

Being instantaneously inspired, I methodically screwed the square bulb into the socket located beneath the black lampshade, and to my sheer ecstasy, light was soon splendidly projected onto the bare wall above and behind the upright piano that Barbara had inherited from her Aunt Mildred. And to my further befuddlement, a wondrous coded message appeared, being revealed partly in hieroglyphics and partly in Egyptian Arabic.

Still being in a trance-like stupor, I assiduously sped into the kitchen, opened the brown rolltop desk and frantically obtained a writing tablet along with an accompanying ballpoint pen. Then without hesitation, I daringly sat-down in the striped chair and very methodically copied the myriad Arabic letter symbols along with the numerous hieroglyphic drawings that had been starkly projected upon the opposite wall above and behind the upright, flatback piano. Ironically, the inimitable square projector-bulb had burned-out a minute or so after I had finished recording my valuable notations.

I never felt obligated to share my almost-miraculous Nerfertiti lamp adventure to my predictably apostate wife. 'I'm just like Daniel in the Old Testament of the Bible during the Israelite captivity in Babylon,' I marveled and lectured to myself. 'I've literally seen the mystic writing on the wall!'

Requesting a "Personal Day" from the middle school's rigid administration, I gladly took the next day off from my teaching responsibility for the purpose of conducting *more relevant and significant* business that definitely required my immediate attention. I drove my red Murano to Stockton State College in nearby Pomona where I presented the carefully recorded Arabic and hieroglyphic information to my dear Lions Club friend, eminent Professor Edmund Evans, Ph.D. Thirty trying minutes later, I was absolutely staggered and almost physically paralyzed at hearing Dr. Evans' impeccable interpretation and magnificent deciphering of the distinguished scholar's revamped coded missive.

"Well John, the Arabic contained in the translated message is written in Masri, a frequent and popular form of Egyptian colloquial language. When added to the associated hieroglyphics, the cryptic passage reads and states, 'Congratulations my dear nephew John: you are about to inherit the sensational sum of 1.5 million dollars currently on deposit at the National Bank of Egypt in Cairo. All you have to do is present your New Jersey driver's license, your passport and your social security number to the NBE in order to firmly secure your well-deserved inheritance. Love always, now and forever: Aunt Genevieve Curtis'!"

'Oh my God!' I exuberantly thought as my heart raced in rapturous appreciation. 'My wonderful inheritance from Aunt Jenny equals that of Cousins David, Stephen and Frank combined. Much to my satisfaction, I now truly consider myself to be an honorary member of the modern-day Illuminati!'

About the Author

Jay Dubya is author John Wiessner's pen name and also his initials (J.W.) John is a retired New Jersey public school English teacher and he had taught the subject for thirty-four years. John lives in southern New Jersey with wife Joanne and the couple has three grown sons. John is the creator of fifty-two books.

Jay Dubya has written adult satires Fractured Frazzled Folk Fables and Fairy Farces and FFFF and FF, Part II. Black Leather and Blue Denim, A '50s Novel and its sequel, The Great Teen Fruit War, A 1960' Novel and Frat' Brats, A '60s Novel are adult-oriented literary endeavors constituting a trilogy.

Pieces of Eight, Pieces of Eight, Part II, Pieces of Eight Part III and Pieces of Eight, Part IV are' short story/novella collections featuring science fiction, paranormal and humorous plots and themes. Nine New Novellas is the companion book to Nine New Novellas, Part II, Nine New Novellas, Part III and Nine New Novellas, Part IV. And So Ya' Wanna' Be A Teacher is a satirical autobiography describing the author's thirty-four-year educational career in American public schools.

Ron Coyote, Man of La Mangia is adult humor and the work is an imaginative satire/parody on Miguel Cervantes' Don Quixote, published in 1605. Mauled Maimed Mangled Mutilated Mythology is a work that satires twenty-one famous ancient tales. The Wholly Book of Genesis and The Wholly Book of Exodus are also adult satirical humor. Thirteen Sick Tasteless Classics, Thirteen Sick Tasteless Classics, Part II, Thirteen Sick Tasteless Classics, Part III and Thirteen Sick Tasteless Classics, Part IV are adult satirical rewrites of famous short fiction.

John has also authored a trilogy of young adult fantasy novels, Enchanta, Pot of Gold and Space Bugs, Earth Invasion. The Eighteen' Story Gingerbread House is a new collection of eighteen diverse and creative children's stories.

Jay Dubya likes '50s rock and roll music and he also enjoys pop' songs by the Beach Boys', Fleetwood Mac, the Eagles, the Rolling Stones, ELO, John Mellencamp and by John Fogerty.

Author Biography

Born in Hammonton, NJ in 1942, John Wiessner had attended St. Joseph School up to and including Grade 5. After his family moved from Hammonton to Levittown, Pa in 1954, John attended St. Mark School in Bristol, Pa. for Grade 6, St. Michael the Archangel School in Levittown for Grades 7 and 8 and then Immaculate Conception School, Levittown, Pa. for Grade 9. Bishop Egan High School, Levittown Pa was John's educational base for Grades 10 and 11, and later in 1960, the aspiring author graduated from Edgewood Regional High, Tansboro, NJ. John then next attended Glassboro State College, where he was an announcer for the school's baseball games and also read the nightly news and sports over WGLS, GSC's radio station.

John Wiessner had been primarily an English teacher in the Hammonton Public School System for 34 years, specializing in the instruction of middle school language arts. Mr. Wiessner was quite active in the Hammonton Education Association, serving in the capacities of Vice-President, building representative and finally, teachers' head negotiator for 7 years. During his lengthy teaching career, John had been nominated into "Who's Who Among American Teachers" three times. He also was quite active giving professional workshops at schools around South Jersey on the subjects of creative writing and the use of movie videos to motivate students to organize their classroom theme compositions.

John Wiessner was very active in community service, being a past President of the Hammonton Lions Club, where he also functioned for many years as the club's Tail-Twister, Vice-President and Liontamer. John had been named Hammonton Lion of the Year in 1979 and in 2009 received the prestigious Melvin Jones Fellow Award, the highest honor that a Lion can receive from Lions International.

John also was a successful businessman, starting with being a Philadelphia Bulletin newspaper delivery boy for two years in the late 1950s in Levittown, Pennsylvania. After his family moved back to New Jersey in 1959, John worked at his grandparents and his parents' farm markets, Square Deal Farm (now Ron's Gardens in Hammonton) and Pete's Farm Market in Elm, respectively. He later managed his wife's parents' farm market, White Horse Farms in Elm for three summers.

Also, in a business capacity, for 16 summers starting in 1967 John Wiessner had co-owned Dealers Choice Amusement Arcade on the Ocean City, Maryland boardwalk and also co-owned the New Horizon Tee-Shirt Store for eight summers (1973-'81) on the Rehoboth Beach, Delaware boardwalk. In addition, "Jay Dubya" was a co-owner of Wheel and Deal Amusement Arcade, Missouri Avenue and Boardwalk, Atlantic City. And then, for 18 summers beginning in 1986, John had been the Field Manager in charge of crew-leaders for Atlantic Blueberry Company (the world's largest cultivated blueberry farm), both the Weymouth and Mays Landing Divisions.

After retiring from teaching in 1999, writing under the pen name Jay Dubya (his initials), John Wiessner became the author of 52 books in the genre Action/Adventure Novels, Sci-Fi/Paranormal Story Collections, Adult Satire, Young Adult Fantasy Novels and Non-Fiction Books. His books exist in hardcover, in paperback and in popular Kindle and Nook e-book formats.